firewo

elizabeth white

fireworks

elizabeth white

ZONDERVAN™

GRAND RAPIDS, MICHIGAN 49530 USA

ZONDERVAN.COM/
AUTHORTRACKER

ZONDERVAN™

Fireworks
Copyright © 2006 by Elizabeth White

Requests for information should be addressed to:
Zondervan, *Grand Rapids, Michigan 49530*

Library of Congress Cataloging-in-Publication Data

White, Elizabeth.
    Fireworks / Elizabeth White. — 1st ed.
      p. cm.
    ISBN-10: 0-310-26224-0
    ISBN-13: 978-0-310-26224-4
    1. Insurance investigators — Fiction. 2. Pyrotechnists — Fiction.
  I. Title.
    PS3623.H574F57 — 2005
    813'.6 — dc22

                                         2005032782

Make-up and hair for cover models by Kim Ricketts

Interior design by Michelle Espinoza

Printed in the United States of America

06 07 08 09 10 11 12 • 18 17 16 15 14 13 12 11 10 9 8 7 6 5 4 3 2 1

To the Lord Jesus—
the picture
of unconditional love.

ACKNOWLEDGMENTS

I would like to express my gratitude to the folks at Zondervan for giving me the opportunity to tell this story. I deeply admire Senior Editor Karen Ball, and I'm humbled that she took a chance on bringing me in as a new author. Diane Noble has been a fabulous editor. I learned so much from you two! Also, appreciation goes to my former agent, Chip MacGregor, who connected me with Zondervan. Alive Communications is a wonderful agency!

The manuscript could not have been completed without day-to-day feedback from my husband, Scott, and my dear friend, Tammy Thompson. When I got off on the wrong track, they steered me back. And thank you to my family who supplied constant encouragement and prayer support.

Several years ago I ran across an article about Christian fireworks designer David Spear of Mandeville, Louisiana. The subject of pyrotechnics fascinated me, so I stuck the article in a file in case I ever needed a good idea. When that day came, I contacted David, and he graciously allowed me to visit his office and warehouse. Over the next two years he patiently answered questions about the business and creative aspects of the special effects industry. If I exaggerated things a bit for the sake of story, it's not his fault!

In developing the plot, Mobile attorney Andrew Clausen spent a day brainstorming ideas. Thanks, Andy, for your expertise in fire and explosives investigation and prosecution.

Also, I received invaluable assistance from Special Agent Michael Knoll of the Biloxi, Mississippi, office of the Bureau of Alcohol, Tobacco, Firearms and Explosives. Mike answered endless questions with thoroughness and good humor. He is a brilliant and generous public servant. Any mistakes in Susannah's investigative techniques are mine.

Thanks go to my friend Warren Helmer, who shared his "weekend warrior" experiences as a top runner in Mobile's Azalea Trail Run. I admire those who use all their gifts to make a difference for Christ.

Members of First Baptist North Mobile will perhaps recognize elements of our fellowship in Quinn's church. I'm grateful for the impact this body of Christ—staff and congregation—have had on my family, my spiritual growth, and my writing ministry. Particularly, I thank Tammy Litton, my friend and fellow pastor's wife—an Arizona transplant who has learned to say "y'all" and drink sweet tea.

William Barrick, PhD, executive director of Bellingrath Gardens in Theodore, Alabama, supplied necessary details about the mermaid—and pictures! Thank you, Dr. Barrick.

Last but not least, thanks to my sister Robin and my nephew Ben, who own the one, the only, the original Bob the Snake. I hope I never meet him outside his terrarium or he will be one dead python.

A NOTE FROM
THE AUTHOR

Within these pages, I have tried to give a flavor of the culture I grew up with, without stereotyping characters. Contrary to what one sees in the movies, all southerners don't have bad grammar, and we don't say "y'all" indiscriminately. However, people really do make three syllables out of a one-syllable word. And yes, many women actually designate a potato salad dish and use it for nothing else. Manners and hospitality, church and family are critical to southern society.

To my southern readers, this is going to sound like overexplanation, but it was brought to my attention—as I worked with editors from other parts of the country—that some of our ways of expressing ourselves are, shall we say, a bit odd. There may be words or phrases uttered by my characters that will clang on the non-southern ear—for example, referring to women, aged eighty or eight, as "girls." Also the word "shoot" is an interjection like "oh" or "well" and has completely lost any association with expletives. I assure the reader with all sincerity that no chauvinism or disrespect is intended.

fireworks
elizabeth white

chapter 1

Quinn Baldwin dove for the pier at Clayton Brothers Drydocks and decided it would be a good thing if Jesus just came to take him on home.

The sooner the better.

Another Roman candle whizzed over his head and detonated like the crack of doom.

Dear Lord, please let the crew be okay.

He squinted across the river. Phillip and Russ were probably halfway through the Bankhead Tunnel by now, on their suppertime quest for hot wings.

Please let them be—

A stupendous concussion smashed his face against the pier again, jamming his goggles into his cheekbone. Flashes of light zigzagged like laser beams over his head, and the acrid stench of sulfur stung his nose.

And Rebecca and Skeet! Ten minutes ago they were sitting on the tailgate of the truck, arguing over who was going to win the NCAA basketball championship next week. But now? He shuddered, thinking what might have happened to them.

Okay, take another look. Gotta be angels around me. Don't seem to be dead yet.

He peered over his shoulder. Smoke from the equipment truck—orange and red and yellow—looked like an illustration from Dante's *Inferno.*

Brain's whacked. What a time for senior English to resurface.

A strobe shell pierced the fog, and he covered his head. Boom followed boom followed boom, numbing his ears. More jags of light. More violent jolts. He clung to the pier, praying for the shaking to stop.

For a split second he considered jumping into the river. But the current was too strong. He'd be slammed into a ship docked downriver or swept into the bay. Maybe speared by one of the trees growing out from the shore. Better take his chances here.

For an eternity, he lay still. Finally the explosions died and the pier stopped quaking.

Shaking, he got up on his knees. Thank God the river breeze carried away some of the smoke, or he would have suffocated. He coughed, then crawled away from the end of the pier until his hand hit cold, grassy mud.

"Skeet!" His voice came out in a croak. "Rebecca! Where are you?"

Then with sickening clarity it hit him.

His show had just exploded in a blaze of premature, misdirected glory. Twenty-thousand dollars' worth of handmade Chinese fireworks destroyed in a burning, blackened, smoking mess. And more still going off in crimson wagon wheels, saffron-yellow glitter palms, green fountains streaking across the river toward the—

"Oh, no!" He stood up without thinking.

The fireworks he'd designed as entertainment for a Mardi Gras charity ball were now headed, with the precision of an assault rifle, straight across the river. Straight toward the eight-story glass front of the Mobile Convention Center.

There wasn't a thing he could do about it.

The wail of sirens split the night. Quinn turned toward the road. Two unmistakable silhouettes were jumping around on top of the hill like Disney *Fantasia* characters—Skeet Lawrence, his friend and part-time employee, and Rebecca Mansfield, his assistant.

"Thank you, Lord," he breathed.

Suddenly a shower of sparks rained down. The smell of singed hair closed his nostrils. If he didn't run, he was going to catch fire.

Staggering toward the road, he dodged sparks spewing sideways from an overturned row of mortar tubes. A burst of adrenaline hit, and he tore up the hill. At the same time, two fire trucks barreled into the gravel driveway between Clancy Brothers' and the field. Firefighters swarmed off the truck.

One grabbed Quinn's arm. "Hey, man, you all right?" he shouted over the boom of exploding shells. "Anybody else over there?"

"No, just me. I'm okay." Quinn bent double, coughing. "You've got to stop it before it hits the—" a crashing explosion and a sudden burst of flames across the river lit up the sky—"Convention Center," he finished weakly.

"Too late." The fireman grabbed his radio. "Dispatch, you better get trucks headed for Water Street on the double."

Quinn heard no more as the fireman ran after the others.

Rebecca got to Quinn before he reached the top of the hill. "I thought you were dead!" she screamed, all but strangling him. "Why are you not dead?"

"Hey, are you all right?" Skeet bounded down the hill and pounded Quinn on the back until his teeth rattled.

"I'm okay, I'm okay. Would you two stop?"

"Sorry, man." Skeet backed off.

Rebecca smeared at tears with the side of her hand. "Quinn, your face is bleeding."

"I'll be okay." He removed his hard hat, goggles, and gloves, then turned to look at the scene of destruction.

One last crossette shell screamed across the river, bursting into a hundred shimmering golden streams just before it pasted the wharf in front of the Convention Center. In the distance a second pair of fire trucks' sirens wailed as they pulled up close to the building. Firemen jumped from the trucks, rushing to connect their hoses. Squinting toward the park adjoining the Convention Center, Quinn could make out the antlike figures of people running from the building.

People in tuxes and evening gowns who had paid him a lot of money to entertain them with a fireworks show. A couple of national political campaign directors who were considering booking him for summer campaign events.

This wasn't exactly the show they had expected.

Quinn's stomach lurched. Even if nobody had been hurt—and he prayed they hadn't—he had just effectively bombed a major public building. Probably incurred thousands of dollars' worth of damage. *Oh, God, maybe millions.*

His truck was gone. His computers fried.

His reputation might as well be at the bottom of the river.

Overcome, he collapsed between Rebecca and Skeet to watch the firemen dousing the whole area with water. A rumble of thunder rolled across the sky, echoing his black depression. Right before that first Roman candle went off, he'd stood on the Clancy Brothers' pier asking God to hold off the rain. Overcast was good; a black sky made a nice backdrop for the fireworks. But a storm would make the crew miserable and chase away the crowd.

Now he hoped it *would* rain. Keep the fire from spreading to the buildings nearby. It had been such a beautiful skyline, with the city's high-rise buildings shimmering in a haze of yellow behind the Convention Center. Chains of light, outlining the bridges and the two tunnel entrances, always reminded him of the geometric design of a giant amusement park. Now everything was obscured by dense black smoke.

Please, Father, let it rain.

Rebecca, who'd been speechless for once in her life, gasped and sat up. "That's Phillip's car! Thank God they weren't here."

Quinn limped toward the souped-up Dodge as it braked with a jerk behind the Suburban. With its huge spoiler and green underbelly lights, the little car looked like a UFO in a B space movie. To Quinn it was a beautiful sight.

Rebecca's brother, Phillip, college freshman and self-appointed linchpin of the universe, scrambled out of the driver's seat. "Dude!" he shouted. "What happened? Are you okay?"

Quinn reached his youngest crew member, and they gave each other a whack on the shoulder. "I'm fine. Pretty big mess here, though. Good thing you two were gone."

"Man, you should've warned us you planned on blowing the place up." Russell Wallace, Phillip's roommate, hovered beside the car, hands stuffed into his back pockets. In the glare of lights from the fire trucks, his square face looked pale and oddly childish atop a hulking football player's physique.

Quinn grimaced. "I'm just glad you guys are okay."

"Y'all don't need to be here," Rebecca said, butting in as usual. "You'll just get in the way. You might as well head back to campus."

Angular chin jutting, Phillip slung a hank of curly dark hair out of his eyes. "Shut up, Rebecca. We're part of the crew too. We're staying to help."

Quinn stepped between the siblings. His head felt like a dragon raged inside it. "The fire marshal's probably on his way. There's really nothing any of us can do except stick around to answer questions." He turned to Skeet. "I need something to drink. Is there another root beer left in the ice chest?"

"Sure, man."

As the five of them trudged toward the Suburban, a jag of lightning slashed the sky over the river, and thunder rolled again. The heavens broke, sending torrents of rain onto the already soggy piles of debris.

Quinn stopped, hands up in surrender, head back to receive this baptism by fire and water. He had no idea what had set off the explosion, but he knew one thing.

His life was never going to be the same.

chapter 2

Montmorency bitterly resented The Cat. The gray and white Manx was called Belshazzar, a name Susannah considered fitting for a creature that could terrorize an eighty-pound black Lab with only a well-modulated hiss. But it had taken nearly a week to find an apartment that allowed pets in this neighborhood. Besides, she'd already signed the lease and lugged her plain brown suitcase up a narrow flight of stairs into Mrs. Elva Kay Shue's attic apartment.

Monty was just going to have to deal.

By the time she'd dragged him by the collar up the stairs, protesting all the way, she barely had the energy to unpack. Fortunately there was a solid oak door at the foot of the stairs, which would keep the canine from attacking the feline. Or, more likely, vice versa.

While her faithful companion settled on the rug beside the canopied four-poster, his nose on a tennis ball, Susannah stowed her collection of jeans and T-shirts in the armoire. Some sensible underwear and thick cotton socks followed.

Hmm, might not need the socks in this climate.

She pulled at the front of her University of Arizona tank shirt. The near 100 percent humidity had sucked all the starch out of her. Kind of reminded her of Dad's navy stint in Korea when she was in high school.

Already dressed in gym shorts, she picked up her running shoes and sat down on the bentwood rocker in the corner. Dilapidated and ugly, the shoes were full of sentimental value. She'd worn them while beating, in eight successive fifty-meter sprints, every male agent in the Tucson field office of the Bureau of Alcohol, Tobacco, Firearms and Explosives.

She didn't know Quinn Baldwin, except from the dossier in her briefcase, but she was pretty sure she'd enjoy taking *him* down a peg too. He was trying to pull a fast one on Independent Mutual Insurance Company, and it was going to be her privilege to keep him from doing so. Plus, the tidy sum she made doing it would go a long way toward getting Dad out of trouble at the hotel. Hey, it was all good.

Susannah snapped her fingers. "Monty, want to run?"

The Lab bounded to his feet from a dead sleep, tail and ears at attention, tongue hanging from a smiling mouth.

"Yeah, me too. Paperwork later." Shoving aside the stack of files she'd dumped on the rolltop desk, she found his leash.

At the bottom of the stairs she laid a hand on the dog's head. "Hold up, let's see if the coast is clear." She peered into the living room. No Tyrannical Beast in sight. It would probably come leaping out at them the minute they weren't looking. "Okay, let's make a run for it."

Susannah tiptoed through the antiques-crowded living room, the dog panting at her heels. Mrs. Shue was in the kitchen making a cake for the prison ministry, whatever that meant. But she had no intention of starting a conversation with her garrulous landlady right now. She had a date with Mr. Baldwin.

He just didn't know it yet.

Susannah gasped for air as she pulled the front door shut and snapped Monty's leash onto his collar. The humidity was so high she could hardly breathe. "Good grief, Monty, I'm gonna have to wear a scuba mask around here." Letting the dog take the lead, she took off at a run.

Careful research of Baldwin's habits had revealed that they seemed to have several things in common, one of them running. And, of course, there was the whole explosives thing.

She picked up the pace and gained on the dog. He sent her an injured look past his flapping tongue. Like most males, Monty didn't like to lose.

Susannah figured this in large part explained why at the age of thirty she was still unmarried, un-hooked up, and pretty much unconcerned about either state. The thing was, all her life she'd known exactly where she was going—a trait which seemed to intimidate prospective love interests.

Phooey, who cares? Men had their uses—after all, she loved her father and brothers—but she sure didn't need one as a permanent attachment. She had a great family and a great dog, thanks to her former ATF supervisor. He'd given Monty to her just before she resigned from the agency. And now she had an interesting six-figure job, which at the moment entailed trying to nail some Alabama hick who'd managed to blow up his inventory and do some major damage to a multimillion-dollar building in one fell swoop.

And she intended to bust his scam wide open.

Doesn't hurt that there's a nice bonus in it for me too.

She hung a left at the corner of the street, where an enormous moss-laden oak tree split the pavement into two lanes. Two blocks down, Murphy High School appeared. Tugging on the dog's leash, Susannah slowed to a walk. Resembling a replica of the Alamo, beautiful Spanish adobe buildings sprawled over three city blocks.

Massive oak trees and full-blown pink azaleas dotted a lawn already greening with spring, and a spiked wrought-iron fence ringed the football practice field and track. Like everything she'd seen of Mobile, the campus was extraordinarily beautiful.

And there was Baldwin flying around the oval track, like that guy in *Chariots of Fire*—head up, knees and arms pumping.

"Here we go, Monty. Let the games begin." She headed for the open gate.

The moment her feet hit the track, she was in her element, the sun on her face so bright it made her eyes water. She ran flat out like she hadn't run in months, laughing at Monty, who galloped like a racehorse trying to keep up.

She caught up to Baldwin and was about to pass him, when he turned his head and caught her eyes. He smiled.

Taken off guard, her pace faltered. Nothing in that smile connected him with the file photo she'd been studying for two weeks. Apparently taken some years ago, the head shot revealed a face built on straight, clean lines and a serious mouth. The eyes had held something in reserve, something dangerous that warned her to be careful.

But what she saw here in the flesh was amazing. Joy radiated out of him in almost palpable sparks.

To her surprise, he didn't speed up and try to show her what those long, well-developed legs could do. He laughed when the dog jerked the leash out of her hand and went streaking past them.

"Montmorency!" she shouted. But Monty kept going. Mortified, she glanced at Baldwin. "He's a little hard of hearing."

"Me too, so don't try to talk into my right ear." Baldwin gave her that quick, open grin again. "Where'd he get a name like that?"

"He—I—" She shook her head, trying to catch her breath. Good gracious, he was tall. Easily cleared six two or three. She could keep up with him, but it was hard to talk at this pace. "It's a long story."

"I'm not in any hurry." As if to prove it, he slowed to a cool-down walk. His cheeks turned ruddy as he said with a slight stammer, "I'm Quinn Baldwin, by the way." Clearly he was having trouble not staring at her.

She suppressed a smile. This was like taking candy from a baby. "My name's Susannah Tait."

"I bet you hear this all this time, but . . . you're not from around here, are you?"

"Arizona. I just moved here this week." For simplicity's sake she elected to ignore the nine states and seven foreign countries she'd called home.

"Oh, yeah, the T-shirt." He grinned. "I like your accent."

She gave him a sideways glance. "I don't think *I'm* the one with the accent."

"I 'magine you're right." *Ooh, what a drawl.* His gaze, sharp steel-gray, flicked across her heated face and sweaty top. "If you're from the desert, the humidity's gonna kill you."

"I'll adjust." She shoved her hair away from her face. It was probably springing in yellow corkscrews in all directions.

Baldwin shook his head as Monty whizzed past on a second lap. "That is one energetic dog you've got there. So what's the deal with that highbrow name?"

"He was named after the dog in this book, *Three Men in a Boat.*" She'd found it in the library last summer and gotten a kick out of it. But she'd heard southerners didn't read much literature. No reason to embarrass the guy. She made a face. "I just call him Monty, except when he's in trouble."

"Looks like that must be fairly often."

"Oh, no, he's actually a—" She caught herself. If she mentioned that Monty was a retired explosives task force animal, Baldwin might start asking the wrong questions. "—an obedience school dropout."

He laughed. The conversation stalled as they walked a lap side by side. Susannah got the impression he was a bit shy, in spite of the big smile. He looked away every time she caught his glance.

She'd just have to figure out how to pry him open. "So ... do you live around here?" Not very original as lines went, but he seemed relieved to have something to talk about.

"Around the corner and down a few streets. How about you?" He chuckled as Monty trotted up from behind and flung himself hard against the back of Susannah's legs. "Hope you've got a strong fence."

"Corner of Old Government and Williams. I'm renting an attic apartment from a lady named Mrs. Shue. Fortunately, she has a nice, big fenced backyard." Susannah smiled. "And a cat, which creates some issues for Monty."

"Miss Elva Kay's my buddy. I cut her grass sometimes."

"Really?" Bingo, now they were moving in the right direction.

"Yeah, how'd you run across her? Are you a relative? I know she's got a sister in Atlanta."

At his expectant look, she blinked. She hadn't gotten around to much personal information about her landlady. "Um, no, I'm not related. An apartment locator hooked me up through the Internet."

"You wouldn't think it, but Miss Elva Kay's a real techno-babe." Baldwin chuckled. "She emails me a recipe about once a week. Guess she thinks somebody needs to watch my nutrition."

Judging by his physique, Susannah would say there was nothing wrong with Baldwin's dietary regimen. She dragged her eyes off those big shoulders. She'd seen plenty of good-looking men, but there was something different about this guy. Maybe it was the gentle expression around his eyes. Or maybe it was the fact that he seemed utterly unaware of how attractive he was. "I can't cook at all," she confessed. "Which is why I'm paying for room *and* board."

"Oh man. You're in for a treat. She made me a hummingbird cake for my last birthday. Best thing I ever put in my mouth."

Picturing tiny beaks and feathers baked into a cake, Susannah's eyes widened. "I'll take your word for it."

"No, it didn't have real—" He squinted at her. "You're kidding, right?"

"I've heard southerners eat some pretty weird things."

He laughed. "I promise you I never had a hog jowl or a possum pie in my life."

"Okay, sorry if I made the wrong assumption. But *hummingbird* cake?"

"Trust me, you'd like it." Baldwin's shoulders were still shaking. "So if you don't cook, Miss Susannah, what *do* you do? Besides chase your dog?"

"Research. I'm a doctoral student at U of A."

His brows rose. "Wow. What's your field?"

"Sociology. My thesis is 'Observable Social Manifestations of Tribal Rites and Rituals in Contemporary Southern Culture.'" Having practiced that line in front of a mirror for five minutes this morning, she managed to say it with a straight face.

"Boy, that's a mouthful." He paused, scratched his nose. "What does it mean?"

"Basically, I want to analyze Mardi Gras. I vacationed in New Orleans one time, and got kind of fascinated by the whole thing. I understand it started here in Mobile."

"Mardi Gras is 'Tribal Rites and Rituals'?" He chuckled. "Well, if you can explain why grown men and women dress up like freaks to throw moon pies and cheap beads off a ten-thousand-dollar parade float, I guess you deserve a PhD. I never finished college myself. Started a business a few years ago and never had time to go back."

A college dropout? That wasn't in the dossier. She had earned a masters in chemistry, plus five different certifications attached to her basic ATF law enforcement training, but a smart investigator wouldn't make assumptions about intelligence based on education.

"What kind of business?"

A little grin quirked his mouth. "I blow things up." Then, quite suddenly, chagrin clouded his expression. "Oh *man*."

Ding, ding, ding. Pay dirt. "What's the matter?"

"I used to tell people that—you know, as a joke." He sighed. "Only now it's not so funny."

"Why? Are you a demolitions expert or something?" Playing dumb was so much fun. She'd never had much chance to do covert work when she was in ATF.

Baldwin shook his head. "I'm a pyrotechnician. I own a fireworks design company, but a few weeks ago we had a bad accident." He reached up to cup his ear. "That's why my hearing's a little messed up right now."

Probably the source of a rather rakish scar on his cheekbone too.

She widened her eyes. "That's terrible." She'd be up for a Best Actress Oscar at this rate. *I'd like to thank my agent, who always believed in me ...*

"Yeah, it was bad. Destroyed most of my equipment and my big truck. And you should see the Convention Center." He looked depressed.

"I've heard of people getting killed in fireworks explosions. I think the whole thing's kind of fascinating." He gave her an odd look, and she belatedly realized how that had sounded. "I mean—your crew were okay, weren't they?"

"Yes, thank God." He shrugged. "I sure wish I could go back and undo that whole day, though."

"I bet." She waited, but he didn't elaborate. *Push him a little more, Susie. You may not get another chance.* "So what do you think caused it? The accident, I mean."

"According to the fire marshal, it was just a fluke. We may never know." He glanced at his watch. "Listen, I've got a gig tonight, so I need to go home and clean up. It was nice to meet you, Susannah." He gave her that sweet smile.

Reluctant to end the conversation, she followed him toward the gate. "I've had enough exercise for the day too. I'll walk that way with you." She produced a piercing two-finger whistle. "Monty! Let's go!"

Baldwin gave her an admiring look as the dog came bounding toward them. "I've never met a girl who could do that before."

"One of my big brothers taught me. I have three. Self-defense, you know what I mean?" They turned onto Williams Street. "What about your family? They here in Mobile?"

"No, they're over in Mississippi." He kicked aside a huge oak branch that had fallen across the sidewalk before she could trip over it. "I've lived here about eight years."

Susannah took a deep breath. Something fragrant was blooming in the hedges, which swarmed with bees. Every yard boasted colorful patches of those brilliant azaleas, purple wisteria, and white dogwood. Here and there fan-leaf palmettos and banana trees lent a tropical atmosphere. Really different from Tucson, where people landscaped with dirt, rocks, and cactus. She'd probably get homesick for the mountains in her backyard before long, but she enjoyed fresh surroundings. "It's such a pretty city."

"It's been my salvation." The sincerity of the deep voice drew her gaze, and Baldwin blushed. "I mean—like I said, I'm doing pretty well here." He grimaced. "I mean, I *was*."

Susannah wondered at the slight melancholy in his expression. Didn't exactly fit with somebody who was about to make a killing off an insurance payout.

Baldwin stopped in front of a small red-brick and clapboard cottage. Ornamental brick columns supported its deep front porch, and a couple of black-painted wooden rockers flanked a barbecue grill at one end.

She pulled Monty in with the leash. "This you?"

"Yep. Home sweet home."

Susannah took a quick survey. Small yard with thick, well-kept grass; a sweeping pecan tree on one side and a full-blown magnolia on the other. He even had a few flowers poking their heads up in the beds under the porch.

"Nice." She knew very few single guys who wanted the bother of keeping up a yard.

"Thanks." He looked away. Awkwardness descended again. "I'm sure I'll see you around. Tell Miss Elva Kay I said hey."

"Sure. See ya."

Like a genie disappearing back into his bottle, Baldwin ducked into the house, slamming the door behind him.

Oh, well. She'd pick up where they left off next time they ran together.

And they *would* meet again.

Quinn took a bottle of red PowerAde out of the refrigerator and gulped down half of it. Boy, what a workout. He had already run five miles before Susannah showed up, then she'd just about worn him out. She didn't run like most girls he knew.

Didn't talk like them either. That clean, crisp cadence to her voice made him want to listen. And he liked the way she laughed. He'd never been much good at talking to women. The things that interested him never seemed to appeal to the girls at church. But Susannah had seemed intrigued by the fireworks topic. He'd found himself talking to her, forgetting to be self-conscious.

He wandered over to the tank on the kitchen table, where his ball python, Bob, lay in a neat coil next to his rock.

"Hey, dude." He wiped his mouth on his sleeve. "What's for dinner?"

Bob apparently wasn't in a chatty mood. He didn't even look up.

"Okay, my turn to cook. How 'bout mouse for you and macaroni and cheese for me?"

He fed the snake first, then went about preparations for his own simple meal. Out of self-preservation, he had gotten to be a fairly good cook over the last few years. Then when Miss Elva Kay started sending the recipes, he'd gotten even better.

Quinn figured anything worth learning was worth learning right—in baseball, fireworks, and life in general. Which was why it had made such good sense when Clint Harrison had told him how to walk with Christ. Like a fallow garden planted with the right seed at the right time, he'd soaked up the good news.

And—call him simple—but he was looking for the rhyme and reason behind that explosion. God didn't just allow things to happen arbitrarily.

The stove timer went off, and he dumped the steaming macaroni into a colander, proud of himself when he burned his hand and didn't swear. *Making progress*, he thought, cutting up a hunk of Velveeta cheese for the sauce.

Once the dish was in the oven, he leaned against the counter to watch the mouse begin its long trek through Bob's digestive system. *"Bon appétit,"* he said, lifting the PowerAde bottle. His musings about divine purpose progressed to the leggy blonde he'd just left on his front sidewalk. "Reckon why God sent *her* along?"

Bob had nothing to contribute to the conversation. The mouse moved a millimeter or so.

"Guess I could have invited her to church."

But that seemed kind of presumptuous since he'd just met her. Maybe he would run into her again, and he could ask her if she had a church home. Wasn't that where you were supposed to start?

Since Bob's gastronomical functions seemed to have absorbed whatever counsel he might otherwise have supplied, Quinn decided to take a shower while the macaroni baked.

The job tonight wouldn't pay much, but after the Mardi Gras explosion cash flow had been a bit of a problem. Especially with the insurance company dragging its feet. To be expected, he guessed, but still disappointing. Providing special effects for a teenage beauty pageant in Satsuma, Alabama, was small potatoes compared to the twenty- and thirty-thousand-dollar country club gigs he was used to.

He was having a hard time getting inventory in too. Should be taking a trip to Taiwan within the next few weeks for an international fireworks exposition, but the travel funds just weren't there right now. He'd made several phone calls to the insurance company during the past month, trying to speed up the payoff on his premium. That was what it was there for, right?

He leaned both hands against the shower wall, letting the spray blast the top of his head. Worry, an old habit, was eating up the lining of his stomach. He knew it was wrong, and he knew how to overcome it.

There'd been a time, when he was working at the docks, that he'd been all but homeless—bumming a place to sleep off of friends and eating at the Salvation Army a few times a week. God had rescued him then, when he least deserved it. Given him a reason to live, good friends, a church family. Even a house, a real place to live. And the business. In spite of the accident, Quinn knew he was born to serve God with fireworks. Crazy, maybe, but he *knew*.

Lord, walk me through this, and I'll see what I can be for you.

chapter 3

Monty slunk through the living room with his tail between his legs. He waited for Susannah to open the door to the attic, then scrabbled up the stairs before the cat could get him.

"Miss Elva Kay, where are you?"

Susannah's landlady was a widow, but southern custom seemed to require addressing one's elders in this pseudo-familiar fashion. She was all for learning to talk like the natives if it would smooth the investigation.

"In here, love."

She followed the sweet elderly voice through the room to her left, which Susannah had yet to explore. Decorated in tones of gold, deep red, and mahogany, it featured a huge table spread with an ivory cutwork tablecloth. A glass-front china hutch, filled with enough dishes to serve a small third-world country, dominated one wall.

Susannah let out an inelegant whistle. Dad had raised her and the boys on plastic utensils and Chinette. If Monty ever got loose in here, it was all but over.

Following the scent of nutmeg and cinnamon, she located her landlady in the kitchen adjacent to the dining room. Sunshine poured through a bank of curtainless windows, across a butcher block table, and spilled onto the honey-toned wood floors. Deep walnut cabinets lined two of the remaining walls; a backyard door and stairs led down to a basement on the third. The effect was warm, practical, and homey.

Mrs. Shue, a little dumpling of a woman dressed in pistachio-colored knit slacks and a flowered top, looked up from her task of smearing icing on a cake. "How's my little Yankee today?"

Susannah grinned. She wasn't anybody's "little" anything, and in her mind Yankees lived in New England. "Pretty sweaty." She looked down at herself. "Is it okay if I take a shower?"

Elva Kay squinted through Coke-bottle glasses decorated with pink rhinestones as she artistically swept the spatula across creamy white frosting. "Certainly, but be careful with the hot spigot. The upstairs plumbing is a little contrary."

Susannah patted herself on the back for having interpreted two sentences with most of the final consonants left off and an extra syllable in every word. She hooked a thumb at the leftover icing. "Are you done with that?"

"Knock yourself out, sugar." Elva Kay handed over the bowl. Squirting detergent out of a bottle covered in a frilly calico apron, she began to wash dishes.

Susannah sat down at the table under the window and popped a fingerful of butter cream frosting into her mouth. Elva Kay might be courting eighty, but she was one happening chick. Remembering Quinn's "techno-babe" comment, Susannah smiled. "Guess who I met this afternoon while I was running?"

"Who?" Elva Kay stood on her tiptoes to peer over Susannah's head. "Oh, me. There's Mr. Hays, wandering down the street in his bedroom slippers again. Let me just give his sitter a call."

While Elva Kay picked up the phone to tattle on her neighbor, Susannah polished off the frosting and watched the truant old fossil shuffle his Dearfoams along the sidewalk. She'd lived such an isolated life for the last few years that the idea of neighbors watching out for one another was rather a novelty.

Elva Kay put the phone back in its wall cradle. "The Hays family has a teenager sit with him on Saturdays. She says she got a text message from her boyfriend and took her eyes off Mr. Hays just for a minute." She smiled at Susannah. "Now—who did you see?"

"Your yard boy."

"Yard boy? I don't have a—oh, you mean Quinn!" Elva Kay flapped her dish towel in delight. "Where did you meet him?"

"The track at the high school. Seemed like a nice guy."

"Oh, you'll never meet a sweeter boy, and he's had such a hard year." Elva Kay clucked like an elderly hen.

"Yeah, he mentioned the accident with the fireworks." Susannah got up to set the empty bowl in the sink. She eyed the virgin expanses of that magnificent cake. It seemed to be begging for somebody to cut a big hunk out of it. "Is that a hummingbird cake?"

Elva Kay smiled. "Matter of fact, it is."

"Could you teach me how to make one?"

"I'd be happy to." Elva Kay put the cake in a Tupperware container and moved it out of Susannah's reach. She winked. "But this one's for the jail inmates' Bible study tomorrow morning."

"You're going to give that to a bunch of convicts? Why?"

"Because Jesus said when we visit prisoners we're visiting him."

Susannah shook her head. "It might be worth going to jail for a slice of that cake."

Elva Kay laughed and began to wipe down the counters. "Tell you what. Come to church with me in the morning and I'll make you one of your very own for dessert tomorrow."

"I like to sleep in on Sunday mornings." Growing up, she'd gone to church with her dad and the boys every Easter and

Christmas. She'd enjoyed the music but hated the long-winded sermons. Be good, don't forget to pray, give lots of money. Blah blah blah. She was a good person. Her dad had taught her to love her country, to treat others with respect, to be honest, and to strive for excellence. You could do all that without wasting time on church. "Nice bribe, but—"

"That's too bad, because I'd like for you to get to know Quinn a little better. He goes to my church."

Baldwin was a church guy? He hadn't mentioned that. What kind of hypocrite would commit crimes like arson and insurance fraud, then have the nerve to show up in church? The quick answer: a smart one. Well, if she had to follow him there in order to nail his cute rear end, so be it.

"I guess I kind of got out of the habit a long time ago, but ..." Susannah stifled a sigh. "Maybe I should give it another try."

"I think you'll enjoy it. Our musicians do a good bit of that rock and roll stuff." Elva Kay lifted her hands and shimmied her skinny hips. "It's quite lively."

Susannah couldn't help laughing. *Techno-babe goes disco.* "Okay. There may be a problem, though. I don't own a dress."

"Oh, nobody but us old fogies wears a dress anymore." Elva Kay gave her a surreptitious glance as she hung her dishrag on the drain. "But we could go shopping for something new. You want to make a good impression."

Susannah would rather have a root canal. "I'm sure I've got something that will work."

"Let's go have a look. I've always had an eye for fashion." Elva Kay charged out of the kitchen.

Who'd have thought her job would have anything to do with her wardrobe? Shaking her head, Susannah followed.

By the time she made it up the stairs, Elva Kay was standing in the open doorway of her closet, hands on hips. She twitched at the one white blouse and khaki skirt hanging there. "Child, this is abysmal."

Abysmal? Whoa, the lady had quite a vocabulary. Susannah didn't think she'd ever heard anybody use that word in a sentence.

She made herself comfortable, cross-legged on the bed. "I just brought those in case there's a funeral."

"What are *these* for?" Elva Kay picked up a pair of purple suede cowboy boots.

"To go with the—"

"You are *not* going to wear this to church tomorrow." Elva Kay lowered her glasses a notch. "Where are the rest of your clothes?"

Hiding a grin, Susannah waved a hand at the armoire. So she was fashion challenged.

Elva Kay poked through the armoire for a few minutes. "Ah. This will work." She pulled out Susannah's favorite jeans and a bright blue ethnic blouse she'd had since her father was stationed in the Philippines. She'd never worn it, just kept it for sentimental reasons. "But not the boots. Or tennis shoes," she added with a glance at Susannah's feet.

"All right." Susannah wrinkled her nose. Her first choice would have been her beige pullover, which would have drawn less attention to her height. But who was she to argue with a five-foot-two octogenarian who had control of the food supply? "As long as you don't make me go shopping."

"Look, I had nothing to do with it." Backstage at the Satsuma High School auditorium, Quinn ran a finger under the tight collar of his rented tux. "Miss Elva Kay called and asked me to pick Susannah up. What was I supposed to say?"

Skeet plugged in the bubble machine. "Elva Kay drives a car the size of the Death Star. Why couldn't she take her?"

"She said she has the jail ministry Bible study, then nursery duty." Quinn shrugged. "I really wanted to invite Susannah to come anyway. Just didn't have the nerve to do it."

"Dude, this is so not like you." Skeet pressed his fingers to his temples à la Carnac the Magnificent. "Let me guess. She's built like Uma Thurman."

"You are so full of it."

Skeet was just fooling around, but sometimes he had frightening bouts of clairvoyance. The first thing Quinn had noticed about Susannah Tait—besides that long, athletic stride—was the fact that she could nearly look him straight in the eye. Second was the pure cobalt of her eyes—the most difficult chemical color to produce, rare and wonderful in a sky painter's palette.

He glanced across the stage to make sure Rebecca was out of earshot. "She seemed lonesome. And she's got a great dog."

Skeet wiggled his brows. "Is that what they're calling it now?" He shoved the bubble machine over an inch with his foot. "You know, missionary dating is a bad idea."

Irritated by a vague sense of guilt, Quinn checked the diagram on his PDA. "Look, we're going to church, not the prom. Besides, for all I know she might be a Christian, and I told you Miss Elva Kay's the one who invited her."

"Whatever you say." Skeet lifted his hands. "Anyway, it's too late now. What time will we get through here? I need to restring my guitar before I go to bed."

Quinn looked at his watch. "Supposed to kick off at seven and finish around nine. Can you and Rebecca handle the computer while I go pretend I know what I'm doing?"

"No problem." Skeet chuckled. "I can't believe they asked you to judge."

"Me either." Physical fitness he understood, but what did he know about poise, talent, and scholarship? The chairwoman of the pageant committee had asked him to judge, and in a moment of total distraction following the Convention Center debacle, he'd agreed.

He headed for the backstage door and found his way blocked by Rebecca. She scowled at him, hands on hips, looking exactly like the chick in the *Scooby-Doo* cartoons — the one with the kneesocks and glasses, not the hot one. "Who's Susannah?"

Nothing like a direct invasion of privacy. The girl had ears like a bat. "My new neighbor."

"I don't know anybody named Susannah." Something about the way she looked at him made Quinn's collar even tighter.

"Contrary to popular belief, you do not know everybody in Mobile County." Which might not even be true. As far as he could tell, Rebecca was related to half of the state of Alabama.

"Touchy, touchy." She sniffed. "So what does she do?"

Quinn gave her a blank look. "I guess she likes to run, that's how I met her."

"No, doofus, what does she do for a living?"

He scoured his memory. "I don't think she has a job. She said she was a grad student."

"Men." Rebecca rolled her eyes. "All you were interested in was her legs."

Skeet's hiked eyebrows plainly said *I told you so*.

"Rebecca." Quinn folded his arms. "I am your boss, and you're not going to talk to me that way."

She wrinkled her button nose. "What are you going to do, fire me? As if."

"Maybe I should," he growled. "Then you'd have to go to college like your mom wants you to." Remembering the title of Susannah's doctoral thesis, he smiled.

Rebecca gave him a suspicious look. "What's so funny? I don't need college. *You* didn't need college."

Stepping around her, Quinn stuffed his PDA into his pocket. He had to get out of here before he said something he'd regret.

Squirming on Elva Kay's living room sofa, Susannah stared at the snooty face of Great-Aunt Josephine, whose portrait hung in dour splendor above the mantel. Why anybody needed a fireplace in a city where the average annual temperature was 67.4 — she'd looked it up on the Internet before moving here — defied explanation.

If Baldwin was going to be late, he could have called. Elva Kay said she'd given him her cell number so that if anything came up he could get ahold of her. She glanced at the antique grandfather clock ticking like a bomb near the hallway door and sighed. It was only nine o'clock, which meant he wasn't late. She was early. According to Elva Kay, her chauffeur was supposed to pick her up at 9:15. Something about stopping for donuts on the way. Everything these people did revolved around food, and the more sugar-loaded the better.

She straightened her top. Goodness knew why she was ready so early. Nerves, maybe. How was it that a woman who could investigate a bomb scene without turning a hair suddenly freaked over going to church? Sometime around seven o'clock she'd heard Elva Kay thumping around in the kitchen right below her bed, singing a hymn loud enough to blow the roof off. She had no idea God got up that early. Unable to go back to sleep, she decided to get up and take a shower.

Maybe it wasn't just church. When Elva Kay told her she'd gotten called on for nursery duty and Baldwin was coming to take her to church, Susannah's pulse took a bounce of excitement. She hoped it wasn't just about being alone with him again. She was a professional, and it made sense to observe him in that context.

Figure out his angle. She didn't know anybody who did *anything* without an ulterior motive.

Except Monty, her only source of unconditional love. She made a face at Belshazzar, draped across the cushion in Elva Kay's antique rocker like a goddess in one of those Egyptian tomb paintings. The cat opened one amber eye, as if to say *Notice who's in the living room and who's banished to the attic.*

She looked at the clock again. 9:02. Sheesh. She needed something to pass the time. Opening her backpack, she took out the copy of the letter the insurance company had sent with her. It was her main piece of evidence that Baldwin was a crook. Laser printed on plain white copier paper, it claimed that SkyPainters Fireworks and Special Events had committed arson with the intent of defrauding its insurance company. In many cases, such a letter, unsigned and a bit vague, wouldn't be taken seriously, but it contained just enough detail to warrant an investigation.

The front door knocker banged. Susannah jumped and stuffed the letter back into her backpack. She bolted for the door.

"Hey! Sorry, I meant to be—" she swallowed—"watching for you." Yesterday's ratty shorts and T-shirt had given her no indication the guy could look this ... this *fine*. Clean-shaven, dark hair attractively rumpled, he had on jeans and a white cotton shirt. The sleeves were rolled up a couple of times, calling attention to bronze skin, strong wrists, and masculine hands.

Something about the way he looked at her created a flutter in her stomach.

"Am I dressed okay? Elva Kay said—"

"You're fine." He smiled. "You ready?"

"I guess." Susannah followed him out to his big gray and black Suburban, which he'd parked on the street. He walked like an athlete. Apparently he didn't just run for the fun of it.

She gave him a startled look when he opened the door for her and held her elbow to help her up onto the high seat. Whenever she got into a car with her brothers, if she didn't hurry she wound up chasing them down the street trying to catch up. She'd learned a certain amount of contempt for women who expected men to open doors and nonsense like that. Baldwin's protective gesture was archaic. And a little bit charming.

"Thanks, but I'm capable of getting into a vehicle by myself."

"I'm sure you are." He winked. "Are you gonna slap me with a sexual harassment lawsuit?"

"A l–lawsuit?" He was teasing, but it was close enough to the truth that it startled her. "Why would I do that?" She reached for the seat belt.

Definitely time to change the subject.

"I can't believe you've never had a Krispy Kreme." Quinn watched Susannah's mouth drop open as hot donuts, oozing white-sugar glaze, meandered down a conveyor belt behind a plate glass window. "You've had a truly deprived childhood."

"I've seen them. Just didn't know what the big deal was." She shook her curly head. "I can't believe people stand in this long a line for donuts." They were about halfway back in a snaking queue that made three turns and ended outside the door.

"Just wait 'til you put one of these in your mouth. This is where the chain started. We're talking the real deal." As always, the odor of yeast, sugar, and hot grease made Quinn's mouth water. The pleasure increased as he watched Susannah anticipate the treat.

"I feel like a pilgrim going to Mecca," she said, eyes glued to that enticing procession down the conveyor belt. "What should I have? Chocolate iced with jimmies? Lemon-filled?"

"Have one of each." Quinn gestured grandly. "My favorite is the crawlers."

"The what?"

"Crawlers." He pointed.

Susannah laughed. "Oh. Crullers."

"That's what I said. Crawlers. Don't tell me you say '*pee*-cans' instead of 'pe-*cahns*.'" He was getting a kick out of teasing her.

"Afraid so. You'll have to translate for me when we get to church."

"Be happy to." At last they reached the glass-front case with its staggering array of deep-fried pastry. He winked at his favorite blue-haired counter clerk. "Sadie, this young lady's from the wilds of Arizona, and she's never indulged. Can you fix us up with a dozen hot ones for here, plus another two dozen mixed to go?"

"A *dozen* for here?" Susannah tugged on his sleeve. "Look, I'm not that big a pig."

"Trust me. A dozen may not be enough."

"'Course I can, cutie-pie." Sadie flashed him a still-charming grin ringed with bright red lipstick. "Cup of coffee too?"

"Make it a large. Susannah?"

"Coffee's bad for you." She shuddered. "I'll have a Coke."

Sadie looked up from punching the order into the computer. "Will that be Coke, Sprite, root beer, or Dr Pepper?"

Looking confused, Susannah glanced at Quinn. "Coke?"

"Gotcha." Sadie waddled off to the back of the store, where she began to plop hot, gooey donuts into a box.

"Down here 'Coke' is generic for anything with soda in it." Quinn smiled as he pulled out his wallet and found a twenty. "I met Sadie when I first moved to Mobile."

Susannah looked distracted. "Look, I can pay for my own."

"My treat." When her sienna-colored eyebrows drew together in annoyance, he sighed. "You can buy next time."

"Okay. So where did you move here from?"

"I was in college at Mississippi State on a baseball scholarship. Blew out my shoulder and had to quit."

He was about to elaborate when Sadie came back with their food. After settling up, he found two stools at the old-fashioned counter, between an old man in overalls and a black family dressed for church. Quinn gave Susannah her soft drink with a straw, then opened one of the boxes of donuts.

"This has got to be illegal." She picked up a donut with two fingers, and it instantly squished into a ball of soft pastry. She stuffed half of it into her mouth, eyes closing in patent ecstasy.

"See, I told you." Watching Susannah's pleasure made his own donuts taste even better.

A smile lit her blue eyes as she watched the farmer flirting with Sadie. After a moment she wiped her mouth and rested her elbows on the counter. She sighed. "I like this place. Thanks for bringing me."

He lifted his shoulders. "One of my favorite spots. I used to hang out here when I worked down at the docks. Sadie was nice to me, gave me day-old donuts sometimes when I couldn't—" Maybe she didn't need to know right off the bat what a loser he used to be. "She's a sweetheart."

"I can tell." She tilted her head. "When you played ball, were you a pitcher?"

"Yeah. How did you know?"

"The way you walk. All three of my brothers played baseball in high school. I went to all the games and kept score."

"I would have thought basketball would be in your family."

"That too. But not me. I ran cross-country."

"Huh. Not surprised." That explained her fine, loping stride the other day at the track. "Where's the rest of your family?"

"Dad's retired navy. Just last month he bought a motel in Tucson." She paused. "My mom died when I was five."

"I'm sorry to hear that." It could explain some of her tomboyish manner, and the independence. "What about your brothers? Are you close?"

"Depends what you mean by 'close.' They're all older. Justin followed Dad into the navy. Jordan's FBI, lives in Virginia; and Jeremy and his wife are in Phoenix. He's a policeman. So we don't get together much."

"And you're a sociologist. The rest of your family seems to be in military and law enforcement. You broke the mold, huh?" Quinn started to wipe off a flake of sugar at the corner of Susannah's mouth with his thumb. Her eyes went wide, and he shoved a napkin at her instead.

Susannah wiped her lips and brushed sugar off the front of her blouse. "Dad always said, 'If you can't eat it, wear it.' What about you? You went to school in Mississippi, right? Is that where your family is?"

"Yep, just across the state line." He didn't go into details. His family was one royal mess. "We should probably go. I'm supposed to have these donuts at church by ten for fellowship time."

"Oh, okay." Susannah got to her feet and helped dispose of their trash.

To his amusement, she charged out the door ahead of him and jumped into the truck before he'd even managed to pick up the two boxes of donuts. He met Sadie's quizzical look.

"Yankees," she said, wiping down the counter. "Always in a hurry."

chapter 4

Susannah had never been in a church where rock-and-roll music was accepted, much less played at ear-splitting levels. Well, it was rock and roll of a sort. She looked at the lyrics, projected onto screens behind the band. They had nothing to do with drugs, sex, or misery.

God this, God that.

But she had to admit it was fun to listen to. Music had always been a big part of her life growing up.

On the third row beside Quinn, she stared in fascination at the bass player, a little shrimpy guy with a wild shock of bleached-blond hair and a tuft of hair under his lower lip. Like an MTV rocker he jumped around his end of the stage—she didn't know what else to call it, since it didn't look like any pulpit she'd ever seen—to a rhythm so captivating she found her own feet moving. Catching on to the chorus after it repeated a couple of times, she self-consciously began to sing along. Fortunately, everybody else sang loud enough to drown her out—even Quinn, and he was sure no Andrea Bocelli.

She felt like ET hiding in Elliott's closet. Afraid somebody was going to realize she didn't belong and throw her out on her tush. She didn't know what to do with her hands. Lots of people waved theirs in the air like they were under arrest. What was that all about? Quinn sang with his hands stuffed in his pockets, but at least he looked relaxed. Comfortable. Happy even.

When she looked up at him, he bumped her elbow with his and leaned over, his voice rumbling in her ear. "Whatcha think?"

"I like the music!" she shouted over the amplifiers.

He laughed and went back to singing.

She looked around as the music ended and they all sat down. This church was different from anything she'd ever experienced, and it wasn't just the southern accents. A few people were dressed up in funeral clothes, but most wore jeans like her and Quinn. It didn't matter that she didn't have a Bible. Quinn had offered to share his, but the text, projected onto the screens, had been translated into modern language that any fourth grader could understand.

It even made sense. God loved people, designed each one for a reason. Maybe she'd known that deep down. Going about her own business, she'd assumed she had it all together enough that words in a Bible couldn't make a lot of difference.

The thing was, she wasn't as together as she wanted everybody to think. Maybe ... maybe there was something a little deeper about this Christianity thing than she'd wanted to admit.

She tuned out the preacher, but her heart still felt heavy. Why? She couldn't think of anything she had to be guilty about.

Except for lying to Baldwin, when he'd been so nice to her.

She sneaked a glance at him. He sat quietly, hands gripping his thighs, eyes closed, and lips moving. Praying, probably. For who? What kinds of things would be on the mind of a guy like that? He'd gone to a lot of trouble to be nice to her today, for no particular reason. Was he praying for her?

A pinch of resentment pierced the bubble of curiosity and lingering guilt. Who did he think he was? *He* was the guy under suspicion of insurance fraud.

And she'd almost felt sorry for him.

A few minutes later he opened his eyes and glanced at her. She gave him a sunny, unaffected smile.

He could act, so could she.

If Elva Kay didn't escape the nursery and rescue him soon, Quinn didn't know what he was going to do. Susannah clearly wanted to bolt out of the room. He'd been watching her, hoping she wasn't bored or turned off. Now that the service was over he couldn't even look at her without blushing.

Maybe the problem was too much physical attraction. Most of the women who entered his orbit—girls with overstyled hair, long polished nails, and multiple layers of Mary Kay—left him cold. But when Susannah, wearing a sleeveless top the same thermonuclear color as her eyes, had yanked open Elva Kay's front door, he'd have been hard pressed to remember his name. He'd always been a sucker for long, curly hair.

He'd managed to talk to her just fine while they were at Krispy Kreme. But the longer they stood here together, the odder the vibes got. She'd seemed to enjoy the music. Sometime during the sermon, though, an invisible wall had gone up between them. Had he done something to put it there? He couldn't think of anything offensive he'd said.

Where was Elva Kay?

Normally, after church a bunch of singles would pile into a restaurant and hang out for a couple of hours. That would help. Safety in numbers. But what if people thought he and Susannah were a couple? He wasn't ready for that. This whole scenario was all no-man's-land. The calendar on his PDA was filled during the week, but he left Sundays open for the Lord. Which was fine as long as things stayed safe and normal.

He had a feeling there was nothing safe about Susannah Tait.

Lord, what do I do now?

Skeet was occupied putting away instruments and sound equipment. No help there.

He glanced at Susannah again. She was watching Dana Carter and a couple of her clones, who were jabbering over on the other side of the room.

Okay, there ya go. Another woman would make Susannah feel welcome—and take the pressure off of him. Dana, a little five-foot munchkin with dimples and big brown eyes, scared him to death. But this was an emergency. Without giving himself time to chicken out, he lifted a hand and caught Dana's eye. She beamed and shot toward him like a bottle rocket, tailed by Katherine and Charlotte Forbes.

"Quinn!" Dana caught her breath. "Hey, I was hoping you'd introduce me to your friend. I'm Dana Carter!" She offered her hand to Susannah. "And here's Katherine and Charlotte Forbes. They're sisters!"

Susannah nodded to the other girls, who backed off in deference to Dana's position as socialite queen. "Susannah Tait."

"We're so glad you came! Are you new to Mobile?" Dana's sparkling gaze moved from Susannah to Quinn. "Where did you two meet?"

"The track at Murphy," Quinn said at the same moment Susannah said, "I'm from Arizona."

Dana giggled. "Aren't y'all cute? Quinn, you should make sure she joins the running club."

Amusement lurked in Susannah's blue eyes. "That sounds like fun."

Dana propped her tiny hands on her hips. "Listen, would y'all like to go to lunch with us? We're going to the Tea Pot."

Quinn froze in horror. He should have anticipated this. Chick food. This had been a very, very bad idea.

But Susannah shook her head. "Thanks, but my landlady's got lunch for us."

Quinn blinked. "She does?"

"I was supposed to tell you and I forgot." Susannah gave him an apologetic look.

"That's okay, maybe next time." Dana didn't seem upset. "Ooh, there's Miss Elva Kay. I wanted to ask her how many women came to know the Lord at the jail this morning." She waved, and Quinn turned around to find his neighbor coming into the worship center from the nursery wing.

"Hello, children!" Elva Kay bustled over, smiling. "Gracious, we must have had fifteen bed babies this morning. I think they're taking this 'be fruitful and multiply' command a little too seriously." Nodding at the Forbes sisters, she took Dana's hand and squeezed it. "The ladies enjoyed your plum cake so much, honey."

Susannah gave Quinn a bewildered look.

"They take food for a Bible study at the jail on Sunday mornings," Quinn said.

"Oh, yeah, the hummingbird cake." Susannah brightened. "Don't I get one of those today too?"

"Yes, indeedy." Elva Kay fished in her purse for her keys. "Which reminds me, I've got to get home and make gravy before you all get there. Dana, why don't you girls and Skeet come too? There's plenty."

"We've already got plans, but thanks so much. Come on, Miss Elva Kay, we'll walk you out to your car." Hooking arms with Elva Kay, Dana twinkled at Susannah. "*So* nice to meet you! I hope we'll see you again."

"Us too," echoed the Forbes duo.

"Thanks." Susannah lifted a couple of fingers as the other women headed for the exit. He couldn't interpret her expression. Cynical didn't quite get it. Bemused maybe.

By now the worship center was almost empty. Quinn looked around for Skeet. "No telling where he is," he told Susannah. "He gets distracted real easy." He pulled out his cell phone and pushed his friend's speed-dial number. "Hey, man," he said when Skeet answered. "Where are you?"

"Right behind you."

Quinn turned around just in time to watch Skeet's hazel eyes widen as he vaulted over a row of chairs.

"You must be Susannah. I'm Skeet."

"The bass player, right?" She smiled down at him and shook hands. "Interesting name. Is that one of those southern family things?"

"It's a long story. My real name is Jedediah, which is even worse. You can call me either Jed or Skeet." Skeet tore his gaze away to look at Quinn. "So what's happenin'?"

"Are you up for some of Elva Kay's pot roast and mashed potatoes?"

Skeet did a little jig. "Is the Pope Catholic? I'll meet you there."

Quinn met Susannah's laughing eyes. No telling what impression she was forming about his friends. *Oh, well, we are what we are.*

Outside, headed for the parking lot, he smiled at her. "I hope we didn't weird you out too much. Our pastor's always interested to know if newcomers feel welcome."

She was silent for a few steps. "I felt welcome." She glanced at him. "I like your friends."

"Dana's kind of a ditz, but she's a nice girl." There was a crack of thunder, and he looked up at the steel-dark clouds hovering over the bay.

Susannah didn't seem to notice, even though the wind was blowing her hair around, turning it into wild, alluring ringlets. "It was different from churches I've been to before."

"Uh, is that good or bad?"

"Well, it sure wasn't *boring*."

The rain started, and they had to run for it. Laughing and wet, they reached his vehicle. The dye from Susannah's blue shirt had started to bleed down her bare arms. She looked like a Maori princess.

A really blonde one.

"Bad choice of clothing." She mopped herself with a towel he kept under the seat. "I told Elva Kay I should have worn beige."

Quinn started the engine and pulled out onto Dauphin Street. "I know not to go anywhere without an umbrella."

"That'll be my first purchase tomorrow morning." She looked out the window. "Monty hates storms."

"I didn't used to be real wild about 'em myself. But the Convention Center would've burned to the ground if it hadn't come a frog-strangler the night it caught fire."

"Really?" She gave him her full attention. "When did the rain start?"

"I don't know. Maybe twenty, thirty minutes after the first explosion? Everything was so crazy that night." He shrugged. "I figure God intervened big time."

He glanced at Susannah as he turned onto Elva Kay's street. There was a residue of something thoughtful in her eyes before she smiled. "Maybe he was asleep when things went wrong, and the blast woke him up."

Quinn didn't answer. He hoped she was kidding.

"My grandmother used to call these cat-heads."

Susannah peered into the basket Quinn passed to her. It was full of massive biscuits dripping with butter. "Hummingbird cakes and cat-head biscuits. What next?"

Skeet winked. "I'm pretty sure the name refers to size, not ingredients."

"Belshazzar will be relieved to hear that, I'm sure." Elva Kay took the basket from Susannah and set it next to a crystal vase full of camellias from her yard. "So how'd you like our church?"

"The music was a lot of fun." She smiled across the table at Skeet. "You ought to be playing in a band."

"Well ... that *was* a band."

"No, I mean—I mean a *real* band. Like on MTV."

Quinn rescued her. "The guys play in a coffeehouse on Friday nights sometimes. They're working on a CD."

Susannah sat up. Live music. "Could I come listen next time you play?"

"Sure, if you want to." Skeet didn't seem offended by her faux pas.

"Skeet's a junior high band director in real life." Quinn passed her the butter. "Somebody should give him a purple heart."

Susannah grinned at Skeet. Besides the wild hair, he sported a couple of small hoops in the top of one ear. "I played oboe all the way through high school and college. You sure don't look like any band director I ever had."

"Yeah, I had a Mr. Dinkle too." Skeet swiped a biscuit out of the basket. "Polyester pants and military shoes wouldn't go over real well where I teach."

Quinn stared at Susannah. "You were in the band at Arizona? I never met anybody who plays the oboe."

"I switched to piccolo during marching season." She shrugged. "Guess that makes me a band geek, huh?"

"Hey!" Skeet scowled in mock indignation. "I make my living creating little band geeks."

"And the world is a much better place for it." Elva Kay patted his hand and turned to Susannah. "What kind of church did you grow up in, dear?"

"We moved around a lot, so my dad thought it was pointless to join a church." Susannah saw Quinn and Skeet exchange glances. Had she just flunked some kind of test? "But on special occasions we went to the chapel on base."

Skeet pushed back his plate. "You should come again next week. Quinn's going to give his testimony."

"Testimony? You mean like witnessing in court?" These people seemed to speak a kind of code language she didn't always get.

"Sort of." Quinn picked up his tea glass and rattled the ice. "I'll just tell how I came to know Christ, and what he's doing in my life now."

Susannah squirmed. Now he was going to start preaching at her.

But he reached for the tea pitcher and refilled his glass. He smiled at her. "Want some more?"

"Just a little. I've already had enough sugar for one day." Susannah relaxed as Skeet got up to help clear the table and Elva Kay went to the kitchen for the cake.

Quinn refilled her glass, then touched it with his in a teasing toast. "If we get too overwhelming, just tell us to back off."

"Okay." She hesitated, trying to puzzle him out. Gentle, intense, self-effacing. So different from her rowdy, often obnoxious brothers. "But you can practice your speech on me sometime ... if you want to."

She hadn't meant it to sound suggestive, but she found herself electrified by a pair of keen gray eyes sweeping her face. Sudden awareness flared between them. "Susannah." He exhaled a long breath. "I hope I'm not sending wrong signals."

Wrong signals? What was he talking about? She'd seen the way he watched her.

She forced a light tone. "Hey, I'm just making conversation. Relax."

Red slashing his cheekbones, Quinn shoved his chair back. "Okay. I just—I just—" He picked up his plate and silverware. "Excuse me. I'll be right back."

Susannah watched Quinn stalk toward the kitchen. Now she'd embarrassed him. How was she going to fix this one?

"Skeet, come here." Quinn shoved open the door to Elva Kay's screen porch without waiting for his friend to follow. He wished he could take off, but his hostess would think he was nuts.

Which he probably was.

Monty, lying asleep on a braided rug in the corner, woke up and gave him a friendly woof. He knelt to scratch the dog's ears and received a tongue swipe across the chin. How did such a confusing woman wind up with such a great pet?

He heard the door screech behind him and turned to find Skeet carrying two china dessert plates loaded with cake. Quinn's mouth watered at the smell of bananas and cream cheese and cinnamon.

"Elva Kay insisted." Skeet grinned. "The equivalent of port and cigars in the library, I guess."

"Why are all the good women either married or eighty years old?" Quinn took the plate and shoveled in a mouthful of cake.

Skeet's eyebrows rose as he sat down in the swing. "What just happened in there? Susannah looks like she swallowed a persimmon."

"I'm not sure. She—she—" Quinn took a breath. "I thought she was hitting on me, and I said the wrong thing."

"Dude, she *is* hitting on you." Skeet set the swing in motion. "You should see the way she watches you."

Speechless, Quinn ate another bite, then two more.

Skeet shook his head. "There's something a little off about her, but I'm not sure what it is."

"You mean like …" Quinn twirled a finger at his temple.

"No. At least I don't think so." Skeet frowned. "Maybe it's that western independent thing. She's just different from other girls around here."

"That's for sure. She doesn't beat around the bush about anything." Quinn sighed. "Maybe I misunderstood her."

"So what did you say?"

Quinn shrugged. "I just told her I didn't want to send wrong signals. You heard what she said about her church background. She doesn't have a Bible, her clothes are on the verge of immodest, and I've noticed her catching some cuss words. I'm pretty sure she's not a Christian."

"Tell you the truth, I get that impression too."

"So what do I do now?"

Skeet's brow wrinkled. "Do what Joseph did with Potiphar's wife, man. Run."

Quinn looked at the pile of moist cake and fluffy frosting, his appetite gone. If he were gut-level honest, he didn't want to run. Susannah was beautiful and confident. Frank and honest and sharp with intelligence. The kind of woman he could imagine dating—that is, if he could ever get up the nerve to ask.

"I tried introducing her to some of the girls at church, Dana and her gang." He looked at Skeet and found him grinning. "What's so funny?"

"I can just imagine what she thought about Yum-Yum, Pitti-Sing, and Peep-Bo." Fluttering his eyelashes, Skeet put his fingers under his chin and sang in falsetto, "Three little maids from school are we ..."

"You are sick, man." Quinn laughed in spite of his confusion.

"Can I help it if my mother dragged me to every Gilbert and Sullivan production within a hundred-mile radius?" Skeet composed himself. "Look, God's gonna have to handle Susannah. Maybe he's brought her into our orbit for a reason. But *you*—" Skeet pointed his spoon for emphasis—"play it straight. And leave your cloak behind if you have to."

chapter 5

Susannah stood at the window watching Quinn and Skeet pull away from the curb. The rain had started to come down in hard, driving sheets, obscuring the front yard and narrow street.

Depressing.

She'd never had trouble developing friendships with men. Why did this one elude her?

Skeet was okay. She understood musicians, and his skewed sense of humor was a kick. But Baldwin ... How could she have so completely misread him?

Sighing, she went out on the screen porch to check on Monty, who was chowing down on the roast beef bone Elva Kay had given him. He ignored her when she sat down on the swing.

When Baldwin had come back inside with Skeet, he'd acted like nothing had happened. Maybe nothing *had* happened. But it sure felt like it did. She could look in his eyes and see the wall.

She'd tried to take his "wrong signals" remark in stride, but it had *hurt*. It felt like he'd been nice to her just to make an impression on a guest at church. She wasn't expecting a declaration of undying love after two days' acquaintance, but the least he could do was flirt back a little.

On the other hand, Susannah, you are an emancipated woman. Your self-esteem is not dependent on every guy on the planet making goo-goo eyes at you.

Susannah jumped when her cell phone went off. Maybe it was Baldwin calling to apologize.

She flipped open the phone. "Yes?"

"Susannah?"

"Jeremy!" Her youngest brother, just nineteen months older than she, was the only one of her brothers she had regular contact with. He called once a week or so. "Where are you?"

"At the station in Phoenix. What's with the attitude?"

She wasn't going to tell him she was pouting over being insulted by a handsome but socially backward southern boy. "It's raining. This is the soggiest city I've ever seen." She made an effort to lighten her voice. "How's Cherry?"

"In blooming health. In fact, she's blooming out of every maternity top she owns. If this baby doesn't hurry up and get here, we're going to wind up on the cover of the *National Enquirer.*"

"I hope you didn't tell her that." Susannah rubbed her foot across Monty's back.

"Well ..."

"Jeremy, you didn't!"

"Yeah, I'm a bit out of favor at the moment. That's why I'm working this afternoon."

"You are such a dork."

"I know." He laughed. "Dad said you had a new job. Where in the world is *Mo*-bile?"

"That's Mo-*bee*-ul," she said, dragging out the three-syllable pronunciation she'd heard from the natives. She was quite an accomplished mimic, and had been listening carefully to Elva Kay. "Not Mobil like the oil company. It's on the Alabama Gulf Coast."

"I stand corrected." He sounded amused. "I was just calling to see how it's going."

"I don't know. I've only been here a week." Though, in a way it seemed like a hundred years. "I'm doing an insurance investigation right now."

"No kidding? What's the case?"

She hesitated. How much to tell him? "I'm checking out a guy they suspect of arson with fireworks."

"Hey, that's cool. Fireworks has always been your hobby. Remember when you lit a bunch of bottle rockets and stuck 'em in your back pocket?"

"That was you, not me!"

"Not as I remember it." He paused. "Are you sure you weren't snarling at anybody specific when you answered the phone?"

Picturing Baldwin, Susannah felt her heart rate kick up a notch. "No. Not really."

"What's his name? I'll come punch his head for you."

"Thank you, Michael Corleone, but I can punch my own heads. Anyway, it was just a misunderstanding. No big deal."

"Okay, but if you need me, just yell. So did you go to church this morning?"

Susannah rolled her eyes. Jeremy, the only religious member of her family, had been after her forever to get involved in a church. "As a matter of fact, I did."

"Come on, Susie, it'll give some meaning to your—what did you say?"

"I said I went."

"That's—that's amazing. I'm not going to ask what kind. It was probably a Buddhist temple or a Hindu shrine."

"No, it was the standard Bible-thumping Jesus-is-the-Way thing." She paused, thinking of Skeet dancing with his bass guitar.

"Maybe a little different in practice. But the message sounded a lot like what you've preached at me since high school."

"I'm glad, of course. So what did you think?"

Susannah hesitated, unwilling to say how pleasantly surprised she'd been. The people she'd met had been friendly, and not nearly as weird as she'd expected. But give Jeremy an inch and he'd take ten miles. "It was kind of interesting, I guess."

"You'll call me if you have questions, won't you?"

"Don't hold your breath. That stuff's personal."

"I know, but … Look, Susannah, I don't ever want to push you into running away from God. But sometimes he makes an extra effort to speak to people. Please just listen for him, okay?"

She sighed. "Okay, okay already. But I'm not doing any whacked-out meditation or anything. I live in the real world."

"I know you do. I think that's part of the problem." Jeremy clicked his tongue. "I'd better go buy Cherry some flowers. Take care, sis, and like I said, call me if you need me."

"Okay. Bye, Jer." Susannah closed the phone.

She couldn't see how things would ever get bad enough that she'd need to resort to praying her way out of a situation.

Susannah awoke from a dream in which she was being chased by a cat with a chainsaw. What a relief to jerk upright and find that the only animal in her room was Monty, lying across her legs and snoring. Miraculous that she'd even heard her phone tweedling "Inspector Gadget."

Locating the phone under a crossword puzzle book, she remembered this time to look at the caller ID. Simon Webster, owner of the Birmingham-based insurance company she was contracted to.

Yikes, what did he want at—she squinted at the clock on the armoire—8:02 in the morning?

"Hello?" She lay back down, propping her feet on Monty's warm bulk. He snuffled in his sleep.

"Miss Tait? Simon Webster here."

Her ear was beginning to adjust to these molasses-like drawls. "Good morning. How are you, Mr. Webster?"

"Doing great, just great, thanks. I'm calling to see if you've gotten settled in, find out how things are going."

Susannah suppressed a yawn. Things would go a lot better if she'd had another hour of sleep. "I found an apartment in the same neighborhood as Baldwin. You'd almost think somebody upstairs likes me."

"Good, good. Have you met our boy yet?"

"Yeah. I found out he likes to run, so I arranged to bump into him at the local high school track. One thing led to another, and he took me to church yesterday morning."

"I'm impressed, Miss Tait. You're a fast worker. If you're as good at explosives investigating, we'll be in business." He paused. "So what did you think about Baldwin?"

He's built like a tree and sounds just like Matthew McConaughey.

Susannah reeled in her straying thoughts. "He's kind of sweet, actually, but I think I made him—" she fished for the right adjective—"uncomfortable yesterday. You didn't tell me he's sort of a prude."

Susannah could feel the temperature lower on the other end of the connection. "Miss Tait, what have you done?"

"I didn't *do* anything. That I know of. It's just this whole religious culture down here. I don't get it."

"You don't have to get it. You have two simple objectives. Interview everybody connected with that accident and reexamine the evidence from the site."

Susannah sighed. "There hasn't been much I could do about that over the weekend. I spent several hours on the Internet last night, looking up articles about the accident, but didn't find much. I'm planning to go downtown this morning. Check out the blast seat and the damage at the Convention Center."

"Good idea."

"Don't worry about the technicalities, Mr. Webster. If Baldwin set that explosion, I'll help you prove it."

"There is no 'if,' Miss Tait. You've read that letter. Independent Mutual is not paying out that kind of money on a fraudulent claim."

"Gotcha. Well, I have to run. Have a great day, Mr. Webster." Susannah closed the phone before she could say anything else to antagonize her client.

One of the first things she wanted to do was discover who had written that letter implicating Baldwin. She doubted it was Skeet. They seemed to be as close as brothers. But there were a couple of other part-time employees, plus the office assistant, Rebecca Mansfield. Susannah was going to probe each of them as soon as possible.

Rolling out of bed without bothering to make it up, she stumbled into the bathroom for a shower. She stood at the mirror staring at her reflection in dismay. Her hair had coiled tighter every day she'd been in this waterlogged city. Another week and she was going to look like Crimp and Curl Barbie.

Dressed in her jeans and a gray T-shirt that said "Wear Your Earplugs," she clomped down the stairs with Monty at her heels. After taking care of his business outside, the dog followed Susannah into the kitchen and scurried under the table. Belshazzar, perched like a vulture on top of the refrigerator, hissed.

Susannah frowned at the cat. "You guys are going to have to come to some kind of understanding. I can't play referee twenty-four hours a day. Howzit, Miss Elva Kay?" Her landlady, gray hair curled and sprayed into place, makeup perfect, sat at the table perusing the newspaper.

Elva Kay looked up and smiled. "'Morning, sugar. Did you sleep well? I saw your light on late. If you're hungry, I made some grits and eggs."

Ignoring the first two comments—her sleeping habits were nobody's business but hers—Susannah lifted the lid of the pot on the stove and picked up a spoon to poke at the steaming whitish substance. It looked a little like cream of wheat. She hated cream of wheat. "No thanks. I don't usually eat breakfast." Besides, all that sugar yesterday, beginning with the Krispy Kreme donuts, had sent her to bed with a headache.

Elva Kay looked scandalized. "But it's the most important meal of the day! At least sit down and have a cup of tea."

Susannah shrugged. "Okay, tea would be nice."

While her hostess put the kettle on, Susannah took the dog out to the screen porch, where she'd left his water and feed bowls and an enormous bag of dry dog food. "Gorge yourself, you big sissy."

Back in the kitchen she found Elva Kay setting two fragile teacups, with beautiful heavy silver spoons nested in the saucers, on the table. "Sit here while I pour." She patted the back of the second chair.

"Thanks, but I warn you I don't know the proper etiquette." Susannah plopped herself down.

Elva Kay picked up the matching pot in the center of the table and poured fragrant tea into Susannah's cup. "Have you never been to a tea party?"

"Nope." Susannah shoved her hair out of her eyes. "Even when he wasn't deployed, Dad had all he could do to keep the boys fed and out of trouble. My oldest brother, Justin, was in charge most of the time." She bent down to sniff the tea. It smelled like oranges. "I was lucky if I got a glass of milk and a cookie after school."

"Poor little girl." Clicking her tongue in sympathy, Elva Kay offered Susannah a tiny pitcher of cream and the sugar bowl. "Don't worry, I'm very informal at home."

"If you say so." Susannah declined the cream. She wasn't going to ruin a good cup of tea, even to please this nice woman.

"I'll have to reserve you a place at my table at our Ladies' Ministry Tea Party." Elva Kay sipped her tea, casting surreptitious looks at Susannah's hair. "Are you going out this morning?"

"Yeah, I have an errand to run." Susannah hoped she wasn't expected to post her comings and goings on a bulletin board. "Why?"

"I just thought if you're looking for a good hairdresser and manicurist, I'd tell you about the salon I go to." Elva Kay looked so sweet and sincere, Susannah couldn't help laughing.

"Thanks, but this mop is hopeless. And I don't have time to deal with fingernails." She curled her fingers to examine her nails. Bitten down to the quick, as usual. One of her few memories of her mother was getting her nails coated with hot sauce — no doubt the cause of her strong affinity for peppers as an adult.

Monty barked at the back door, and Susannah gulped down the contents of her cup. "Thanks for the tea. I'll have my cell with me if you need me."

Of course she didn't expect any more phone calls, now that she'd talked to Jeremy and Mr. Webster. Baldwin wasn't likely to call, after the way he'd reacted to her yesterday. Maybe she should spin by the library to look for a book on relating to the modern southern male.

Quinn had been staring at the computer for the last hour trying to figure out how he was going to pay for a trip to Taiwan. Asian fireworks expos were the best in the world. He always came away with good deals on materials and cutting-edge design ideas.

But a couple of his major venues were behind on settling up, and he'd be thousands of dollars in the hole if he didn't book something big. And soon. Time to call the insurance company again.

"So how was your date with the Arizona Amazon?" Rebecca peered over the top of her computer monitor.

"It wasn't a date. We just went to church together."

"Didn't you pick her up?"

Quinn wished he had someplace else to go. But their desks faced each other less than three feet apart in the front section of the warehouse he called an office. It was separated from the design and storage area by a couple of folding screens he'd picked up at a yard sale. Rebecca had decorated her side with a bunch of Thomas Kincaid prints that gave him claustrophobia every time he looked at them. One day he was going to redecorate. *Dogs Playing Pool*, maybe.

"Yes, but—" He frowned. "How'd you know that, and how'd you know she's from Arizona?"

"Dana Carter teaches kindergarten across the hall from my cousin Sheree who called me while her class was in P.E."

Rebecca went to a large Methodist church in west Mobile but had relational tentacles in every church in town. "I wish you'd mind your own business, Rebecca."

"Quinn, Quinn, Quinn." She tapped her pen against her blotter. "How old are you?"

"Twenty-nine. Not that *that's* any of your business either."

"And how many serious relationships have you had?"

"Rebecca—"

"Come on, how many? One? Zero?"

He frowned. "I'm taking my time."

"I rest my case. You know zippo about women. And you also didn't answer my original question."

"All right, Barbara Walters. I picked her up, and we had a nice time." At least, they had at first. He couldn't squelch a memory of Susannah's face when he'd given her his "wrong signals" warning. She'd been hurt, and it was his fault. *Why* was he so inarticulate around women? "We had an okay time. Church is always good."

"Then how come you've been so moon-eyed all morning?"

"I'm just *busy*. I have work to do. And so do you, for that matter."

"So are you going to ask her out again?"

"I didn't ask her out in the first place." Quinn cracked his knuckles. "I might," he blurted to his own astonishment.

"Aha! I knew it."

"You knew *what*? Will you please answer that phone? We just happen to be running a business here, and you *are* the receptionist."

"Executive assistant." Rebecca picked up the handset. "It's a great day at SkyPainters!" she chirped, though he'd told her a hundred times how goofy that sounded. "This is Rebecca! How can I help you?"

Quinn went back to his spreadsheet.

He heard Rebecca huff in irritation. "Skeet, you have played that dumb joke so many times, would you please get a life!"

A few seconds later he looked up when his "executive assistant" leaped to her feet behind her desk. She pressed the phone to her shoulder and looked at him wide-eyed. "Quinn," she whispered, "I think you'd better take this call."

"Ha ha. If it's the president, tell him I'm busy."

"Quinn." She swallowed hard. "It *is* the president. Of the United States." Thrusting the phone at him, she rushed off toward the restroom.

chapter 6

Not sure what to expect, Quinn put the phone to his ear. "This is Quinn Baldwin."

"Hey, Quinn. Will Fletcher here."

"Will! Man, what's going on?" Further confused, Quinn sat down in Rebecca's chair. He had met Skeet's longtime friend, a Nashville Christian entertainment lawyer, several years ago. The three men played golf together a few times a year when Will came to Mobile to enjoy the beautiful Gulf Coast courses. Quinn turned to look at the closed bathroom door. "You shook Rebecca up, you goofball. What did you say to her?"

"I told her I was calling from the White House. She kinda smarted off."

Quinn laughed out loud. "Good one."

"It happens to be true." Will chuckled. "Zoë and I moved to D.C."

"Huh? When did that happen?"

Will, the grandson of U.S. Senator Bart Fletcher from Mississippi, had for years avoided family pressure to enter politics.

"A few weeks ago. Grandpa's the chairman of the president's reelection committee, and he's had me do some work for him for the last couple of years. I'm, uh—" Will laughed sheepishly. "I'm the new campaign manager."

"Will, that's great!" Quinn smiled. "We need more believers in our government."

"Thanks. The timing was just right. Listen, I wanted to catch up with you, but there's another reason I called. A business reason."

"Okay, shoot." Quinn settled into the chair.

"I need some special effects, fireworks and confetti and stuff, for campaign speeches and—can you keep this on the QT?"

"Sure."

"Okay, I'm going to suggest they award the fireworks contract for the Republican National Convention to you. You've got a reputation for real artistry, and I need somebody I can trust." Will paused. "And when we win, I'd like you to handle the special effects for the inaugural celebration."

Quinn felt his jaw drop. "Will, you wouldn't kid me about something like this, would you?"

"Of course not, what kind of jerk do you take me for?"

"I'm—I'm—" Collecting his scattered thoughts, Quinn picked up his PDA with shaking hands. "I'm honored. Of course I'll do it. Do you have any initial dates and the venues to give me?"

"Sure, but I'll get back to you later about that. I think there are some background checks and things like that with Secret Service we have to handle first. Hang on, my secretary will give you the fax numbers you'll need, okay?"

"All right." Dazed with excitement, Quinn listened as Will put him on hold and "Walking on Sunshine" filled his ear. "Thank you, Lord," he whispered.

Maybe he could book that flight to Taiwan after all.

A few minutes later Quinn looked up from packing his portfolio as Rebecca came out of the restroom, makeup and self-assurance restored.

"There you are." He'd been afraid she would spend the rest of the afternoon in the bathroom. Rebecca didn't like to look foolish. "Listen, I've got a SERPA meeting in Biloxi." The Southeast Regional Pyrotechnics Association rotated its meeting locations monthly. As a founding board member, Quinn's presence was required. "I'll be gone all afternoon. Probably go straight to baseball practice."

"Fine." Rebecca scooted her chair up to her desk with a screech and flicked open her computer screen. "So what was that phone call about?"

Quinn picked up his keys. "That, my fine young executive assistant, was about us scoring the biggest contract in pyrotechnics history."

"It's about time. So what's the job?"

"Are you ready for this?" He leaned toward her. "They want us to do the national convention and the presidential inauguration!"

She adjusted her glasses. "I see two major problems."

Quinn sighed. "You would. I'm sure you're going to enlighten me."

"I would be happy to." She ticked off a manicured finger. "For one thing, there's no guarantee the president's going to win. It's only March, and a lot could happen between now and November."

"Come on, Rebecca, we're talking about one of the most popular presidents in recent history. If he runs, he wins." An avid political junky, Quinn read the paper every day and kept up with C-SPAN and the cable news.

Rebecca gave him a skeptical grimace. "And they want to hire *us*?"

"Didn't you hear me? They've already tapped me. That's what Will called about just now."

"You mean I might get to meet the president?" Dawning excitement widened Rebecca's eyes.

"Well, I'm not sure about that." Quinn handed her his PDA. "Copy down these fax numbers. They want names and addresses, Social Security numbers, all that stuff on you, me, Skeet, Phillip, and Russ."

"Okay, but what for?" Rebecca opened a new document on her computer.

"Security check, I think. Standard procedure for—"

"Security!" she squeaked. "What do you think's gonna happen when Homeland Security hears about the Convention Center blowup?"

"Would you tell me why you're being such a cosmic killjoy?" He frowned. "The accident wasn't my fault. The fire marshal confirmed it."

"Yeah, but what if they interview Russ and Phillip, and one of them says something stupid? They're liable to make something up that'll make us look bad, just for a joke."

Quinn looked at the ceiling. Her worry-wart attitude was going to drive him right over the edge. "Rebecca, breathe. It will be okay."

She scowled. "But what if the feds find something the local people didn't?"

"That's not going to happen. Whose side are you on, anyway?"

"Yours, of course. But if they ask me questions, I can't swear I was with you the whole time. I'm not telling lies even for you."

Quinn took a breath. "I don't expect you to tell lies, and I can't believe you think I'd want you to. Just—just be careful, okay? This contract may make the difference in us being able to stay in business."

Rebecca's brown eyes flickered. "Of course I wouldn't do anything to jeopardize my job. Goodness knows why, but I like working here—even if it *is* a run-down office in an abandoned air force hangar." She blew at her bangs. "I'm sorry if I seem ubernegative.

Phillip's been driving me crazy. I found out he lost his cell phone and put this expensive new one on Mom's charge card. Now he's racked up a bunch of text messages we can't afford to pay."

"Okay, I'm sorry for snapping at you." Some of the panic that had been seeping into Quinn's gut gave way to compassion. Between working full-time and shepherding her younger brother, Rebecca had had a lot of responsibility since her teens. "Look, why don't you take an extra hour for lunch today. Go shopping or something. You can set the voice mail to transfer calls to me."

Rebecca gave him a suspicious look. "You're not trying to buy me off, are you?"

Quinn closed his eyes and counted to ten. "Nobody with half a brain cell would try to coerce you into anything." He snapped his portfolio closed. "Before you leave for lunch, I want you to get hold of the insurance company. We've *got* to get them to pay our claim."

Rebecca reached for her Rolodex.

"And Rebecca—" Quinn paused in the doorway—"would you please be nice to anybody else who happens to call or come by? We can't afford to lose any contracts."

After slinging her backpack into the backseat of the Jeep, Susannah removed its windows, folded the top back, and cranked up the radio as she headed downtown.

She hated to leave Monty whining in the backyard, but he'd be fine once she was out of sight. He had a nice shady spot next to the back step, with plenty of water and food, and Elva Kay had promised to check on him during the day. Her landlady had planned a jaunt to the Junior League thrift store, where she volunteered once a week, and then a hair appointment.

Elva Kay had paused on her way out the door. "Are you sure you don't want me to ask Tricia to work you in, dear?"

"No thanks." After wadding her hair into a ponytail, Susannah had stuck a baseball cap on her head and called it good enough. No sense worrying about your hair when the wind would tear it to pieces in five seconds anyway.

And boy, was it a glorious day. Yesterday's rain had swept across the skies and disappeared over the bay, leaving a bright spring morning with nary a cloud in its wake. Susannah was in the mood to explore.

She'd found a map of Mobile on the Internet and spent an hour studying it last night. The city was laid out in a seashell pattern, with four main thoroughfares—Government, Dauphin, Old Shell, and Springhill—fanning westward from the point where the Mobile and Tensaw Rivers dumped into the bay. A grid of smaller streets cut across those four, with exotic French and Spanish names like Joachim, Conception, and Conti alternating with the more prosaic Jackson, Hamilton, Franklin, and Claiborne. Saints Joseph, Louis, and Anthony also found representation in the cultural mishmash of the antiquated little city.

Driving down Dauphin Street without the distraction of Quinn Baldwin's charismatic presence, Susannah found herself paying attention to the beautiful two-story French architecture. It reminded her of New Orleans. The warm red-brown brickwork of the oldest buildings crumbled in places, and scaffolds and tarps provided occasional eyesores but the hope of restoration. She found the ornamental wrought-iron railings, balconies, and grills charming.

Dad would love this place. Whenever he was on leave, he took Susannah and the boys on every historical tour within a five-hour drive—and sometimes farther. They'd explored New Zealand, Japan, Guam, Korea, and all parts of Europe.

In fact, if she hadn't had such a strong head for math and science, she'd have chosen historical studies for her lifework. A mile-wide practical streak convinced her she should make her living in a technical field, and indulge herself with history for a hobby.

As she passed the police precinct, then Baldwin's church, she thought about Jeremy insisting she "listen for God." Did God have anything to say to someone like her, who had pretty much ignored him most of her life? Did the Almighty just wake up one morning and say, "Hey, I think I'll go down and visit with Susannah Tait today. She looks like she could use a friend."

The thought, silly as it was, took her off guard.

You've got plenty of friends. The guys in Tucson ATF, for example, even though she hadn't heard from any of them in several months. After all, they were busy. And she exchanged Christmas cards with three different college roommates—when she happened to remember.

Yeah, and she had a great family. Sometimes she missed her mother with a fierce, aching need for someone to put loving arms around her. But Dad was solid as a rock; she could call him at any time and get good advice or a loan or whatever. The boys, as she thought of them collectively—Justin, Jordan, and Jeremy—were there too, if she got in a pinch.

She'd never been one of those women who needed girly, slumber-party type friendships. So what was up with this sudden itchy suspicion God had something to say to her?

Maybe turning thirty last Christmas had done something to soften her brain.

She stopped at a traffic light at the end of Dauphin Street, where it met Water Street. To her right she could see the glass and steel structure of the Convention Center with its massive three-level tower. Breathtaking, at least from the front. Squashed between Water Street and the river, it rose in a series of soaring green-roofed atriums with a flavor of the nostalgic in its design.

Baldwin's explosion had damaged this place, and if the insurance didn't cover it, he was going to have a heck of a time paying for it.

As she turned right onto Water Street, putting the river on her left, she noted a freight train lumbering along the riverbank. Beyond the train were the hulks of ships in dry dock, hoisted on cranes like dinosaurs in a museum. Farther downriver the colorful flags of a cruise liner snapped in the wind. Overhead a covered pedestrian bridge connected the Convention Center to an impressive high-rise hotel.

She smiled.

Ignoring people honking at the out-of-state yahoo wandering around well below the speed limit, she cruised on past the Convention Center. Just before ramping onto the interstate, she screeched into the parking lot of a steelworks and pulled into a slot marked "Employees Only." Catching herself looking for her ATF parking card to stick on the dash, she let out an irritated breath. She wouldn't be here long.

Crossing the railroad tracks, she came to a railed fence which opened into a beautiful terraced riverside park. She couldn't resist checking it out. Great place to run, if they'd let her bring Monty. At nine in the morning there wasn't much traffic, just a few young moms and the occasional bum sleeping on a bench.

Susannah leaned over the railing at the river side of the park. She stood there for a minute listening to the seagulls, the chug of motors along the waterfront, and traffic from the interstate nearby. A deep breath pulled in the scents of fish and salt and something fresh she couldn't put her finger on. Peaceful.

At least it was until she turned and saw the riverside view of the Convention Center.

Holy guacamole. It looked like a bomb had gone off. Which, in essence, she supposed, it had. A whole bunch of colorful bombs full of black powder and perchlorate stars.

Interesting, from an investigator's viewpoint, that the broken glass had been swept from the terraces along the outside of the building. Every pane of the glass that made up the outer walls had been replaced by plywood boards.

She walked back toward the entrance to the park and circled the courtyard until she encountered another barricade. Ignoring a sign posted "Danger: Keep Out," she stepped over the yellow tape and headed for the rear terrace.

No wonder Independent Mutual was reluctant to pay off this claim. She spent another ten minutes walking around the building, trying to peer into the charred interior. The electricity in the damaged section was off, of course, but by the daylight filtering in from outside, she could make out what had once been an exquisite carpet and a glint of brass chandeliers. She would have loved to take a closer look, but yellow barrier tape prevented her.

You're no longer ATF, lady. You're gonna have to get permission.

"I'm sorry, Miss, but you cain't park there," drawled a masculine voice behind her.

Susannah whirled to face a stocky middle-aged man in a hard hat. He had a mustache like a janitorial broom. She put a hand to her chest. "Goodness, you startled me!"

He hitched his tool belt under an impressive paunch. "I apologize for that, but you parked in my place. You're gonna have to move your car."

Susannah sighed. Whatever happened to southern hospitality? "I'm sorry. I'll move it in a minute. I couldn't get into the—"

"You ain't from around here, are you?" The man grinned.

"No, I'm a grad student from Arizona, and I was only going to look around here for a few minutes." She blinked at him as she'd seen the girls at church do yesterday, which lost something in translation as she towered over him by at least an inch. Leaning back against the terrace rail, she glanced at the name patch on the man's denim work shirt. "Listen, Jesse, you seem like a guy who pays attention to details. I'm interested in the fireworks explosion that messed this place up a couple of months ago. Were you anywhere nearby when it happened?"

"Yes, ma'am, I sure was." Looking gratified, Jesse folded his arms. "Dangedest thing I ever saw. Looked and sounded like an air raid." He squinted at Susannah. "Guess you saw me in the news. They had me on Channel 4."

Susannah had talked to a couple of reporters last week. But she didn't remember seeing this guy, famous as he was in his own mind.

"I guess I didn't recognize you. I can't remember where you were."

Jesse gestured over his shoulder with a huge callused thumb. "I was up in the office, just about to clock out for the night. Heard this humongous boom about six thirty when the truck exploded, then the fireworks started to go off. Looked out the window and dang if they wasn't shootin' straight across the river!"

"Wow, that must've been something else."

"You ain't kiddin'." Jesse's beefy face became more animated. "At first I thought the shells were gonna hit the mill, but then you could hear glass shatterin' over at the Convention Center. People in fancy clothes—beads and sequins and feathers out the wazoo—they started runnin' out the front doors, screamin' like the Tribulation done started."

"The Tribulation?" Susannah raised her brows. "Never mind. So how long did the fireworks last?"

"Oh, man, it was a full-fledged show, just headed in the wrong direction. Must've gone on a good fifteen minutes. Crazy thing was, the fire department got here pretty quick—I was the one called 'em—but the lady that answered the phone already knew about it. There wasn't much they could do at first. Every time they'd put out the fire, another shell come screaming across the river and started another one." Jesse chuckled. "It was almost funny."

"I bet the fire chief didn't think it was funny." Susannah had worked her share of bomb scenes, and she'd never seen anybody in a place of responsibility laughing.

"No, ma'am, of course not." Jesse looked abashed. "But it coulda been a lot worse. The Good Lord made sure everybody was upstairs in a banquet room. Otherwise somebody woulda been hurt bad."

Susannah nodded, though the image of an angel herding drunk party animals up an escalator to keep them from being the target of a fireworks show made her want to giggle. "Do you happen to know Quinn Baldwin?"

"The poor sucker that accidentally shot off all that stuff? No, ma'am, but he was in the news a lot the next couple of days. Seems like a nice guy." Jesse's mustache twitched downward. "Hey, I got to get back to work. Are you gonna move your car or not?"

Figuring she'd extracted everything she was going to get out of the Hard Hat Hero, Susannah nodded. "You bet. Thanks, Jesse." As she accompanied him back to her Jeep, she began to line up her next plan of action.

Baldwin was more than a nice guy. She just had to figure out what that "more" was. Maybe a surprise visit to his place of business was in order.

Yeah, there ya go. When in doubt, attack.

chapter 7

Quinn entered the front door of Xtravaganza Events and smiled at Adam Brown's beautiful auburn-haired wife. Julie sat at a small receptionist's desk containing nothing but a telephone and a bayberry candle in a crystal saucer. The rival company had relocated last year to a stand-alone building just outside the Biloxi, Mississippi, city limits. It boasted a big warehouse, a private entrance off the highway, and twenty-five acres of land in which to expand.

Nice digs, but Quinn wouldn't have traded his converted air force hangar. *Remember where you've come from, boy.* He returned Julie's welcoming smile.

"Quinn!" She removed her headset and got up to give him a brief hug. "Adam said you were coming by. You're looking well." She let her eyes travel down him.

His face flamed. Good thing he'd worn his best khakis and a new golf shirt. He'd once worked for Adam, and couldn't help feeling a little like a country cousin around Julie. He had to keep reminding himself she wasn't his boss's wife anymore.

"Adam's out in the warehouse playing with a new computer." Handing him a black mug emblazoned with the Xtravaganza logo, Julie gestured toward the coffeemaker behind her desk. "Help yourself while I buzz him to let him know you're here."

She walked by a mirror on her way back to her desk, stopping to fluff her hair and adjust her diamond-drop necklace. Her suit must have cost three hundred bucks, and the smooth, unwrinkled skin—no telling how much *that* cost. Julie had to be in her mid-fifties, but looked thirty.

For a second he couldn't help comparing that sleek, polished look to Susannah Tait's natural brand of beauty. Susannah would still be gorgeous in her sixties.

Yow. Dangerous train of thought.

Coffee in hand, he wandered around studying the award plaques lined up on the office walls. He'd collected a few awards of his own over the last couple of years, but it was because of Adam he had chosen the fireworks industry as a career. Watching an Xtravaganza Fourth of July show in Pascagoula, Quinn had decided what he wanted to do with the rest of his life.

"How are ya, Rocket Man?" Adam barreled into the foyer. He shook hands, then led the way back to his private office. "Thanks for making the trip over here." He dropped into the executive chair behind his desk. "I know you must be busy, but we need to get some details down for the regional meeting coming up."

Quinn couldn't help a small smile as he took a leather-upholstered chair. Adam was old-school Brooks Brothers embodied: crisp white shirt, striped tie, and expensive cuff links. "No problem. I needed a little distraction today."

"So how's it going over in L.A.?"

Adam's Lower Alabama joke was getting stale, but Quinn went along with it. "Doing our best to move into the twenty-first century." He sipped his drink. Julie made good coffee. Maybe he could get her to set up a training session for Rebecca.

"You recovering from that mess at the Convention Center?" Adam's shrewd brown eyes were warm with sympathy.

"It's been slow. Seemed like it took forever for the fire department to complete the investigation, then they still couldn't determine the cause of the explosion. At least they didn't try to pin it on me, so I still have my license."

"That's good. I've had my share of accidents. Happens to all of us sooner or later." Leaning back in his chair, Adam laughed. "Maybe not as spectacular as yours ..."

Quinn grimaced. "It was spectacular all right. I still can't figure out how it happened."

"You may never know." Adam shrugged. "Just clean up and move on. If there's anything I can do to help, let me know." He pulled a legal pad out of a drawer. "Listen, I've been keeping track of most of the major national venues. What have you heard about the political events for the summer? With the election coming up in the fall, I figure it'll start heating up soon."

Quinn hesitated. Adam had developed a strong client list on the foundation of sheer organization and reliability, but Quinn's business had tripled in the last year. People said they came back to him because of his innovation and creativity. He didn't give a flip about corporate intrigue, but for the first time he seemed to have insider information.

He owed Adam a lot. Still, what Will told him had been on the QT.

"Don't know anything specific, but I'm sure there'll be plenty of business to go around for all of us."

Adam leaned in. "*I* heard Bart Fletcher's a big dog in the re-election this go-round. I'm hoping he'll favor Mississippi companies when it comes to campaign contracts."

"I guess that could happen." To avoid Adam's eyes Quinn fiddled with his PDA. "He's a good man. I admire him a lot."

"I'm southern enough to be loyal to my state, and Fletcher's been good for our economy. But he makes me nervous with his 'family values' policies." Adam's lip curled.

Quinn shook his head. "That's one of the main things I like about him. I've never seen any reason to think he isn't exactly what you see on the outside."

"Trust me—" Adam tapped the tip of his heavy gold pen on his blotter—"*everybody's* got something to hide."

Quinn blinked. "That's a pretty cynical outlook, brother."

Adam shrugged. "Keeps me from getting burned." He pointed the pen at Quinn. "But whoever wins, we've got to watch each other's backs. If anybody needs a reference, buddy, you send 'em to me."

Heading southwest of I-10 into Mobile's old Brookley Field area, Susannah found herself in a neglected neighborhood where peeling clapboard shotgun houses alternated with apartment complex projects. Reminded her of the worst parts of Tucson. She supposed every city had its eyesores.

A broad four-lane avenue took her to the entrance of an industrial plant, where she recognized the military origin of the offices and warehouses. Generic red brick, serviceable aluminum siding, plain white blinds or no coverings at all on the windows.

Déjà vu.

Baldwin's office was a corner building separated from its neighbors on both sides by a couple of two-acre empty lots surrounded by chain-link fence. Looked like an old airplane hangar.

She pulled into the crumbling parking lot and stopped beside a dark blue sedan. Baldwin's truck was nowhere in sight, but this had to be the right place. Next to the garage-style door was a standard door bearing a gold-lettered sign. "SkyPainters, Inc., Fireworks and Special Events."

"Fabulous," she muttered, getting out of the Jeep. "Could we *get* any farther out in the boonies?"

She knocked on the metal door and waited, shifting from one foot to the other. She'd elected not to call first, hoping the element of surprise would turn up something useful. She was ready to give up and pull out her cell phone after all when two fingers separated the blinds. A pair of brown eyes, framed by trendy little horn-rimmed glasses, appeared between them.

Susannah did her best to look harmless.

A dead bolt clicked back, then the door opened a crack. "Hi, I'm Susannah Tait." She smiled. "I'm looking for Quinn Baldwin."

The door opened further to reveal a young woman dressed in a short black skirt with a pink knit blouse that looked about a size too small. Her smooth brown ponytail and bangs, along with the round face, gave her an ingenuous look heightened by a slight widening of the brown eyes. "*The* Susannah Tait?" She stepped back, giving Susannah the once-over. "Quinn's not here."

Disappointed, Susannah stepped into the office anyway. "When will he be back? I need to talk to him. About church." Would Baldwin's employees be religious too?

The girl raised a skeptical brow. "Sometime this afternoon. Maybe. He went over to Biloxi for a meeting, but he has to be back in time for baseball practice."

"Baseball?" Susannah wandered over to look at the artwork on a folding screen that separated the entry area from a couple of metal desks. She recognized one of the prints from Elva Kay's living room. "I thought he'd messed up his shoulder and didn't play anymore."

"He coaches a kids' Dixie League team. Would you like to leave a note or something? I was just about to eat my lunch." The young secretary sat down at her desk and rummaged for a notepad, then looked up, her mouth curled in a little grin. "Oops. Forgot I was supposed to be nice. I'll be glad to share my sandwich."

"Thanks, I just ate. But you go ahead." Susannah looked around for an extra chair, but the only one she saw was behind Baldwin's desk. "Would it be all right if I wait for him?" She sat down before the girl could answer. Leaning back, she winced when the old chair's springs let out a loud squawk. "Now tell me your name again?"

"I'm Rebecca Mansfield, Quinn's executive assistant." She opened a drawer and pulled out a brown paper sack, from which she extracted a sandwich on white bread, a bag of corn chips, and a Twinkie. She went to the drink machine in the corner and came back with a diet Dr Pepper.

"I haven't known him very long." Susannah scanned the desk. No pictures whatsoever, except for the computer screensaver, a photo of a kids' baseball team. Scrawny little bodies, big grins full of crooked teeth, half of the kids kneeling, half standing. There was Baldwin on one end, and a long-haired young man who looked a lot like Rebecca on the other.

"So how did you meet Quinn?" Rebecca pulled the crust off her sandwich. Susannah noted the perfect pink nails and a silver and pearl ring on Rebecca's right hand. No engagement or wedding rings.

"We're neighbors." Susannah clasped her hands over her stomach. "We met on the track at that big high school down the street."

"Oh, yeah, Murphy. My alma mater." Rebecca opened the chips, dumped them on a napkin and spread them out in single-layer rows.

What we have here is a card-carrying obsessive-compulsive. Susannah tipped her head. She was pretty good at guessing people's ages. She gave up on Rebecca, young of face and old in heart. "Are you a college student?"

"No. I started as part-time work-study in high school, but I'm full-time now." Rebecca folded up her lunch sack into a neat square, then laid it in the trash can under her desk. She heaved an odd little sigh. "Quinn and my mom go back a long way."

Susannah waited, hoping Rebecca would elaborate. Baldwin didn't seem like the kind of guy who'd go for a December-May love affair. She was beginning to get a very muddled picture of the guy. Religious nut who shot fireworks for a living, cut an elderly neighbor's grass as a hobby, and coached kids' baseball in his spare time.

Rebecca opened her Twinkie and began to nibble it, first at one end, then the other. She obviously had nothing else to say about her mother.

Man, this is one strange chick. Susannah stood up. "Listen, while I'm here, is there any way you could give me a quick tour? I've always been fascinated by fireworks."

Rebecca frowned, making Susannah wonder if the girl was onto her. Then the wistful gaze went to a bridal magazine lying on her credenza.

Oh. I'm interrupting maiden fantasies.

"I'll be glad to." Rebecca closed the computer screen again. "Come on back to the warehouse. There's nothing to see here in the office."

"Are you getting married?" Susannah followed Rebecca through the opening between the screens.

"I wish. I'm helping my cousin plan her wedding."

Susannah could think of few things more boring than organza and flowers and candles and birdseed. She focused her attention on Baldwin's design and storage space.

Rebecca spread her hands, indicating the large concrete-floored room. "This is pretty much it."

The first thing that struck Susannah was the rigid orderliness of the room. A worktable against the far wall held a computer and phone, with the usual office supplies organized within arm's reach. A couple of five-drawer file cabinets flanked the table, with the computer's accessories—printer, fax, and copier—underneath. Metal shelving lining the two long walls contained a variety of hardware: five-foot containers with heavy-duty hasp locks; electric matches, orange six-volt batteries, neatly coiled cables hanging on spikes; hammers, nails, shovels, and buckets; and most important of all, several industrial-quality fire extinguishers.

The whole building had been insulated with nonsparking foam, and there wasn't a speck of dust, dirt, or trash in sight.

Susannah put her hands on her hips. "This is amazing. Nobody should be this neat."

"Scary, isn't it? The boys call Quinn 'Flylady,' just to give him a hard time."

"Flylady?"

"The Internet housekeeping guru."

Susannah grinned. "Housekeeping's not on my radar screen. Who're the 'boys'?"

"Phillip and Russ, the part-time guys. Phillip's my younger brother."

Susannah walked over to the back wall where Baldwin had stored a few shells.

"Don't touch that stuff back there," Rebecca warned. "We could get in trouble with our permits."

"It's okay, I'm a certified—" catching herself just in time, she turned and gave Rebecca a goofy smile—"a certified idiot. I should know better than to get too close. Didn't you guys have an accident not too long ago?"

"I'll say." Rebecca shook her head, setting her long, gaudy earrings to swaying. "That's why this room is so empty. We haven't had the money to replace all the equipment that blew up with the truck that night."

Susannah walked back to the worktable, wishing she could get into the computer. She glanced at Rebecca. "Were you there?"

"Oh yeah." Rebecca squeezed her eyes shut as if blocking out the image. "I was so scared. I thought Quinn was in the explosion too, until he walked out of it. He looked like somebody coming out of hell."

Having witnessed the aftermath of too many bomb scenes, Susannah had no trouble picturing it. Made her sick to think of somebody endangering people's lives by setting off a bunch of fireworks—especially with the intent of making money. But why would the idiot have put *himself* in harm's way?

Cover, that was why. What better way to deflect suspicion?

"Boy, that must have been something else. Amazing he got out alive. Any idea what set it off?"

Rebecca's open expression shut down. "You'll have to ask Quinn about that." She shrugged. "He's the fireworks guy. I just do what he tells me. All I know is, one minute Skeet and I are sitting on the tailgate of the truck arguing basketball, the next we're watching World War III going off." She clapped her hands. "Ka-*boom*!"

I just do what he tells me. Would that include setting up an explosion?

Susannah decided to risk a couple more questions. "Where were the other two guys? Phillip and Russ?"

"They'd gone across the river to get hot wings." Rebecca made a face. "Phillip's *always* hungry. I couldn't believe Quinn let them go when we only had four hours to get everything set up, but he's such a marshmallow sometimes."

"So … you and Skeet and Phillip and Russ. That's not a very big crew to set up and run a show of that size."

If Rebecca wondered what Susannah knew about running fireworks exhibitions, she didn't say so. "First off, Quinn knows what he's doing. He plans way ahead of time, goes out to the site and marks everything, so it's just a matter of painting by numbers, you know?"

"Huh?" Susannah was having a good time playing dumb.

"Come here, let me show you one of his diagrams." Rebecca went to the computer and booted it up. "They're really cool."

In a matter of moments Susannah was sitting in Baldwin's chair staring at a fireworks design on his PowerMac. She couldn't believe it. The only problem was, Rebecca was looking over her shoulder.

What a great design too. Quinn had made notations about the music—the soundtrack from *Star Wars*—with specific fireworks and colors noted. If he could do this kind of work, why would he need to blow up his business to collect the insurance?

There was no way to hack further into the computer with Rebecca standing right here, so she'd better get out before the girl got suspicious. "This is amazing. I'd love to see one of your shows. When's the next one?"

"Let's see. There's the May Day battleship thing coming up with the Mobile Bar Association, if you're going to be around that long."

"I'm not sure." Susannah moved aside so Rebecca could shut down the computer.

Rebecca flicked shrewd brown eyes at Susannah. "So you're just killing time with Quinn?"

"Killing time?" Susannah laughed. "I guess you could say that. I just met him a couple of days ago."

"Well, I hope you won't take this the wrong way. But Quinn's more than my boss. He's like my big brother, and I don't want to see him get hurt."

This little chick had some nerve. "What are you saying?"

Rebecca gave her a cool look. "You're attracted to him enough to chase him all the way out here without even calling first to make sure he's in the office."

Susannah felt her blood pressure go up. "Are you warning me off?"

"I don't dislike you, Susannah, since I don't know you at all." Rebecca shrugged. "I'm just telling you Quinn isn't like most guys. You're the first person he's expressed any interest in, in a long time. He's very tenderhearted and shy. Don't lead him on. 'Kay?"

Susannah doubted she could lead Quinn Baldwin anywhere he didn't want to go. On the other hand, she wasn't going to let some interfering little office clerk barely out of her teens tell her what to do.

"He's a big boy. I think he can take care of himself." She pulled her car keys out of her pocket. "Listen, I've got to go. Thanks for the tour. When Quinn comes back, tell him I came by."

All in all, a productive afternoon. She should treat herself to a run. Besides, Monty needed to stretch his legs. And she needed to think.

chapter 8

Quinn repositioned the bat in Trevor Ballard's hands and stepped back before the little chunk could whack him in the chest with it. For the last thirty minutes he'd been watching Rebecca. What was she doing up in the stands, making conversation with Alden Makin's mother?

After he'd left for Biloxi, he'd driven straight to the field. So he hadn't seen her all afternoon. She usually went straight home after work to care for her mother. Maybe she'd come to harass Phillip, who was helping Quinn coach the SkyPainter Braves. Squinting against the sun, he found Rebecca's brother in the outfield demonstrating how to hold a glove while catching a pop fly.

His attention was yanked back to the field when Jacob, his first-string pitcher, let loose with a fast ball that zoomed toward the inside corner of the plate. Trevor swung late and missed, turning himself into a tubby corkscrew.

"Trevor! Get ahead of the ball next time. Good pitch, Jake." He grinned at the boy as he caught the catcher's return throw. "But this is fielding practice. Go a little easier on 'em, okay?"

"Okay, Coach." Jacob wiped his nose on his sleeve and wound up to throw again.

Quinn checked his watch. Time to let the kids go for the day. Two hours twice a week was plenty for nine-year-olds this early in the season. The first game was coming up Saturday, and he knew not to push too hard. Sportsmanship and teamwork were just as important as winning. He planned to take the team to the double-A BayBears game afterward to celebrate, win or lose.

"Okay, guys, once around the bases and we'll head for the house." He waved toward the outfield. "Send 'em in, Phillip!"

Pandemonium ensued as fifteen sweaty, smelly, and dust-covered kids shoved into a straggling line. Like John Wayne directing a cattle drive, Quinn waved his cap and whooped encouragement.

Everybody made it around the bases and lined up for post-practice popsicles. Quinn took a red-white-and-blue Bomb Pop out of the ice chest, then walked over to Rebecca. She was helping Cindy Makin pass out BayBears wristband tickets.

"Any more calls while I was out of the office this afternoon?"

"Nothing that won't wait until tomorrow." Rebecca smiled at freckle-faced Alden Makin, who stuck out his tongue and ran off. "Hello, what'd I do to deserve that?"

Quinn sat down on the tailgate of his truck and tore the paper off his popsicle. "Alden's a little mad at the world right now. His dad just ran off with the secretary and left the family high and dry."

Rebecca winced. "Oh, man."

He sighed. "All but three of these kids live with just a mom or a grandmother." Rebecca was quiet for a moment, watching Jacob and Trevor squabble over the last sherbet push-up. He nudged her with an elbow. "Why don't you go get it and end the argument?"

"Nah, let 'em duke it out." She nudged him back. "You're a good guy, you know that, Quinn Baldwin?"

"I gave you a long lunch today. You can't have another one."

She rolled her eyes.

"And I can't afford to give you a raise."

"Lighten *up*. I don't want anything."

"Then what are you doing here?"

Rebecca sighed. "I missed your charming, suspicious nature and couldn't wait until tomorrow morning. How's Phillip doing? He never talks to me."

"I can't understand why he wouldn't talk to someone who pesters the living daylights out of him." Quinn bit into his popsicle. "He just made the dean's list."

"That's good. I kept telling him if he'd go to bed at a decent hour, he'd do better in his morning classes."

Quinn glanced at his young assistant coach, who was flirting with Trevor's pretty teenage sister. Phillip kept his back to his own sister. "Speaking of lightening up—"

She waved away the interruption. "Susannah Tait came by the office this afternoon."

"*Susannah* came by? Why didn't you tell me—"

She huffed. "I just *did*."

"What did she want?"

"She said she needed to talk to you about church." Rebecca rolled her eyes again. "We chatted for a while and I gave her a tour of the warehouse. Your lips are turning blue."

Quinn pitched the melting popsicle into a nearby trash can. "You gave her a *tour*?"

"Yeah. She seemed impressed, but you know, I'm even more convinced she's not your type."

"And *you* know that's none of your business—"

"Hey, Coach Quinn, see ya Friday night!" Tacy Stevenson, one of the twin girls who took turns at first base, waved wildly as she locked arms with her sister. At least, he was pretty sure it was Tacy who'd waved. Maybe it was Toni.

"Okay, don't forget to put your game face on!" He demonstrated. Both little girls giggled and ran off toward their mother's car.

Phillip wandered over with a surly look for Rebecca. "You ask me if I made up my bed this morning, and I'm going to deck you."

Quinn sympathized. Rebecca, who had helped raise her younger brother during their mother's recurring bouts with leukemia, didn't know when to let well enough alone.

"Good practice today." He reached out to bump fists with Phillip. "We might even win."

Phillip started dumping bats and balls into a mesh bag in the back of the truck. "How come a guy who knows how to coach baseball like you do gets stuck with this bunch of leftover kids?"

"I picked 'em myself." Distracted, Quinn looked at Rebecca. "So what did you and Susannah talk about?"

"Girl stuff." She lifted her shoulders. "I wanted to find out if she was into you, or if she was, you know, just playing you."

He folded his arms, mostly to keep his hands from going around Rebecca's neck. "Please tell me you didn't ask her that!"

Phillip chunked the equipment bag into the truck. "What'd you do, Rebecca, give her a *Cosmo* Love Quiz?"

Rebecca ignored her brother. "Frankly, I don't see the appeal. The girl has no idea how to dress, and her hair's a mess. She carries a backpack instead of a purse, for heaven's sake!"

Phillip struck an exaggerated hand-on-hip pose. "The *What Not to Wear* crew would just be appalled."

"Anyway—" Rebecca sent him a dirty look—"I was very subtle."

Quinn stood up, wiping his sticky hand on the seat of his pants. "Rebecca, you have got to stay out of my—my—" He wasn't going to say "love life." He *had* no love life. "Personal business."

"I was just trying to help. You *said* you might ask her out again."

"I changed my mind. Susannah's not a Christian, and I can't start something—"

"Who made up that rule, anyway?" Rebecca wore her you-can't-tell-me-anything scowl. "Seems to me we should take every opportunity to make friends with unbelievers."

"That's true, but when you're a guy and the other person is a beautiful woman, you shouldn't—" Quinn lowered his voice when he noticed Phillip was looking back and forth between him and his sister like a spectator at a ping-pong match. "It's a lot more effective if the friendship comes from a person of the same s—uh, gender."

"Come on, Quinn, you can say the word." Rebecca rolled her eyes. "Sex. God invented males and females, and he won't strike you dead if you acknowledge there are two of them."

Phillip lifted his hands. "See what I've had to live with all my life? I'm outta here." He slouched off toward his car, to which he'd recently added racing stripes and new taillights.

"And you see what *I* have to live with?" Rebecca stomped her foot. "I work like a dog to make sure he gets to go to college, and he spends every penny he earns on that stupid car!"

Quinn didn't know whether to laugh or throttle her. He'd spent nearly an hour this morning praying for wisdom in dealing with his employees, but instead he seemed to be losing ground.

Or maybe his mind. "You didn't take the afternoon off like I told you to, did you?"

She lifted her chin. "I had too much to do."

"I appreciate your diligence, but you don't do anybody any good when you're all stressed out like this. How's your mom today?"

"Fine," Rebecca snapped, then her shoulders drooped. "Her blood work came back this afternoon. It's bad, Quinn. Her spirits are down."

He touched her shoulder. "You know I'm praying for her, right? Are you getting help from people at church?"

"Yes." She sucked in a breath. "Everybody's been great, bringing food and staying with her while I work. I just wish Phillip would go by and see her more often. It was good for him to move into the dorm, but he's just so ... so self-absorbed sometimes."

"Come on, Rebecca, he's young. He'll make mistakes and do stupid things, but you've got to give him time to grow up. Be his sister, not his mother." He wanted to hug her, but she was so prickly. "I'll talk to him, but you take care of yourself, okay? Promise me you'll take the day off tomorrow."

"The whole *day*? In the middle of the week? I can't do that!"

"Sure you can. Stay home with your mom, read a book, give yourself a manicure, whatever girls do. I swear I won't let the place go to rack and ruin."

"If I know you, you won't even be there."

He laughed. "I do have a bunch of meetings in the morning, but I'll have my cell phone. Anybody who needs me can get me."

"Okay, but I'll be a nervous wreck worrying about what I should be getting done." Rebecca took a step back. "I'd better get home to relieve the lady staying with Mom this afternoon."

Quinn walked her to her car and opened the door. "Good night, kiddo. See you Wednesday." He watched her drive off, then stood there alone in the empty parking lot of a deserted elementary school.

The joy of the Lord is my strength, he thought, trying to head off a frustrating attack of loneliness. Rebecca cared about him in her own twisted way. The meeting with Adam Brown had produced a couple of new job leads. His Braves were shaping up into a decent little team. *So get over yourself, Baldwin.*

He dumped the ice out of the chest, slid it into the back of the truck, and started for home. What in the world had brought Susannah out to the SkyPainters office today?

Susannah never would have believed it of her own dog. But the evidence was right there in front of her.

Monty, with that big, happy doggie grin on his face, almost jerked her arm out of its socket, pulling on his leash in an effort to bound up Baldwin's porch steps. Somehow the dog knew where his idol lived, and he seemed determined to pay homage.

Clearly he *adored* the man. The traitor.

After dinner Elva Kay had gone to a women's Bible study, leaving Susannah to her own devices. Of course she'd been invited to go.

"No, ma'am, but thank you." Susannah was beginning to get this southern manners thing down. "I have some work to do."

She'd sat cross-legged on her bed for an hour, compiling a list of people she still needed to interview. Inevitably, though, her thoughts had strayed to Quinn, the centerpiece of the investigation. He just did not match the profile of the typical arsonist.

He wasn't married, therefore could not be conducting an illicit affair. No drinking problem or gambling addiction she could see. Of course, she knew nothing about his family background, but the business seemed to be holding its own.

From what she could tell, he just wasn't a screwup. He was serious and responsible and likable.

And really good-looking.

Catching herself fanning her face instead of working, Susannah had decided Monty needed another walk, even though they'd run five miles that afternoon.

She knew exactly when it first occurred to her there might be something fishy about that letter to the insurance company. She'd been passing old Mr. Hays as he shuffled along on his walker, with his harried daughter on his heels, when the idea had jumped fully formed into her head. What if . . .

What if the letter was somebody's clumsy attempt to discredit and ruin Baldwin?

Who would benefit from such a thing? None of it made any sense. Rebecca, the snarky young secretary—*executive assistant, yeah right*—seemed to have a well-hidden case of hero worship for her boss. Besides, what would she have to gain if her job went kaput?

Same thing for the two college students, one of them Rebecca's brother, who worked part-time for SkyPainters. Susannah had yet to meet either one, and she'd added that to her list of things to do.

Skeet. Her instincts said to rule him out. Not only was he Baldwin's best friend, with no apparent motive to harm him, but anything underhanded seemed out of character—judging by the short amount of time she'd spent in his company. However, the least likely culprit often turned out to be the person with the most secrets. Skeet's name stayed on her mental list.

And then there were the company's competitors. What better way to eliminate a rival than to ruin him financially and publicly embarrass him? A quick Internet search of pyrotechnic companies had yielded several possibilities. She'd begin tracking them down tomorrow.

Of course, she still had to presume Baldwin could be guilty, as much as she liked him. It happened all the time. Ambitious young entrepreneur starts a promising business, finds the daily demands of running said business more than he can handle, and decides to get out from under the burden by cashing in on a lucrative insurance policy.

One of the most compelling pieces of evidence against him was the fact he'd made sure all his employees were out of the line of fire.

Oh, rats, Monty had started barking. Somebody was going to call animal control.

"Come on, buddy, let's go," she groaned, tugging on his leash. "I'll give you a nice treat when we get—"

Too late. The front door opened, and a tall, dark-haired figure appeared, a set of dumbbells in each hand. Then she saw the yellow and brown snake slithering across his bare shoulders.

Susannah shrieked.

"Susannah? Is that you?" Baldwin peered out into the dark, the snake's head wobbling beside his ear. He flipped the porch light on. "What are you doing out here this time of night?"

She had flung her hands over her face, letting go of the leash. Monty bounded toward Baldwin, barking with joy. Either he didn't see the snake or it didn't bother him. The jury was still out on what the snake thought.

"Y—you didn't tell me you have a s—s—snake! Monty! Shut up and get back here!"

"The subject never came up, I guess. Hold on, let me go put Bob back in his tank." Baldwin disappeared, shutting the door to block Monty from surging after him.

A minute later he was back, wearing a white T-shirt in place of his serpentine friend. Which, in Susannah's mind, was a relief in more ways than one.

"I wasn't going to bother you." Breathless, she grabbed Monty's collar. "I know it's late, but I was sick of TV and the moon's so pretty and Monty needed to—" She was babbling. "Never mind." What was it about him that made her feel like a teenager with a crush on the quarterback? *You're a professional investigator. Chill.*

"It's okay, I was just getting in a workout before Letterman comes on." He walked over to sit on the top step. "You want to sit down?"

She should go home.

"Sure, why not." At least she hadn't been invited into the house with the cobra, or whatever it was. She perched on the concrete seat beside the steps, letting Monty wriggle close to Baldwin's knee. "What were you doing with that thing, anyway? Is that some kind of religious ritual?"

He laughed. "Where do people get this stuff? Bob's a ball python—very friendly and totally nonvenomous. He belonged to a kid on my baseball team from last year, but I adopted him when the mom threatened to execute him. The snake, I mean, not the kid."

Susannah shuddered. A couple of years ago she'd come face-to-fang with a diamondback rattler in her garage. Though diamondbacks were a protected species in Arizona, the snake had somehow managed to commit suicide on the end of her shovel.

"I sympathize with the mom." She looked over her shoulder. "Are you sure he's locked up?"

"You want to come see?"

"No, thanks. I'll take your word for it." She watched Monty slobber on Baldwin's hand. "I went by your office today."

"Rebecca told me." He scratched the hard-to-reach spot under the dog's collar. "I'm sorry I missed you."

Backlit as he was by the porch light, Baldwin's face was in shadow. She wished she could see his expression. "I was just driving through the neighborhood—"

"Susannah." He sounded amused. "Nobody goes to Brookley without a reason. Why didn't you call first?"

"I was afraid you'd tell me not to come. I wanted to apologize for embarrassing you yesterday." She'd been thinking about it all day. If she wanted to get to know him, she was going to have to play on his turf. Carefully. "It's just that you hurt me when you snubbed me like that, and I didn't ..." She sighed. "When we were at Krispy Kreme, I thought you were flirting."

"Okay. I can see that." He nodded. "I accept responsibility. Just goes to show you how out of practice I am—with girls, I mean." When she shot him an incredulous look, he spread his hands. "I don't know what you think, but I haven't had a serious relationship in four or five years."

"Are you gay?" Wouldn't that just figure?

"No!" He laughed, shoving his hand into his hair. "I'm about as ungay as they come. Look, Susannah, this may make absolutely no sense to you. But if it makes you feel any better, I find you way more attractive than I can deal with at the moment."

Susannah stared at him. "Then you *were* flirting."

"If that's what you want to call it."

He looked so uneasy she smiled. "Forgive me if I don't know what to do with this information."

"Me either." She heard the smile in his voice. "Are you still mad at me?"

She shrugged. "I was feeling a little manipulated about coming to church. By you and Elva Kay." Although, come to think of it, *she* was the one doing most of the manipulating. *Hypocrite,* said her conscience.

Shut up, she told it. *This is business.*

He hesitated, pressing his lips together. "If you had a favorite restaurant or something—wouldn't you tell everybody about it? Take people there?"

"I guess. That seems a weird way to talk about church, though."

"I don't know any other way to make you understand. It's the most important part of my life. Well, not the church building. The people there. And the Lord, of course."

Susannah shifted her shoulders again. "Well, it makes me uncomfortable." She gave him a sideways look. "How about inviting me somewhere else?"

He considered for a moment. "You can help me chaperone my baseball team Saturday night at the Hank."

"The Hank?"

"Hank Aaron Stadium. It's where the BayBears play double-A baseball. Our first game of the season is at five. After that we're going to watch the big boys play."

"If you bribe me with Cracker Jacks."

His white grin flashed. "Cracker Jacks we can do."

There was another awkward pause, during which Baldwin stared at his hands and Susannah tried not to stare at him. There had to be something wrong with him. A tall, intelligent, ungay guy with sexy eyes and a killer smile who didn't understand a single one of the rules of flirtation. Or maybe he understood them and simply chose to ignore them.

Monty broke the ice with a loud, contented snore. He had squeezed his big muscled body onto the step beside Baldwin's foot and had fallen sound asleep with his nose across Baldwin's running shoe.

Baldwin laughed. "I think you've got him up past his bedtime."

"I know. I should get home. Elva Kay will be worrying about me." Susannah smiled. Kind of a strange and pleasant thing, being worried about, actually.

"Okay, at the risk of sounding like my buttinsky secretary—"

"Executive assistant."

"Oh, yeah, whatever." He smiled. "Anyway, it would make me feel better too if you wouldn't run in this neighborhood by yourself after dark."

"I've got Monty."

Baldwin looked down at the Lab, drooling in puppylike abandon on his foot. "Come on, Susannah, promise me you won't—"

"All right." She lifted her hands. "But only if you'll agree to come with me a couple times a week. I can't stand being cooped up in the house all the time."

He tapped his fingers together for a minute. "I usually run in the mornings after my quiet time. I guess I could make an exception once in a while, though. But not too late. I have to get up early."

Quiet time? She wasn't going to ask. She figured she'd already gotten a major concession out of him.

"Cool. Tomorrow night at nine, then." She bounced to her feet before he could change his mind. "Come on, Monty, old buddy, let's go chase the cat."

Baldwin stood up too. "Oh, no, you don't. I'm walking you home."

"Quinn—"

"Didn't you hear what I just said? This may look like a quiet place, but we're not far from the projects. Gangs and druggies and all kinds of lowlife." He walked down the steps, snapping his fingers for Monty, who, fawning sycophant that he was, came instantly to heel.

Susannah heaved a long-suffering sigh and fell into step too. Alarming how much she was beginning to enjoy being protected.

chapter 9

I talked to your new girlfriend last night." Dana Carter brushed her bangs out of her eyes with a purple-feathered pen, then sneezed. "I like to've never caught her at home."

Mentally focused on his meeting with the Bar Association's May Day committee this morning, Quinn hadn't been paying much attention to the conversation. It was Wednesday afternoon, and he and Skeet sat with Dana on the back patio of a midtown coffee shop known as He-Brews. Drafted as part of a community outreach team, he'd agreed to the meeting when Dana bribed him with a caramel espresso. He had a serious coffee addiction, but, hey, it was a minor vice.

If he didn't tune in, though, she was going to stick him with some lame job like whitewashing the county dog pound. "What did you say?"

"I said I called Susannah last night."

He did a double take. "Were you talking to *me*?"

"Yeah, I was talkin' to *you*." She giggled at her terrible DeNiro impression. "I thought she might like to help out with the water table for the Azalea Trail Run."

"Okay, back up the truck." Quinn intercepted Skeet's amused look. "First off, Susannah is not my girlfriend."

"I told you so." Skeet banged on the iron table with a couple of coffee stirrers.

"But you brought her to church." Dana blinked. "I assumed—"

"We're just neighbors." How many times was he going to have to explain that?

Her mouth formed a perfect pink O. "I have to say I'm a little bit relieved."

Surprised, Quinn frowned. "Why?"

"She's perfectly nice, of course, but she didn't seem to want to talk about anything spiritual." Dana let out a little sigh, genuine concern puckering her brow.

"Well, thanks for trying." Quinn drained his coffee. "Susannah needs another girl sharing the Lord with her." He hesitated. "I'd appreciate it if you wouldn't give up on her."

Dana's bright smile reappeared. "You really like her, don't you?" Before he could deny it, she laughed. "Have you ever known me to give up on anything? Never fear! We shall persevere!"

Arguing with Dana was pointless. "What did she say about helping with the water table?"

"She thought it was a great idea. Said she'd be glad to help."

So Susannah didn't plan to participate as a runner. He'd signed up for the race on the opening day of registration. It was scheduled for a week from Saturday.

"Anyway," Dana scrawled in her notebook with her ridiculous pen, "that's our project for this month. We just need about six other people to help. Who else can you recruit?"

"I'll ask the other guys in the praise band," said Skeet.

"Perfect!" Dana scribbled again, tongue between her teeth. "Oh, and one other thing. Quinn, you're good at advertising. Can you get us a nice banner and frame to go over the table? And make sure we have enough church brochures printed up?"

"Sure." To Quinn's relief, the conversation veered away from his imaginary love life as Dana went on to other details for the project.

Later Skeet popped him on the arm as they walked toward the parking lot. "What's the matter, man? You haven't said a word in fifteen minutes."

Quinn hesitated as he pulled his keys out of his pocket. Maybe it wouldn't hurt to get his frustration off his chest. "It's been a real weird day."

"Until you've heard a beginner oboe player squawk through 'The Banks of Loch Lomond,' you don't know what weird is." Skeet leaned against his Honda. "Come on, man, spill it."

"Okay." Quinn propped a foot on his front bumper. "I met with the May Day committee this morning. Three months ago they booked me to do the battleship thing. Now they're talking about backing out, and I've already put over a hundred hours into planning it."

"Don't you have a contract?"

"Of course I do." He shrugged. "But if they want out, I'm not gonna hold them to it. I mean, this is a civic organization, and I've already got a shaky reputation in town." Quinn grimaced. "Here's an example. I'm in Pet-o-Rama Saturday morning, buying Bob's dinner, and the guy that kills the mice says—"

"Wait, wait." Skeet held up a hand. "The pet store pays somebody to kill a mouse for you? On the spot?"

"Bob likes 'em fresh, and I don't have the heart to do it myself." Quinn folded his arms. "Anyway, this was a new guy—apparently there's quite a bit of turnover—"

"I can't imagine why."

"—so I walk in the store and he goes, 'Dude! I know you! You're the guy that blew up the Convention Center back in January. High five!'"

Skeet laughed. "See, you're a legend in your own time."

"I have no desire to be a folk hero to some headbanger punk who assassinates mice for a living!"

"Come on, man, where's your sense of humor? This'll all blow over by summertime and—"

"But I don't have 'til summer." Quinn looked down to mask his anxiety. "SkyPainters is in the running for some major national political events."

Skeet stared at Quinn for a moment, his sharp brain patently revolving all the implications. "You mean, like presidential campaign stuff?"

Quinn shrugged.

Skeet whistled between his teeth. "Sounds like you're in the big leagues now."

"It's an unbelievable opportunity. Plus, you know how much I like politics."

Skeet pulled on the tuft under his lower lip. "Okay, here's what I think. Which part of this whole scenario is actually under your control?"

"What do you mean?"

"For example, can you go back and undo the explosion?"

"Well ... no."

"Can you make people quit talking about it?"

"Come on, Skeet—"

"I'm serious. Looks to me like you have two options. Worry until you give yourself another ulcer, or let go and rest in whatever the Lord's doing here."

"Easy for you to say," Quinn muttered, looking away.

"I know. But when you think about it, who gave you the business to begin with?"

"God did, of course."

"Then you can trust him with it." Skeet aimed his remote key at the car door. "Now run for your life, before Yum-Yum chases us down with the purple pen."

Rain drizzled from a leaden sky as Susannah parked behind the newly renovated GM&O Railroad Station, home of the Mobile ATF office. The building's hundred-year-old facade looked gray from a distance, but close-up she could see the taupe-colored brick and concrete ornamentation. Susannah knew next to nothing about architecture, but ornate little turrets marching across the front of a flamboyant red-tile roof gave it the look of a Spanish castle. The waterfront location was beautiful, but in Susannah's opinion, security stank. Nothing but a four-foot chain-link fence separated the parking lot from the street on one side, and a board fence ran along the riverside railroad tracks on the other. Not much to keep the bad guys out.

Fortunately, it wasn't her problem. She turned off the windshield wipers and cut the ignition. Rats, she still hadn't gotten around to buying an umbrella. With a sigh, she locked the Jeep and dashed for the entrance.

She found herself in a soaring atrium-style lobby with marble floors and cold plaster walls. The air-conditioning practically turned her damp clothes to ice. Shivering, she looked for the directory and found it next to the elevator.

Bureau of Alcohol, Tobacco, Firearms and Explosives — Suite 300. She punched the button and headed up.

With a quick phone call that morning, she'd arranged to meet with agent Beverly O'Neal. Laying her issues on the line with a female agent could be either a good thing or it could dig her into an even deeper hole. Depended on the cat quotient.

Please, God, let me find out what I need to know.

The prayer startled her so much she grabbed the rail behind her. Why would God have any interest in whether or not Susannah Tait nailed an insurance fraud suspect? And why should it suddenly occur to her to ask him for help?

With a slightly creepy feeling sliding across the back of her neck, she got off the elevator and found herself in a dim hallway facing a generic brown steel door. *Here we go, open the chute.*

Susannah signed in with a guard—Earl "Peabo" Fontaine, according to his name tag—who buzzed Agent O'Neal to make sure she was expected. He then told her to step through the scanner frame and run her backpack through an X-ray machine. Standard procedure, but it was the first time in nearly six years she'd had to do more than flash a badge to get into a government office.

Shrugging off her irritation, she gave Fontaine her widest smile. You never knew when an ally would come in handy. "So where can I find Agent O'Neal?" She grabbed her backpack off the conveyor belt.

"Last office on your left," he rumbled in a basso profundo that could have projected across a football field. "Tell her she still owes me twenty bucks on the Braves pot."

"You got it." Susannah winked at him and headed for a row of cubicles. As she reached the wall separating the last two offices, she paused just long enough to note Beverly O'Neal's outdated bleached-blonde hairdo before the agent looked up from a pile of paperwork. Dressed in khakis and an ATF polo shirt, she stood and extended a bronzed hand to Susannah.

O'Neal smiled, the deep sun-wrinkles around her pale green eyes placing her in her late forties or early fifties. Experience was traced into every line around her mouth. "How are you, Ms. Tait?" She indicated a chair for Susannah.

Susannah took it, dropping her backpack onto the floor. "Call me Susannah. I'm good. How 'bout you?"

"Covered over at the moment." O'Neal glanced at a towering stack of files on one corner of her desk.

Susannah sympathized. She'd been there before, and it was one of the main reasons she'd looked for a job elsewhere. "Thanks for taking time to see me this morning."

"No problem." O'Neal crossed her legs and leaned back. "So you're here about the SkyPainters case. Like I told you, we closed it a couple of weeks ago. What's your interest in it?"

You mean besides the good-looking suspect? "I represent Mr. Baldwin's insurance agency."

O'Neal uttered a deep smoker's laugh. "Poor guy. Good thing he *had* insurance. Lost just about everything in that explosion."

"He's covered—if it really was an accident. That's why I'm here. I'd like to hear your version of what happened."

"Sorry, but I can't give you any information until you submit the Freedom of Information request." O'Neal tapped the ends of her long maroon nails together.

Susannah sighed. "I sent it in a couple of weeks ago, but I was hoping you'd go ahead and talk to me. Did I tell you I was with Tucson ATF for five years?"

"No, you didn't. Not that it makes any difference." O'Neal studied Susannah from under half-closed lids. "How come you left?"

"I wasn't fired, if that's what you're asking." Susannah leaned forward and lowered her voice. "I liked the challenge of being in the field—the science, the interviews, the travel. Using my brain." Seeing she had O'Neal's attention, she looked around to make sure nobody else was within earshot. "Somewhere along the way I realized the only route to the next pay grade was in management, and—" she spread her hands—"that's just not me. You know what I mean?" Susannah glanced at the stack of files.

O'Neal gave Susannah a bland look. She might look like an escapee from a country-western jubilee, but she was no dummy.

"I know what you mean, but I still can't tell you anything specific about this case."

"Okay, then maybe you'd consider an exchange of information."

"I doubt you have any information we haven't already investigated. We searched the perimeter of the blast seat, sent all the debris to the lab, and nothing abnormal—" O'Neal clamped her wide lips together. "I'm not saying anything else about it."

"Take a look at this." Susannah pulled the anonymous letter out of her backpack and handed it to the agent.

O'Neal laid it on the desk. With a little huff, she pulled a pair of reading glasses out of her desk drawer and stuck them on her nose. She perused the letter for a minute or two, then looked at Susannah over the glasses.

"When did you get this?"

"It came in the mail three weeks ago. No return address, and it was sent from a huge post office in Pensacola."

"This could be a crock. A competitor who's jealous of Baldwin, just trying to get him in trouble."

"Sure it could. But you can see why the insurance company has to take it seriously. The payout's enormous."

"Tell you what, Ms. Tait." O'Neal took off her glasses and slid them back in their case. "You come up with evidence there's something to that letter, and I'll consider reopening the case."

"I don't want you to reopen the case; I just want you to let me have a look in the vault." Susannah felt like banging her head against the wall. "Look, could you at least tell me what you think about Baldwin and his company?" She leaned over to put away the letter—and to hide the embarrassing extent of her interest in SkyPainters' CEO.

"I guess that's no big secret. I've done his annual inspections twice. Baldwin's a nice kid, and he complies with safety codes to an almost fanatical degree. You're gonna have a hard time pinning anything on him—except maybe a Boy Scout badge."

Susannah stared at the agent. Baldwin seemed to have snowed this woman but good. She wasn't even open to new information.

Admit it, Susie. You're just a little bit snowed yourself.

"You know what? I hope you're right." She grabbed her backpack as she stood up. "Will you give me a call as soon as that information release form is approved?" She handed one of her business cards to the agent.

O'Neal tucked the card into her Rolodex. "Okay, but don't hold your breath."

It was still raining that night when Quinn came by to pick Susannah up for their run. She opened the door to find him standing under an enormous maroon and white golf umbrella. He was dressed in gray running shorts and a white muscle shirt.

She peered past him at the deluge. "Um, I thought you might cancel."

"What's the matter, you Arizona Gila monster? Can't take a little damp weather?" He grinned.

"You're not serious?" She looked down at herself. She still had on her jeans and T-shirt from her trip to ATF.

He laughed. "Yeah, I'm serious, but I won't make you run in the rain. We're going to the Y."

"Oh. In that case, come on in while I change." She stepped back to let him in.

He propped the umbrella in the old-fashioned walnut stand by the door and wiped his wet running shoes on the rug. Picking up the cat, he dropped into the rocker. "No hurry," he said, stroking Belshazzar's fluffy back.

Susannah scooted up the stairs to her room. It was so weird seeing Quinn after she'd spent all day investigating him. She wondered if Mata Hari had ever had attacks of conscience like this.

Twenty minutes later she and Quinn were jogging side by side around the quarter-mile perimeter of the Moorer YMCA gym. As they ran the second-floor track, Susannah kept an eye on the gym floor below, where a rough-and-ready pickup basketball game was being waged by a crowd of middle-aged men in baggy shorts. Fascinating in a train-wreck kind of way.

"How's your research going?" Quinn rounded the corner, falling a step behind to let Susannah go first. "You never say much about it."

Susannah stumbled. "Research? Oh, you mean the sociology paper."

"Yeah. What did you think I meant?" He gave her an eyebrow-raised look as he caught up to her.

"Oh, I was just thinking about something else." About what a gentleman he was. And how much she did *not* want to discover he had blown up his fireworks on purpose. "It's going fine. Today I talked to a woman who knows you. She said she's done your inspections a couple of times. Beverly O'Neal?"

"Agent O'Neal? Why were you talking to her?" He didn't look suspicious, just curious.

"She's actually a pretty big Mardi Gras enthusiast."

"Hmph, no kidding. How did my name happen to come up?"

"Oh, I …" Susannah thought fast. "I got the usual 'you're not from around here' question. I was just telling her about how nice everybody's been to me." She gave him a sidelong look. "Even you."

Quinn seemed to take that at face value. "She's a nice lady. Very thorough." He grinned. "And she always passes me on inspection."

Susannah laughed. "She says you're squeaky clean."

"I believe in doing things right." After another lap, Quinn eased his pace, and Susannah slowed to match his stride. His expression turned pensive.

"What are you thinking about?"

"My grandfather. He's the one who taught me that ethic. I used to follow him around when I was little. Before my family kind of fell apart."

"Tell me about him." Susannah found herself hungry to know more about Quinn. Maybe she could figure out what made him such an enigma.

"Nothing special about him, I guess. Just a country businessman. Grandpa runs a little feed store over in Jackson County, Mississippi." Quinn glanced at her, smiling. "He's always had a garden and a few animals, and I used to help him throw seed in the spring. Then all summer he'd put me to work shelling purple-hull peas until my thumbs looked like I'd soaked 'em in grape Kool-Aid."

"Do you still—I mean, is he still alive?" Susannah could grill perps 'til the cows came home, but somehow conducting this backstabbing sort of interview felt strange.

The sudden cloud in Quinn's gray eyes took her by surprise. "Yeah, but I haven't seen him in quite a while. Like I said, there's been a pretty serious rift in the family."

What kind of rift? she wanted to ask. She thought about Elva Kay's neighbor, Mr. Hays, whose family treated him like minor royalty though he wasn't even cognizant of their care. What would keep a Christian man like Quinn from visiting an aged grandfather whom he obviously admired? Some previously unsuspected streak of sensitivity prevented her from asking.

Besides, she needed to be delving into his methods of conducting his fireworks business rather than his personal life.

But the opportunity was lost when a couple of the men on the basketball court below shoved into one another and wound up sprawled on the gleaming floor.

"You think we should call the paramedics?" Quinn winked at her.

Laughing, Susannah nudged him as they circled the short end of the track. "Look out, you'll be bald and slow one of these days too."

He tugged her ponytail. "And you'll be running circles around me."

Susannah wondered if he heard the implication behind his words. Once she got this case settled, she'd go back to her Arizona desert and never see him again.

The thought was depressing beyond words.

chapter 10

Twelve feet in the air on top of a giant inflatable slide, Quinn watched Susannah hand her ticket to the attendant at the entrance to Gaslight Park. The picnic and children's area of Hank Aaron Stadium was full this afternoon, swarming with peewee ball teams, families, and church groups. Susannah disappeared into the crowd.

Sending little black Kenny Pettway zooming down the slide, he contemplated jumping off the back way.

Susannah. Every time he got around her she managed to extract things from him he'd just as soon stay bottled up where they wouldn't bother anybody but him. Why had he even mentioned his grandfather? Now he felt guilty he hadn't talked to the old man since he'd called Quinn to say Jana and the kids were coming home.

And rightly so. That had been two months ago. First thing tomorrow morning he was going to call Grandpa at the Farm and Feed—wait, no, tomorrow was Sunday. The store would be closed. Okay, then tomorrow afternoon he'd call him at the house.

He looked for Susannah and found her watching some kids in the ball pit, with her face mashed up against the mesh enclosure. The aggravating thing was, she seemed so interested in asking *him* questions, he really didn't know anything important about her.

"Hey, Coach Quinn, are you gonna slide or are you just gonna stand there?"

Quinn turned around to find one of the Stevenson twins hopping up and down with impatience. He squinted at her, trying to remember which one wore her dark hair parted on the left. "Okay, Toni, I'm going. See you at the bottom."

"I'm Tacy!" she screamed as he jumped.

Climbing to his feet, Quinn made his way toward the gate. Skirting pavilions and picnic tables, he looked for Susannah in the crowd of parents, coaches, and kids swarming all over the park. On a beautiful Saturday evening, it was a great place for families to hang together. Man, he loved the smell of a ballpark. Popcorn, cotton candy, peanuts, and a bunch of other stuff he couldn't readily identify. He'd never get tired of it. Maybe one day he'd have his own kids, and bring them to the games. After he got a wife, of course.

He spotted Susannah, wearing an orange T-shirt and khaki shorts. She had a flowered handkerchief tied around her hair, and bright purple socks peeked out above her sneakers. The bizarre look somehow suited her. He didn't want to consider what that said about her personality.

Waving, she hurried toward him. "I found you! I'm sorry I couldn't make it to your game. Did you win?"

"Sure did." Quinn fell into step with Susannah. "Got a bunch of happy little guys and girls running around here."

"I bet. What was the score?"

"Eighteen-five. Hey, can I put you to work? The kids have been pestering me for hot dogs since we got here."

"Sure, what can I do?"

"Come on, I'll show you." He led the way to a pavilion near the fence, where a couple of covered metal catering tubs and an ice chest had been stashed. "We're gonna just let the kids come by and load up their plates. If you'll give each one a hot dog and a bag of chips, I'll handle the drinks."

"That sounds easy enough."

"Good. I'll go round up the kids."

She got the plates and napkins ready while he located the twins, who ran to help him find the rest of the team. Within two minutes they were all gathered in a jumping, jabbering knot of energy in the pavilion. Susannah squirted mustard, handed out napkins, and generally organized the feeding of fifteen grade-school hobbits. Quinn took charge of the ice chest. Like a horde of locusts, the team tore through the kid-style feast. Susannah laughed and dealt with spills and whines and hurt feelings with unexpected aplomb.

He didn't know what he would have done without her.

When the last chocolate chip cookie had been doled out, she wiped her hands on the seat of her shorts and turned to Quinn with a smile in her blue eyes. "I'm just curious. Who paid for all this?"

"Uh, me." He grabbed a hot dog, a bag of chips, and a drink, handed them to Susannah, and then gathered his own meal. "Come on. Our turn to eat." He led the way to a picnic table vacated by the kids.

Susannah sat down across from him and tore open her bag of chips. "You do this kind of blowout party for the team often?"

"No, just once at the beginning of the season and once at the end. It's no big deal, I have a college buddy who's the manager here. He lets us in the game free. Besides, I have as much fun as they do." He picked up his hot dog. "So what have you been up to?"

She looked at him for a minute, smiling, then shrugged. "Not much. Had another interview this morning."

"So you're finding what you need for your thesis?"

She dropped her gaze and concentrated on wiping a blob of relish off the table with a napkin. "It's going pretty slow." She cleared her throat. "I want to hear about the game. How old are these kids?"

He accepted the abrupt change of subject, though it was getting peculiar she didn't want to talk about her project. Maybe Rebecca was right, and she *was* a corporate spy. *Ha ha.* Like he had any big secrets worth stealing. "They're nine- and ten-year-olds. Big enough to start grabbing some of the concepts of strategy, and still young enough to have respect for a coach."

"How'd you get roped into coaching Little League, when you don't—" Susannah's cheeks reddened. "You *don't* have any kids of your own, do you?"

He laughed. "Nope, no skeletons in my closet. I just like to stay busy and give back some of what athletics has given me over the years." He paused. "It's a sort of a spiritual project too."

"A spiritual project?" Susannah looked intrigued. "How's that?"

"Well ..." Quinn despised bragging, and he'd never told anybody why he'd taken on this team. "About a year ago, a bunch of guys at church were sitting around after a Bible study, trying to figure out how to apply what we'd been learning—"

"And what was that?" Susannah watched his face with intense blue eyes.

"Oh—a Scripture out of Mark." This was so embarrassing. He was never any good at explaining the Bible to anybody else. "We'd been talking about being leaders. You know, where Jesus says to be great, you have to be the lowest of servants."

"Huh?"

He took a breath. "Okay, well, nearly everything Jesus taught is backwards and upside down from the way the world operates. For example, if you love your life, you lose it."

She had such an expressive face, he could almost see the thoughts chasing through her brain: *The guy's insane. Humor him.*

"So what does that have to do with coaching baseball?"

"Not much, you'd think. But I got to thinking about how much time and energy I'd spent trying to build my company, and how God's blessed it. So I looked around for ways to serve with it, and somebody suggested sponsoring an inner-city team." He laughed. "Turned out it's a tax write-off. How's that for providence? Then I found out the team I wanted to sponsor didn't have a coach, so I thought, why not." He shrugged. "Guess I'm fairly well qualified."

"Cool." Elbow on table, Susannah propped her chin on her fist. "So is that your testimony?"

He blinked. "My testimony?" Oh, the conversation at Elva Kay's house on Sunday. "Part of it. You could come tomorrow night to hear the rest of it."

She wadded up her trash. "Maybe. Isn't it time for the game to start?"

Quinn looked at his watch. "Yep. Help me gather up the kids, would you?"

Oh well, he thought, beginning the roundup. So he wasn't destined to set the world on fire with evangelistic zeal. But at least he'd given it a stab. Maybe Dana would follow up later.

At the moment he had fifteen hyperactive miniature baseball players under his care. That gave him plenty to worry about.

Jumping to her feet, Susannah put two fingers to her lips and blasted out a whistle as the BayBears' left fielder leaped to catch a fly ball just before it sailed over onto BayBear Mountain. She turned to slap hands with Quinn. "Third out!"

He was laughing at her. "That whistle is amazing."

"I was well taught." They sat down again as the home team trotted into the dugout for the change of innings, and Susannah reached down for the box of Cracker Jacks Quinn had bought for her. "How about you? Do you have brothers and sisters?"

"One younger sister." Quinn poked through his bag of sunflower seeds. "I haven't seen Jana in several years, but she's coming back to Mississippi this summer. I'll get to meet my niece and nephew for the first time."

Susannah stared at him, intrigued by this unexpected confidence. Talking about his grandfather the other night had seemed to surprise him as much as her. He spit out a sunflower husk and popped another one into his mouth. After a moment he looked at her, a smile she didn't understand pulling at the corners of his eyes. Shades of color there, as complex as the ocean, drew her until she had a completely inappropriate urge to touch his face.

She tucked her fingers between her knees. "Where's she been?"

"It's kind of a long story." He slid down on his tailbone, propping his feet on the seat in front of him. "When Jana was eighteen—I was in college by then—she ran off with this loser from down the road. Just disappeared, and nobody heard from her until a few years ago when my grandpa traced her to Knoxville, Tennessee. Her husband had died, and she was finishing up college. She graduates from vet school in May."

Susannah had a hard time deciding which track to follow and went for nonconfrontational. "Sounds like a smart lady."

"There's no doubt Jana's a bright girl, even though she made some dumb decisions as a teenager." He smiled. "She was always an animal nut, even when she was small. I'll never forget the summer she raised an albino fawn. The interesting thing is, she became a Christian right about the same time I did."

Susannah frowned. "You talk a lot like my brother Jeremy. He thinks I should 'convert' too. I keep telling him I'm already a Christian. I mean, I'm not a Hindu or Muslim or anything."

Quinn was quiet for a moment, then reached down to grab a giveaway bat that Kenny and Jacob, seated below them, were wrestling over. "Knock it off, guys, or we'll go home early." He stuffed the bat under his seat along with three others he'd already collected, then glanced at Susannah. "I can see where you'd get that idea."

"But you think I'm wrong?"

"Let's just say it's a whole lot simpler than that, and a little more complicated."

Susannah had to laugh. "Not according to my brother. He thinks if you're not a Jesus Freak, you're going to hell."

"What do you think? About Jesus, I mean?"

In one of those stinging flashes of crystal awareness, Susannah realized she'd never had to articulate the answer to that question—at least as an adult. As a child she'd parroted some of the traditional Christmas themes of Jesus as the Prince of Peace, the King of Kings, Wonderful Counselor, et cetera. On Easter she would put on a pretty dress and take Communion, making faces at the dry, unsalted crackers and warm grape juice. But the rituals never penetrated beyond momentary thoughts.

The BayBears' shortstop whacked a triple into center field, the crowd around her erupted into roars of approval, and she sat glued to her seat, hardly aware of the noise and movement around her. Up to now, she hadn't considered that her opinion about a man named Jesus mattered one iota.

But what if Jeremy was right? What if Quinn had just asked her a question of far more significance than anything she'd studied in school? He sat beside her munching sunflower seeds, not looking at her. But she somehow knew his entire focus was on her.

"I guess ... I guess I don't know him well enough to have an opinion."

"That's honest at least." He smiled and offered her the bag of seeds. "Maybe you should check it out so you can give your brother a good argument."

Susannah took a handful of seeds, wrinkling her nose. "You don't know Jeremy. He's like a bulldog when he gets on that subject."

"I'm guessing you can hold your own in a debate," Quinn said with a grin.

"So why aren't *you* cramming it down my throat?"

"Because I don't have to."

Now what did he mean by that? She narrowed her eyes at him, hoping to shake his confidence, hoping not to. He gave her that full-on, high-wattage smile. Flustered, she turned her attention to the game, savoring the salt on her tongue as the BayBears scored a run.

When the crowd settled down again, Susannah looked at Quinn. "Did you put Dana Carter up to calling me?"

"Nope." His eyes twinkled.

"She said you're running in the race."

"Uh-huh. I'm gonna win it."

She gave a startled laugh. "How do you know that?"

"I've trained and I'm ready. I'll be pressin' for the prize."

"You are something else, Quinn Baldwin. I don't know what to think about you either." She folded her arms. "But win or lose, I'll be there to give you a cup of water."

"Reckon why she's got two tails?" Clint Harrison leaned over the Little Mermaid Pool, staring at its graceful terra cotta fountain with a puzzled squint wrinkling his good-natured face.

Quinn laughed. "One of those unexplained mysteries of life, I guess."

He'd asked Clint and his wife to come with him after church to Bellingrath Gardens to pray. With a camouflage fishing hat covering his bald head, the big, bearded, dry docks supervisor looked more like a shrimper than anybody's spiritual mentor.

But when Quinn needed somebody to pray, the Harrisons were the first ones he called. That morning during church he could hardly concentrate on the service for worrying about his testimony tonight. What would he say? What if he sounded like a redneck? There were a bunch of educated, articulate people in this church, and he had a horror of letting the Lord down.

He didn't advertise how often he came here. A lot of his male friends would consider his love for gardens a weird quirk. But since the first time Elva Kay had brought him to Bellingrath, he came whenever he needed a place to get away and think. A couple of hours lost in the beauty and variety of color and texture of God's creation always set him straight.

Today he needed it bad.

Located on Fowl River just southeast of Mobile, the Gardens had once been the country estate of Coca-Cola magnate Walter Bellingrath. Over a forty-year period in the first half of the twentieth century, Bessie Bellingrath had transformed her husband's fishing camp into a botanical showplace. Now it was a major tourist attraction, the setting for scores of weddings throughout the year. Which was great for Quinn's business.

Though the rose garden was his favorite spot on the estate, he'd towed Clint and Julianne past it without going in. It was still a little early for the roses to be in full bloom, but the azaleas lining the walkways were going crazy this year. He was glad the gardeners quit pruning them into flat, puritanical hedges, instead letting them grow into their natural shapes—some nearly six feet tall, and all loaded with flamboyant blooms. Pink and white petals littered the walks like a bridal path. He couldn't help thinking how much Susannah would like this place. Maybe Elva Kay would bring her here sometime.

Clint whacked him on the arm, jostling him out of his reverie. "Come on, man, Julianne's got the fried chicken out over there. Let's eat, and you can tell us what's bugging you."

He followed Clint to the bench where Julianne had unpacked a wicker picnic basket. Midforties, red-haired, and comfortably cushioned, she looked up and smiled. She wasn't quite old enough to be Quinn's mother, but she'd filled the role just the same. Though it was a second marriage for both her and Clint, they'd learned from mistakes and moved into a strong and deep mutual walk with the Lord. Quinn loved to watch them together.

"White meat or dark?" Julianne offered Quinn the cardboard bucket.

"Dark." He helped himself to a drumstick and sat cross-legged on the ground while Clint landed on the bench. "Thanks for bringing this."

"Long as I didn't have to cook and clean up, I'm happy. The Colonel and I have a long-standing relationship." She smiled and poked Clint's broad middle. "Frequent too."

"Now, Mama." Clint's laugh rumbled. "You're gonna hurt my feelings. Where's the potato salad?"

"Here." Julianne opened a quart container and gave him a plastic fork. "Just leave a little bit for Quinn and me." She glanced at Quinn. "Clint said you wanted to pray about your talk tonight."

"Yeah. I want to be open to what God wants me to say. I don't want the focus on me—but on him." He hesitated. "If there happens to be somebody there who doesn't know him ..."

"Sounds like you might know someone like that who'll be there."

"There's a friend of mine who said she might come. Actually, I wanted you two to be praying for her."

Julianne's bright green eyes lit. "A young lady?"

"Her name is Susannah." He opened his hands, staring at a blue hydrangea on the opposite side of the fountain. It was just about the color of Susannah's eyes. "She's renting Elva Kay's upstairs room for a few—" What, weeks? Months? He didn't even know how long Susannah planned to stay in Mobile. "For a while," he finally added. "So she's getting that influence every day."

Julianne laughed. "Then she doesn't stand a chance. Okay, baby, we'll pray. You just let the Lord put the words in your mouth."

Quinn couldn't have explained the peace that flooded his spirit just then. But he was grateful for it.

Lord, help me glorify you tonight. And please draw Susannah to yourself.

chapter 11

Susannah took Monty with her across the river. She'd always thought it would be fun to live in a city near the ocean, and she enjoyed the Sunday afternoon drive down Government Street with a strong river breeze blowing across the Jeep's open top. There were two tunnels under the river, and she chose the older Bankhead Tunnel.

Halfway through, Monty sat up in the backseat and his excited barking echoed off the rounded tile walls.

Susannah laughed. "Kind of like singing in the shower, huh, big guy?"

Once they were out in the open, the dog quieted again, laying his nose on the back of Susannah's seat. She reached back to pet him as she turned left onto the eastern bank of the river.

To her left was a series of industrial and shipping complexes composed of vast concrete and aluminum warehouses, steel silos, and cranes. Across the river she could see the Alabama State Docks, a train bumbling down the riverside tracks, and the messed-up Convention Center.

Susannah had to admit that, despite a mixture of funky odors, Mobile was a charming little city. A fresh breeze off the Gulf alleviated some of the heat, and the cry of seagulls wheeling along the shore filled her with a melancholy sort of peace. There was a sense of permanence about this place.

The landscape on this side of the river was different, though. Raw and desolate, quiet as a graveyard. She'd have to come back during the week to interview the owners of the property where the explosion occurred. First, however, she wanted to check it out for herself: get a feel for the slope and texture of the ground, distance from the river and the road, composition of the surrounding buildings.

According to archived newspaper articles and the TV reporters she'd interviewed, Quinn had set up his shells and equipment on an empty lot next to Clancy Brothers Drydock and Repair. He'd parked his van and truck near the road, then carried the cases of fireworks to the field.

There was the dry dock, a big 3,000-square-foot aluminum building with the name of the company on a sign near the road. A chain-link fence bordered the property, with only a simple yellow-painted iron chain across the opening. Apparently the Clancy brothers weren't overly concerned about trespassers.

Susannah parked outside the chain. The place was deserted. She got out, letting Monty leap out with her. He pressed close to her side, and she gave him a pat as they approached the opening in the fence. There was a big yellow sign fastened to the chain: "All visitors report to the office." She stepped over it as Monty ducked under.

Oyster shells and gravel crunched underfoot as she walked toward the river. The strong odors of oil and diesel fumes carried up from the boatworks all along the river. Not the best surroundings for a fireworks display. Could some fuel oil have leaked from somewhere, accelerating the ignition of the fireworks?

It was possible, but from what she could tell as she walked around the property, everything was tight and dry. Of course it would be, after an explosion of this magnitude.

Susannah inspected the exterior of the dry docks building and the entire perimeter of the parking lot. Walking down to the river, she stood listening to the lap of the water. Peaceful. Quiet. Hard to imagine the staggering effect of the blast that had caused major damage to a building all the way across the river.

Where had the fire department been? Police barricades were usually set up, with a couple of squad cars for enforcement. If Quinn had failed to secure proper barricades and fire safety, he could be liable.

Bringing Monty to heel with a whistle—he loved water and was likely to jump in—Susannah moved to the end of the pier, where Quinn had been when the explosion went off. With her back to the water she studied the dockyard. The fire marshal would have been first to arrive on the scene, and he would have called in ATF. Starting from the blast seat, they would have worked the scene as a team, gathering explosive debris in sterile bags. No question, she was going to have to see the fire marshal's report. Pulling out her PDA, she made a note to call for an appointment.

Monty shoved against her knee, panting. Leaning down, she scratched under his collar.

"Quinn must be in deep trouble if he did something like this on purpose," she muttered. She'd picked through the aftermath of enough explosions that she had no trouble imagining what he must have felt like, lying flat on his face while thousands of dollars' worth of fireworks self-destructed right over his head.

Of course, people would do insane things for money. She'd seen it happen over and over.

But *Quinn*? She'd watched him with the children last night. Endlessly patient, he'd answered questions, listened to knock-knock jokes, performed bathroom sentry duty, bought popcorn and sodas, and even arranged for them all to get into the Stadium Club for ice cream.

It occurred to her that lately she'd been thinking of him by his first name. Not just Baldwin, the suspect. The more she got to know him, the more personal this investigation became.

Connecting him to this crime scene took a greater leap of faith than believing him innocent.

Which would not make Simon Webster happy.

But it was still early in the investigation. Tomorrow was soon enough to worry about all the people she still had to interview.

She gave Monty a last squeeze and stood up irresolute. The dog looked up at her, as if to say, *Okay, now what are we going to do?*

"Want to go play with Belshazzar?" Monty's ears went flat, and Susannah laughed. "Okay, we can do better than that, huh?" The thought of spending Sunday night shut up in her room with a book was depressing.

Back in Tucson she had friends she could have called up, but here the only people she knew—Elva Kay, Quinn, Skeet, Dana, even Rebecca—went to church on Sunday nights.

Church? Quinn had invited her to come.

She should go running. That was the way to dust off cobwebs and cleanse the spirit. She wasn't dressed for it now, but she could go home and change into her shorts and running shoes, take Monty out around the neighborhood before it got dark. She grinned. Wouldn't want to make Quinn frown at her.

She snapped her fingers at Monty and headed for the car. Maybe other people needed religion to deal with their loneliness. *Not me.* She could make her own peace.

Quinn blinked when Susannah walked through the door into the worship center. He stood on the platform in front of the congregation, waiting for the worship leader to turn the service over to him—and trying to pretend he wasn't about to throw up from nervousness.

How many business presentations had he made over the last few years? How many times had he stood in front of young ballplayers, demonstrating techniques for swinging a bat or throwing a ball?

But boy, this was different. He'd promised Julianne he wouldn't worry. But claiming the Lord had changed his life, trying to articulate what those changes were ...

Made his stomach churn to think about it.

Susannah took a seat on the back row, separating herself from everyone else. Even though he'd asked her to come, he couldn't believe she was here. Was she that curious?

He smiled a little, the knot in his stomach relaxing. Susannah couldn't be still for five minutes. She'd been on her feet during most of the game last night—except for the awkward discussion about Jesus. He should have kept his mouth shut, waited and let somebody like Dana, who had had real evangelism training, talk to her.

The kids on the team had loved Susannah. She didn't know any better than to talk to them like grown-ups, and she understood the language of the game.

Whatever her reason for coming tonight, he hoped God would do something beyond his own ability. *Father, I give myself to you ...*

The worship leader offered a prayer, then the musicians laid down their instruments and microphones and sat down. Everyone looked at Quinn.

He took a mike off a stand and walked to the edge of the platform. Skeet had sat down with several other single pals, about three rows back from the front. Wow, and there was Rebecca too. He'd had no idea she planned to come. Skeet must have told her about it. These were his friends, his family. Time to grow up. Stuffing his free hand into his pocket, he cleared his throat.

"I'm no public speaker, but there's a couple of things on my mind tonight. Not too long ago, somebody asked me what a testimony was." His gaze found Susannah. When her eyes widened, he smiled. "I guess it's just telling about what you've witnessed or experienced. Most of you know that about ten years ago I was wandering around like a dog without a collar. Didn't have enough education to keep a decent job, and too proud to ask for help. Finally somebody told me they were hiring down at the State Docks. So I went over there, and who should I wind up working with but good old Clint Harrison."

There was a general hoot across the congregation, because everybody knew and loved Clint. Holding hands with Julianne, he beamed like a giant southern variety of Santa Claus.

Quinn shook his head. "There are some trials nobody should have to bear." He winked at Julianne, who blew him a kiss. "Anyway, it took Clint about a week to get me to the point where I agreed to read the gospel of John just to get him off my back. And all the time he kept telling me God loved me and had good things in mind for me — if I'd just get over my pride and let Jesus be my boss. I decided to come to church here to see what made this guy so different from all the other knuckleheads down at the docks."

He swallowed, sudden emotion thickening his throat. "For the first time since I had to leave college, I felt like I belonged someplace. I wanted what you people had. You loved me to Christ. I think that's what the church is supposed to be.

"Most of you know things haven't been easy lately. God gave me my business, but I almost handed it back when this accident happened. It's been embarrassing, but I just keep hanging onto the Psalms — especially the one that says God is our refuge and strength, an ever-present help in trouble. So I won't be afraid, though the earth gives way and the mountains fall into the heart of the sea, though its waters roar and foam—he's there."

Quinn found his voice strengthening. He didn't know where the words came from, but he felt like shouting. "You know what, he's so good! I don't know what he's going to do with me, but I know I'll never go back to what I was before. I've got a lot to learn, I just hope—I hope you'll all be patient with me while I'm in the process." He caught Susannah's gaze. He couldn't have interpreted her tense expression if his life depended on it. "I just want you to know, because of you I've found real purpose in my life. I understand what I'm on this earth for. I think ... that's all I have to say."

He shrugged, walked off the platform, and collapsed on the front row.

When a round of applause went up, Quinn sat dazed, feeling drained and exhilarated all at once. Maybe that hadn't been too terrible.

Pastor Martin, sitting beside him, smiled and shook his hand, then stepped onto the platform to wrap up the service. The musicians returned and began a soft altar-call chorus. All Quinn could do now was pray.

A few minutes later, as the music ended, he opened his eyes and looked for Susannah again. She was gone. He shouldn't be surprised. She'd probably been unable to stomach another open profession of Christ.

Skeet came over to pump his hand. "Dude, that was awesome. I can't wait to talk to Susannah."

"She left."

"No, she didn't. She walked down the aisle to talk to Martin, and he handed her off to one of the girls. Dana, I think."

"What? Where are they?"

"You mean you didn't see?" Skeet laughed and shuffled into a hyper dance step. "They went to one of the counseling rooms."

"No way."

"Man, you got about zero faith sometimes. Haven't you been praying for her?"

"Of course I have, but ..." Quinn lifted his hands. "She's just been so cynical and disinterested about Christianity. It just seems too ... I don't know, *easy*. That she would make a commitment of faith like this out of the blue. I'm sure she's just asking questions. That would make more sense."

Skeet gave him a long, thoughtful look. "You got a pretty wide cynical streak yourself, man. Don't sell the Holy Spirit short. Look, I've got to catch Martin about the Japan mission trip before he gets away. When Susannah comes back, tell her I'm happy for her."

"Okay." Quinn stationed himself outside the door to the counseling area to wait. He tried to imagine Susannah taking seriously anything Dana had to say.

Lord, help my unbelief, he thought, shaking his head.

Susannah could see no way out of the room short of leapfrogging over Dana Carter. So she sat with her head bowed, letting herself be prayed over as she replayed Quinn's words in her mind.

She'd walked down the aisle to talk to him, but had been headed off by the pastor—a nice guy who misunderstood everything Susannah said and passed her off to Short Stuff here.

I don't know what he's going to do with me, Quinn had said, *but I'll never go back to what I was before ... I hope you'll be patient with me while I'm in the process.*

He had been looking at her. *In the process of what?*

She had so many questions about where he'd come from. He seemed like such a normal kind of guy. If he'd dropped out of college and gone to work at the docks, where had he gotten the capital to start up a business that, in the short span of five years, seemed to be doing very well?

"Amen." Squeezing Susannah's hands, Dana looked up and beamed. "I'm so happy you came forward. Are you ready to pray?"

"Pray?" Susannah snatched her hands back. "Um, to be blunt, no. I just wanted to talk to Quinn."

"But ..." Dana looked ready to cry.

Susannah regretted that, but she wasn't going to sell her soul so easily.

"Look, Dana." She shouldered her backpack. "I appreciate your concern, but I'm already a Christian in my own way. Believe me, my brother's as gung ho as you are, and he's on my case all the time about coming to church more often."

Dana bit her bottom lip. An astute gleam appeared in her big brown eyes. "I bet he says you need to do more than come to church. Sitting in an oven doesn't make you a biscuit, you know."

Susannah laughed. "Especially a cat-head." Dana looked confused. "Never mind, I get your point. But I think you guys are off on some things. There's more than one way to get to heaven." She rose and started to walk off.

"Not unless Jesus was just kidding."

"What?" Taken aback, Susannah frowned.

"Well, he claimed he was God's only Son and that he was the only way to connect with God." Dana sat with her hands folded in ladylike fashion in her lap.

That sounded like something Jeremy had spouted at her a number of times. She'd never paid attention, because after all, what did her *brother* know about anything? Always up for a debate, Susannah put her hands on her hips. "Is that in the Bible?"

"Yes. John 14:6."

"Okay, I believe in Jesus. So I'm covered, right?"

"Susannah." Dana's kittenish face softened along with her voice. "Would you sit down for a minute? You're giving me a crick in my neck."

Startled into laughter, Susannah complied. "Sorry."

"It looks like you're getting defensive, and the last thing I want to do is make you think people at church are judgmental and hypercritical." Since that was exactly what Susannah had been thinking, she clamped her lips together. Dana smiled. "If I give you my Bible, will you read what Jesus had to say for himself?"

"I can't take your Bible," Susannah said gruffly.

"Sure you can. I've got another one. I promise there's lots of good stuff there, to help you with whatever happens to be going on in your life."

Susannah doubted anything in the big hardback book in Dana's lap would help her figure out Quinn Baldwin. But she'd wasted enough time in here. Quinn would have left by now, which was too bad. She'd wanted to talk to him.

"Oh, all right." Heaving a deep sigh, Susannah held out her hand. "Let me have it."

"I'm so happy!" Eyes shining, Dana handed over her Bible.

Having done her good deed for the day, Susannah started to get up again, then sat back down with a slight grin. "Mother may I?"

Dana dimpled. "Yes, you may."

chapter 12

Susannah came out of the counseling area holding a Bible, and Quinn considered doing a handspring.

Then he caught the expression on her face. Reality check. She didn't look like a person who'd just given her life to Christ. She spotted him and stopped dead in her tracks. Then Dana Carter poked her head from behind Susannah, and they looked so much like a totem pole Quinn stood up, grinning.

"Hey!" he said. "You didn't tell me you were coming tonight."

"I decided at the last minute." Susannah stuck the Bible under her arm. "Didn't have anything else to do tonight, and I hate TV."

He winked at Dana, who sidled past Susannah, a pleased little smile curling her lips. "What's up, Dana?"

"Great job tonight, Quinn," she said, lighting up. "I love to hear how God speaks to people in different ways. My story is so boring. I've been in Sunday school since Cradle Roll, and I never have anything interesting to share."

"What's Cradle Roll?" Susannah unzipped her backpack and dropped the Bible in.

"Tell you the truth, I don't know." Dana wrinkled her freckled nose. "My grandma always said that. I guess she meant Mama brought us kids to church when we were just babies."

"Don't sell yourself short." Quinn thought of all the years he'd wasted before he'd met Christ. "People can look at you and see how walking with the Lord for a long time saves them from a lot of unnecessary heartache."

Dana blushed. "That's very sweet, Quinn. Thanks." She smiled at Susannah, who had begun to inch toward the door. "Can you meet me for lunch one day this week, Susannah? We can talk about any questions that come up as you read."

Cornered, Susannah backed toward the door. "I don't know, I'm pretty busy this week."

"Come on, you've got to eat! I know this darling place called Miss C's Sippy Tea Room, we could even wear a hat and a boa and gloves—"

Susannah started to laugh. For the first time Quinn noticed the rips in both knees of her jeans, the well-worn Birkenstocks, the black T-shirt that read "Love the Skin You're In." Her hair was drawn out of her face with a red shoelace.

"I could come up with a baseball cap," Susannah said, still chuckling, "but I'd stick a pencil in my eye before I'd wear a boa *or* gloves."

"In that case, we'll just take a lunch to the park or something. I can make pimento cheese sandwiches and—"

"Dana." Quinn had caught Susannah's beseeching look. "You two can work out the details later, but Susannah and I have to go. Give her your phone number and she can call you, okay?"

Dana's eyes widened, and Quinn realized too late he'd implied more than he meant.

"Ohhh." Her eyebrows arched. "I gotcha." Pulling the purple pen and a flowered notebook out of her handbag, Dana printed her number, then handed it to Susannah.

Susannah stuffed the paper in her pocket and backed toward the door. "I'll give you a call this week. I have to get home and let my dog out."

"A dog?" Dana gasped. "What kind of dog?"

"Monty's a black Lab."

"I have a Shih Tzu named Bubbles! I can't *believe* we have so much in common!" Dana put her pen and notebook back into her purse. "Give him a hug for me!"

Quinn gave Dana a quick thumbs-up and took off after Susannah. Those long legs could eat up distance. He caught up to her in the empty lobby. "Susannah! Wait up!"

She turned and grimaced. "Under no circumstances will I wear a boa."

He laughed. "I have to tell you, I find that reassuring." He held the door for her. "You should probably start in John."

"What?"

He followed her to the parking lot. "The Bible. Start with the gospel of John."

"I like to go from the beginning of things."

Good night, she didn't like to be told what to do. "You can always go back and do that later. But if you're interested in the claims of Christ, you'd be better off to read the story of his life."

She reached her Jeep, which was parked next to his truck, and leaned against the door looking up at him. "I liked what you said tonight. I was coming to tell you so, when the guy with the beard grabbed me."

"Pastor Martin." He cleared his throat. "I was pretty nervous. I'm not much of a speaker."

"Yeah, but you were sincere. See, that's what's important. You're okay as long as you believe what you've experienced."

"I thought that for a long time too." Quinn paused, groping for a gentle way to tell Susannah she was dead wrong. "But reality is, experiences and feelings can lead you way off base."

He saw something click in her brain. She started to comment, then looked away. "I've got a busy week, so I'd better get home."

Her gaze skated past his again as she opened the door of her Jeep. "Let me know if I can help with the team again. I've done a little coaching before."

"Okay. 'Night, Susannah."

He waited until she'd driven off in the direction of their neighborhood before he got in his own vehicle. He sat there a minute feeling let down. Then his own words hit him.

Feelings could get you off track in a hurry. Most of the time the Holy Spirit worked behind the scenes when things were looking their worst. Best thing anybody could do was pray and trust God to handle the details.

And that goes for me too.

When Susannah got home she found Elva Kay sitting at the computer, finishing an email to her sister, who lived in an assisted-living facility in Peachtree, Georgia. The women corresponded often, though they only visited once or twice a year.

Susannah sat down on the living room floor so Monty could flop across her legs. He whined until she scratched him under his collar.

Elva Kay swiveled her computer chair around. "What have you got there?" She nodded at the book in Susannah's lap.

"A Bible. A girl at Quinn's church gave it to me."

"Oh, lovely! I should have thought of that, but I assumed you had one."

"I do. My brother gave it to me for Christmas, but I left it in Tucson. Didn't think I'd have time for it."

"Ah." Susannah halfway expected Elva Kay to launch into a sermon, but she smiled instead. "I'd like to meet your brother one day. What does he do?"

"He's a policeman." Susannah remembered telling Quinn about her brothers. She almost wished the two men could meet. They'd have a lot to talk about. Like Susannah the Heathen Infidel. She grinned. "He and his wife are about to have their first baby. I can't wait to see what it looks like."

"All babies are beautiful." Elva Kay's smile broadened. "Even when they look like Yoda."

"Do you have children, Elva Kay?"

"No. We wanted them, but back in those days infertile couples didn't have all this fancy medicine and in vitro stuff that's available now. Dr. Shue and I just had each other."

Susannah smiled at her landlady's charming old-fashioned way of referring to her late husband. "Was he a medical doctor?"

Elva Kay nodded. "He was an army surgeon stationed in England near the end of the war, and I went over as a nurse. We married right after VE Day."

Susannah stared. "Boy, that was a quick romance."

"We didn't want to waste a minute apart. Time's precious."

Susannah squirmed a little. She didn't have much time in Mobile, which was too bad. She was just beginning to feel strangely at home.

"Vancleave Farm and Feed." The irritable gravelly voice in Quinn's ear reminded him of why he waited so long in between phone calls. His grandfather threatened every month to disconnect the phone in his store. Said it interrupted business.

"Hey, Grandpa, how ya doing?" He sat at the Krispy Kreme counter, sipping coffee and playing a game of checkers with Mr. Thibodeaux. The old man reminded him a lot of his grandfather. In fact, Grandpa was pretty fond of checkers too.

"This Quinn? Where are you, boy?"

Quinn smiled. The irritation level had dropped to mild annoyance. "Mobile. I'm headed to work, here in a little bit, and I thought I'd call and check on you." He'd meant to do it yesterday, but thinking about Susannah and his testimony had sent his intentions to call Grandpa clean out of his mind.

"Check on me? I told you two months ago I was fine. I'll let you know if something changes."

"King me." Mr. Thibodeaux cackled. He had just jumped three of Quinn's men and landed on his back row.

He scowled at the old man to make him happy and covered his king. "Did you cheat when I wasn't looking?"

"Cheat?" said Grandpa. "You know I run a legitimate business and I wouldn't—"

"Sorry, Grandpa, I wasn't talking to you."

"Then what'd you call me for?"

"I told you—" Quinn sighed. "I was just thinking about you the other day and wanted to tell you I love you. I'm going to drive over there when Jana gets home this summer. Spend a few days with y'all."

There was dead silence over the line for a few seconds. Quinn looked at his cell phone to make sure he was still getting a signal.

Finally Grandpa said, "Are you feeling all right, boy? You're not dying of some gosh-awful virus, are you?"

"No, I'm fine." He rested his forehead in the heel of his hand. Grandpa would cut out his tongue before he ever said "I love you" to another man, even his own grandson. "I just wanted to tell you I'm practicing my checkers, so you'd better brush up before I get home."

Grandpa snorted. "The day you beat me in checkers is the day I'm puttin' on my pine pajamas and layin' down for a long sleep. Now let me go 'cause I got a customer, and there's a delivery truck out to the warehouse." There was a brief pause. "You can call closer to the time, let me know exactly when you'll be here. I'll have to change the sheets."

That was about as close as he was going to get to a declaration of affection. Smiling, Quinn said goodbye and closed his phone. He moved one of his checkers into Mr. Thibodeaux's back row and grinned at the wily old man's chagrin. "Crown me, Mr. T. I'm not giving up yet."

After spending most of Monday wangling her way into the fire marshal's office, where she received the same response she'd gotten at the ATF office—"We'll mail you a report, Ms. Tait, after you fill out the appropriate forms"—Susannah drove over to the junior high school where Skeet taught. She'd never known a band director who didn't hold sectionals every afternoon after school.

Locating the band hall by listening for the cacophony of instruments, she found Skeet standing in front of a semicircle of clarinet players honking their way through a simplified Aaron Copeland overture. She stood in the doorway, fond memories of her own junior high days crowding her mind.

At the end of the piece Skeet cut the group off with a slash of the pencil in his hand. "Okay, troops, that's enough for today. Put 'em up and promise me you'll practice at home. Contest is in two weeks."

As the rehearsal disbanded with a clatter of stands and a few reedy squawks, Skeet waved Susannah over. "Hey, lady! What brings you out to the wilds of middle school land?" He closed his conductor's folder, stuck the pencil behind his ear, and started moving chairs back to concert setup.

"Hey, Tiffany, Mr. Lawrence has finally got a girlfriend!" squealed a skinny young girl with a mouthful of metal and rubber bands.

Her friend stared openmouthed at Susannah. "She's too tall for him." The two of them followed the crowd into an open instrument storage room.

Pretending not to have heard the loud exchange, Susannah pitched in to help Skeet.

"Sorry about that," Skeet said when all the students had left. "Manners and inhibitions get closer to extinction every year I teach."

"It hasn't been that long since I was fourteen." Susannah laughed. "Girls that age have only one thing on the brain."

"Don't I know it. I'm glad you came in. Old Aaron's probably rolling in his grave." Skeet hopped onto his director's stool and tipped it back against the wall. "One day I'm gonna retire and go on the road with the guys in the praise band."

Susannah chose a chair that looked like it might not topple with the first false move and sat down. "I could see you doing that."

Skeet's hazel eyes twinkled. "In the meantime, I do my part to reestablish cultural dignity in the South."

Susannah smiled. "You're kidding, but I admire you and Quinn a lot. You don't sit back and let things slide. You make a difference in your community."

Skeet regarded her with a wry twist to his fine mouth. "Says the sociologist?"

"Says a person interested in your religion." Susannah reached down to pick up a wooden metronome balanced on a stack of music on the floor. She slid the weighted pendulum free and let it tick a few times before putting it back. "Did you and Quinn meet at church?"

"Yep. We were both going to the big church out by the interstate. Martin, our pastor, wanted to start a church that would reach people like—" he grinned a little—"people who wouldn't understand the lingo and music of the traditional-style church."

"People like me?" she guessed, and Skeet laughed. "I think it works. You've made me listen."

"That's good." He took the pencil from behind his ear and started tapping it against his music stand. Man, the guy was a live wire. "Susannah, I'm glad you're interested in our church, but don't make a decision just for Quinn's sake, okay?"

"I promise you I don't let anybody else dictate my personal beliefs." She hesitated. How could she slide the conversation in the direction she needed it to go? "Have you been helping Quinn with the fireworks stuff for a long time?"

"Pretty much since he started the business five years ago. Rebecca and I got certified at the same time, along with a couple of other people who work off and on. Schoolteachers don't make much money, and fireworks gives me a good income during the summer."

"So the business is doing well?" An impertinent question, but somehow she had to find out. "I mean, Quinn seems anxious sometimes, when he thinks nobody's looking."

Skeet's eyes narrowed. "I noticed that too. But he's not real good about sharing his problems. Likes to handle things himself." He shook his head. "Dumb, if you ask me. I mean, that's what Christian brothers and sisters are for, sharing the load."

Something about the way he said that tugged at Susannah's heartstrings. She wished she were in a position to help Quinn, rather than to create more problems for him. "So has he always been like this? Hiding his problems, I mean? Or do you think it has something to do with the big ka-boom at the Convention Center?"

Skeet's shrugged. "Maybe it does. That put a pretty big hole in the company, no pun intended. Wouldn't *you* worry? He told me he's had people threatening to back out on contracts. Maybe they're not confident he can produce a show without accidents. There was even a rumor the Mardi Gras krewe might sue him. He'll have to rebuild his reputation. Of course ..." He leaned in. "There's a *big* contract on the horizon—if it pans out."

Susannah waited, but Skeet didn't elaborate. "What kind of contract?"

"I can't say. But I mean it's a *major* deal." Skeet's eyes gleamed.

"That would be great, of course." Susannah made a mental note to fish for information from Quinn. Or maybe Rebecca. "But maybe the problems at SkyPainters started before the big explosion. Did Quinn seem discouraged about anything?"

"Maybe. But I was pretty busy with football season and Christmas parades and Mardi Gras stuff back then. I wasn't paying attention. Anyway—" Skeet's gaze sharpened—"I don't know why you're asking that."

She gulped. Maybe she'd gone too far. "Don't you think you can help people more if you understand what's at the root of the trouble?"

"I can't make Quinn confide in me. And guys don't always talk to each other about stuff that matters anyway." Skeet flipped the pencil into the air and caught it in his teeth, a neat trick that made Susannah laugh. "We'd rather give each other a hard time." He got up and stretched his back. "I've got a rehearsal tonight, so I'd better get home and gather up my stuff. The girls have a Bible study going on at Dana's house, if you're interested."

"I'll think about it."

She wasn't sure how much she'd learned, but one thing was clear. Skeet cared a great deal about Quinn and had no apparent reason to wish him harm.

Quinn was watching Russell Wallace install some new design software onto his computer when his cell phone rang.

"Hey, man, where are you?" said Skeet. "I need to talk to you."

"I'm at the office. Come on down. I want to show you this new program."

"Sorry, don't have time, I'm headed to rehearsal."

In the background Quinn could hear the screaming guitars of a popular Christian band coming from Skeet's end of the line. "Okay, then just let me have it. Is something wrong?" Skeet hated telephones and had been known to leave his cell in a drawer uncharged for weeks at a time.

"No, at least I don't think so. I just thought you ought to know Susannah came by the band room just a little while ago."

"She did?" Quinn tamped down the spurt of his pulse. He'd had Susannah on his mind since they parted ways in the church parking lot Sunday night. He wondered how she was getting along with Dana's Bible. "I've been praying for her."

"Yeah, well, I think you should up the ante a bit."

"What do you mean?" Distracted, Quinn peered over Russell's stocky shoulder as he tapped a code into the computer. The kid might look like a linebacker, but he was a genius with electronics. "You gonna show me how to use this when you get done?" he said to Russell.

Russell grinned. "This is so simple even *you* can do it, Flylady. I'm almost done; hang on and I'll give you a lesson." His fingers rattled across the keyboard.

"What are you doing?" asked Skeet. "I'm trying to tell you something important."

"Everybody wants a piece of me," Quinn sighed. "I've been stuck in the dark ages of last week's technology, and Russell's bringing me up to speed." He walked into the office and sat down at his desk. The photo of his team reminded him he needed to pick up popsicles before practice that afternoon. "Now what's this about Susannah? What was she doing at the school?"

There was a pause. "I don't know, she never did say. She just sat around and talked for a few minutes, then said she had to go. But she seems fascinated by Christianity, especially our church." Skeet chuckled. "And she obviously thinks a lot of you."

"Skeet—"

"All right, I'll leave you alone. But, listen, you'll tell me if there's something bugging you, right?"

Quinn hesitated. There were a lot of things bothering him, but nothing Skeet could do anything about. "Just ... just pray for me to have wisdom around her, Skeet."

"That goes without saying. I mean—you know the stuff we talked about the other day? About your business? I know I told you not to worry, but if there's any way I can take some of the load off you—"

"Oh, no, I'm fine." Just knowing his friend had his back in prayer lightened Quinn's heart. "Have a good rehearsal. Are y'all playing this weekend?"

"Friday night at He-Brews. You should come."

"I will if we get through with baseball practice in time."

"Cool. Take care, man."

"You too." Quinn closed the phone and laid his head against the back of the chair.

Thank you, Lord, for good friends.

His thoughts cruised to Susannah. *Wonder what she's up to right now.*

chapter 13

Susannah sat crossed-legged on her bed with Dana's Bible in her lap, the overhead fan whirling hard enough to lift off the roof and whipping her hair into knotted ringlets. Not only was Elva Kay's plumbing "contrary," but the air-conditioning never quite caught up with the heat that collected at the top of the house. She should have gotten up a long time ago to put her hair in a ponytail, but she kept reading just one more page.

This guy John, whoever he was, was some kind of writer. She'd gotten mixed up and started with First John, until Elva Kay explained it was one of three letters to some first-century church members, not the story of Jesus' life—*gospel, good news*, according to Elva Kay.

The lady was a walking encyclopedia of information about the Bible. Susannah kept asking her questions, just waiting to hear the words "I don't know" come out of her mouth. Good grief, the woman could go on *Jeopardy* and win a million dollars in the Bible trivia category.

Susannah, on the other hand, had never felt so ignorant in her entire life, but she'd decided to keep reading the letters. She had this thing about finishing what she started.

How could words on a page do such strange things to her heart and mind? Right in the first chapter, the words jumped out at her as if a giant spotlight focused on them: *"God is light; in him there is no darkness at all. If we claim to have fellowship with him yet walk in the darkness, we lie and do not live by the truth."*

Chewing her fingernails, she read those five short chapters again and again, trying to puzzle out the paradox of condemnation of sin operating within the context of Father-love. As a former federal law officer, she recognized darkness and deceit when she saw it in others. The concept of justice made perfect sense. But did God consider her own minor faults to be just as bad? Was lying to Quinn about who she was a direct affront to God? How could it be? It was her job!

She put her finger on a verse about halfway down in chapter two. *"If anyone loves the world, the love of the Father is not in him."* What did that mean, anyway? Of course she loved the world. She loved being alive and she loved plenty of other people.

Questions, questions. She flung her head back and let the breeze from the fan cool her hot face and shoulders. She wanted answers right now, but Elva Kay was still working at the thrift store.

She closed the Bible, tossing it on the nightstand in frustration. What good was a procedure manual when you couldn't understand it?

Then she remembered. Skeet had said Dana and "the girls" were having a Bible study tonight. The very idea scared her silly. She'd walk in, feeling tall and stupid and out of place, and they'd all know more than she did. Bet they were all Cradle Roll babies like Dana.

But Dana was kind, even if she was giddy as a Shih Tzu puppy.

Should I, shouldn't I, yes, no, maybe.

Yes, something told her. *You should.*

She had no reason to be afraid of a roomful of sweet-tea southern girls who wore their white gloves to bed. Impatient with this inexplicable attack of timidity, she went searching for the jeans she'd had on Sunday night. Finding them on the floor between the wall and the armoire, she turned all the pockets wrong side out until she located three pennies, a jelly bean, and the scrap of paper with Dana's phone number. She stuck the jelly bean in her mouth as she punched the number into her cell phone.

And jumped when "Inspector Gadget" shrilled in her hand.

"Hello?" She sat down on a pile of dirty clothes in the rocker.

"Susannah? This is Rebecca. I hope this isn't a bad time."

Susannah was so startled she nearly sucked the jelly bean down her windpipe. "Rebecca? You mean Quinn's Rebecca?"

"He doesn't own me yet." Rebecca laughed. "Hey, I was wondering if you might want to come eat supper with me and my mom tonight. I mean, if you didn't already have plans. The ladies from our church made this gargantuan pot of dumplings and we'll never be able to eat it all by ourselves."

"Dumplings? Tonight?" Now, this was interesting. Rebecca hadn't seemed particularly friendly the day Susannah had showed up at Quinn's office. But she had to admit to curiosity about Quinn's relationship with the girl's mother and her younger brother, Phillip. And it would be a good chance to find out about the "major deal" Skeet had mentioned. "Sure, that sounds great. What time should I come?"

Bible study with the girls would have to wait.

On the way home from practice, Quinn drove by Elva Kay's house. Susannah's Jeep wasn't in the driveway or parked on the street. Not that he would have stopped anyway. He wanted to get home and watch *Hardball*. Will's grandfather, Senator Fletcher, the head of the president's reelection campaign, was supposed to be on tonight, and Quinn was dying to know what he had to say about the presidential race. Will had called again that morning to tell him the security check was in process. Just a matter of time before he could be offered a contract.

He sat in his driveway with the engine running for a minute, wondering where Susannah was. Interesting that she showed up at Skeet's school this afternoon. Of course, as a band director Skeet helped out with Mardi Gras parades all the time. Maybe she was interviewing him for her thesis. A little prick of something needled under his skin.

Lord, not jealousy. How dumb would that be? Skeet had no interest in dating Susannah. Not that Quinn did either.

Of course, he was *interested*, but a person didn't have to act on every impulse that came along. Shaking his head, he cut the engine and got out to unload the truck.

Later he made himself a couple of peanut butter and banana sandwiches and ate them in front of the TV. On the first commercial break, he muted the set and picked up his phone. He should call Elva Kay and see if she needed her grass cut this weekend. He'd have to work it in around the Azalea Trail race, but he could manage if he got up early Saturday morning.

Okay, admit it. What he really wanted to know was if Susannah had forgotten their running date tonight.

He punched Elva Kay's number before he could talk himself out of it.

She answered on the third ring, sounding breathless. "Quinn! How are you, sugar?"

"Fine. Did I catch you at a bad time?"

"No, no. I was just—" She laughed. "Belshazzar had Montmorency cornered behind the stairs, and he obviously needed to go outside. So I had to put the cat on the porch and drag that poor dog ... never mind. You don't want to hear about the Hatfields and McCoys. What are you doing tonight?"

"Just finished baseball practice. I was wondering if you needed your yard mowed."

"You just did it last week. I think it's fine." She sounded amused. "Susannah will be sorry she missed your call."

He gulped. "I didn't—"

"I know, but she left a note saying if you came by to go running tonight, to ask you to wait. She went to have supper with Rebecca and her mother. She should be back anytime now."

"She did? She will? Then that's all I—I mean, that's good." Could Rebecca have invited Susannah over to eat? What was that all about? "Okay, tell her to call me when she gets home. I'll come get her."

When Susannah opened Elva Kay's front door, Quinn's warm smile dispelled some of the melancholy that had enveloped her since leaving Rebecca's house. Equally thrilled to see him, Monty barked a noisy welcome.

"Hey!" Squatting down to ruffle the dog's ears, Quinn took a slobbery tongue across his cheek. "How was dinner?"

Looking down at the crown of Quinn's head, Susannah hesitated. Dinner with the Mansfield women had been a revelation, but not the sort she'd hoped for. The subject of fireworks contracts never came up.

She wrinkled her nose. "I'm not a big fan of dumplings, but somebody made a decent cheesecake."

Quinn looked up at her, eyes twinkling. "The church ladies always come through." Curiosity filtered into his expression. "So Rebecca invited you over? I'm sorta surprised."

"She said they had way too much food and wanted to share."

"Hmm. I'm proud of her." He sobered. "How was Miss Alice doing tonight?"

Susannah had been dismayed to discover Rebecca's mother was ill, probably dying. "I liked her a lot. She reminded me of ..." She shrugged. "My mother had a form of cancer they couldn't treat back then."

Quinn's eyes softened. "You said you were five. That's awful young to deal with something like that."

"I don't usually let it bother me. It was just, this lady is so nice, and I almost wish I hadn't met her." Susannah put her hand over her mouth. What had she just said?

Quinn didn't seem shocked. "You don't want to run right now, do you?"

"Not really. Maybe I'm just tired."

"You want to sit and talk for a while? The doctor is in. Consultations five cents, and worth every penny."

She laughed. "Okay, sure." She dropped onto one of the concrete retaining walls beside the front steps. "But I'm probably not very good company right now."

Quinn settled on the opposite wall with Monty's snout across his feet. The dog let out a big snuffle of contentment. The street was quiet, soft in lamplight, fireflies blinking in the yard. They sat in silence for a few minutes before Quinn cleared his throat.

"Tell me about your mom."

"I don't remember her being well. But near the end I'd lie in the hospital bed with her. She wanted me to read to her, so I picked *Hop on Pop*, over and over." Susannah swallowed a wad of sudden tears. "She had such soft arms, and she smelled like roses."

"She sounds awesome."

"Yeah. She always told me what a smart girl I was, learning to read so fast. Then she went away—to stay in heaven, they said.

Daddy told me she wouldn't ever come back, but he'd take good care of me."

"Did he?" Quinn's voice sounded tense.

"Sure. I always had everything I ever wanted."

"Except your mother."

Susannah hated people feeling sorry for her. She took a breath. "I didn't mean what I said a minute ago. Wishing I hadn't met Rebecca's mom."

"Alice used to work at the docks. When I started there I was basically homeless. Lots of times she'd bring an extra sandwich and share lunch with me."

Alice hadn't mentioned that tonight. More of Susannah's assumptions about Quinn's relationships went tumbling.

"What I meant was, it's hard to let go of people who mean something to you."

"Nobody likes death, Susannah. You don't have to explain it away."

"Aren't you going to tell me not to be sad, because she'll be in heaven?"

He didn't answer right away. "I don't think you're ready to hear that. Although it's true."

A surge of bitter resentment rocked Susannah. "They said that about my mother. I didn't want her in heaven; I wanted her with *me*. I guess that's pretty selfish."

"Sounds normal to me. I think you'd be sick if you *didn't* miss your mom. Rebecca's going to miss Alice too. I hate it for her. It makes me mad."

For some reason, the gritty, bald statement eased Susannah's turbulent feelings. "So it's ... okay to be mad at God?"

"I sure hope so, because I spend a good bit of time telling him exactly how I feel." Quinn let out a breath. "He hasn't struck me with lightning yet, so I guess he's cool with it."

"Huh." Susannah had a lot to think about. For once she wasn't focused on Quinn, or even herself. The concept of a real, living God had begun to penetrate her fog of self-absorption. She could suddenly see herself very clearly.

I'm not sure I like the view.

On Tuesday afternoon Susannah staked out Phillip Mansfield in the University of South Alabama library. She'd followed him from class to class all morning, listening in on his conversations with friends. She could hardly believe the kid spent time in a building containing anything that didn't look, smell, or sound like a car.

But there he sat, all by himself at a table in the stacks, studying what looked like CliffsNotes. Perfect opportunity.

She approached the table and chose a chair across from him but not too close. Slinging her backpack onto the table, she pulled out a copy of *Super Street* magazine and laid it on top of her notebook. She pretended to study a book she'd picked up in the local history section.

After a few minutes she caught Phillip looking at her.

She gave him a wry grimace. "Too bad to be inside studying on a pretty day like today, huh?"

He smiled in return, a good-looking kid just out of the gawky high school stage. "Yeah, I got a paper due tomorrow." He showed her his book: cheat notes on *Portrait of the Artist as a Young Man.* "You know anything about James Joyce?"

Susannah wasn't about to get roped into coaching freshman comp. "Sorry, I'm a sociology major."

"Dude. I'm sorry *for* you." Phillip glanced at the magazine on top of Susannah's notebook. "I have that issue. That's my car on the cover."

Trying to look impressed, she gave him a flattering once-over. Lean and well-built, he had curly dark hair that hung around his ears and into the ice-blue eyes. "Do I know you from somewhere?"

"I don't know." He shrugged. "Maybe a car show."

"No ..." She tapped a finger against her cheek. "I know where it was! You're Rebecca Mansfield's brother, aren't you?"

He frowned. "Yeah. How'd you know that?"

She laughed. "I'm a friend of Quinn's, and I saw your picture in the photo of his baseball team."

"That's cool. As long as you're not big buddies with my sister."

"We've met, but I don't know her well." Better not tell him she'd had dinner with the Bad Seed last night. "I went to the Bay-Bears game with Quinn last weekend. He told me what a big help you are with the team."

"It's fun." He shrugged. "Not so much as cars and fireworks, though. And girls." He gave her that lady-killer smile. "What's your name?"

"Susannah Tait."

Phillip's eyes widened. "The *Cosmo* Love Quiz Susannah Tait?"

"Excuse me?"

He laughed. "My sister thinks you're out to do an *Erin Brokovich* on Quinn. She told him you're a corporate spy."

It took Susannah a second to get her breath back. "Oh, right. Like I know anything about fireworks."

"Rebecca has a conspiracy theory about everything, even me. You can tell her I was studying this afternoon, huh?"

Susannah hid a smile at the hint of vulnerability beneath the boy's hubris. "Sure. So how long have you been working for Quinn?"

"With the fireworks, you mean? Since I turned eighteen last—I mean, a few years ago. Quinn wouldn't let me help until I was old enough for the permit. He's such a grandpa about following rules."

This time she did smile. Quinn didn't look or act like any grandpa she'd ever known. "So why do you think he had that big blowup at the Mardi Gras ball back in January? Was there a glitch in the process somewhere?"

"I don't know, accidents happen." Phillip's beautiful icy eyes met Susannah's with apparent sincerity. "Sometimes you get a defective shell. All I know is, Russ and me went to get hot wings and we came back to find the fire department crawling all over the place, with the Convention Center on fire across the river. It was crazy."

"Guess nobody wanted hot wings after that."

"Not so much." Phillip grinned. "Hey, you wanna come see my car? I'm parked right outside the library."

"Sure." Susannah slammed the history book shut. The fireworks conversation was over, but she could talk about cars all day long. She'd spent many a Saturday morning under the hood of her brother Justin's Camaro. "Sociology is for geeks anyway."

Quinn treated Phillip to a Whataburger after baseball practice, with the intention of broaching the subject of family responsibility. He didn't see himself as much of a counselor, but he'd promised Rebecca.

He understood Phillip's reluctance to face the seriousness of his mom's illness. Susannah's sadness Monday night had brought the feeling home. Whether you were five years old or twenty, losing your mother was a knockdown slam.

They found a clean table in the crowded dining room and sat down with their trays. Phillip, six feet tall and lanky as a lamppost, had supersized everything; Quinn had no doubt he'd eat every bite.

"Guess who I ran into at the library today," Phillip said with his mouth full.

Quinn jammed a straw into his drink. Generally he had to pry information out of Phillip. "Who?"

"The evil woman."

"*What* evil woman?"

"The one Rebecca got her drawers in a twist about the other day."

"You mean Susannah? You saw her at the library?"

"Yeah, but I didn't see what the problem was. The girl's a babe, and she understands cars."

Quinn frowned. "I didn't think you two had met before."

Phillip unwrapped his second double cheeseburger. "We happened to be sitting at the same table up in the stacks, and she introduced herself. She said she'd seen the picture of the ball team on your computer."

"That's interesting." Quinn had been wondering if Susannah ever spent time conducting research for her paper. It seemed she did. "What'd you talk about?"

"Cars. Fireworks." Phillip's mouth curled in a sly grin. "You better jump on this one, dude. She's pretty hot for you."

"Don't talk about her like that."

Phillip wiped his mouth on the sleeve of his T-shirt. "Oh come on, Flylady, don't be such a prude. If you're not into her, I'm gonna ask her out. I could tell she liked me."

Quinn took a couple of deep breaths. Phillip was just an ignorant kid who spouted off to make himself sound cool. But what had Susannah said to make Phillip think she was "hot" for him? The very idea was ... embarrassing.

"Can it, Phillip," he said, tamping down his annoyance. "Tell me how your classes are going."

Phillip shrugged. "Okay, I guess. Economics makes me want to hurl."

"Then why are you majoring in business administration?" Quinn hadn't been all that fired up about computer courses when he'd been at State, either. Some guidance counselor had talked him into majoring in a field wide open with job opportunities. Maybe that was why he hadn't pushed to go back when the bottom dropped out of his scholarship. Just didn't have a passion for it.

"I don't know. I want to own a business like you do." Phillip squirted ketchup on his fries. "Something to do with cars." He looked up from under that mop of hair. "*You* never had to slog through economics."

"Not in college, but I study the business section in the paper every day and watch the finance reports on the news shows. And I learned the hard way by recovering from my mistakes." Quinn sighed. "You don't want to have to do that."

"No, I guess not. But I also don't want to waste a bunch of time shut up in the room studying, like Russell. I've got a *life*."

Quinn wadded up his trash and crammed it into a paper sack. "You're right, in a way. We only get one life to spend, and you're smart to think twice about what you do with it. But think about baseball. You spend hours and hours practicing. Listening to your coach. Getting yelled at when you screw up. Then when the big game comes and you're up to bat—you're ready."

Phillip sat for a minute with a french fry poised in front of his mouth. Finally he grinned. "Dude, that's profound. Dr. Phil better watch his back."

"I should have known you wouldn't take me seriously. Whatever. Just go see your mother this weekend. She misses you."

"All right, all right. I'm running out of clean underwear anyway." Phillip slurped the last of his drink. "So when are you gonna do another show?"

"We've got your cousin Sheree's wedding coming up the first weekend in April. Why? Didn't know you were so eager to work."

"I need the money. Mom hasn't had much to give me lately because of all the medical bills. I gotta buy gas soon."

He debated how far to go. "You know, Rebecca has a certain point. If you wouldn't blow everything on accessories, you could afford gas."

A mighty scowl crossed Phillip's otherwise good-looking face. "Don't *you* start. I can take care of my money. Just holler at me when you need me to come wire, so I can arrange my schedule."

Quinn shook his head. Had he been that pigheaded at eighteen?

chapter 14

Iodine deficiency is rare in areas where iodized salt is used, but in other parts of the world, IDD is the leading cause of preventable mental and physical retardation. As many as one-point-five billion people are at risk, especially young children ..."

Quinn ate a piece of rubbery key lime pie as the United States Surgeon General—a man of education, experience, and character, but sorely lacking in rhetorical skills—continued to drone. He dreaded the inevitable moment when the distinguished doctor would wind down.

Mayor Posey, across the table at the monthly Kiwanis meeting, had been sending him dirty looks for the last twenty minutes. It was enough to give anybody indigestion.

And the day had not started well. First thing this morning he'd called the insurance company again. After being passed from operator to clerk to office assistant to agent to supervisor, he finally learned his policy hadn't been canceled. His claim was being processed, and he'd have to be patient.

Big surprise.

He chased a curled lime slice across his plate and stabbed his fork into it. Death to all insurance agents.

Brother, that was a Christlike thought, wasn't it? *Just kidding, Lord.*

He looked up and caught the mayor's fulminating dark eyes. A trim, middle-aged black man with an aristocratic hairline and an impeccable Italian suit, he was a notorious member of the Krewe of Vulcan—whose social event Quinn had bombed. Which made the man even more rabid to complete repairs to the Convention Center. Tourism and social and cultural events had been major planks in his campaign platform.

Quinn blinked in surprise when everyone around him applauded the Surgeon General. The speech was over, and he knew little more about Iodine Deficiency Disease than he had when he sat down.

I've really got to get over this worry thing, Lord.

Joining in the applause, he started to get up, but Mayor Posey touched his arm.

"I need a moment of your time, Mr. Baldwin," said the mayor in his slow, sonorous voice. "If you don't mind."

A million things awaited his attention back at the office, but it was an order, not a request. Quinn sat back down. "Yes, sir. I don't mind at all."

"The Convention Center is finally up and running, but summer tourist season is almost here, and we still don't have use of Exhibit Hall A." The mayor touched the tips of his fingers together. "The one ruined by your accident."

"You know how sorry I am about that." Quinn picked up his fork again. He'd already apologized a million times. What else was he supposed to say?

"The city council is screaming about having to pay for the repairs out of the budget."

"I understand, sir, but—"

"Your insurance company has yet to reimburse the city for lost revenue while we complete repairs to that exhibit hall."

Quinn tapped the fork against his plate. "I have no control over my insurance company, sir. Unfortunately."

"I just thought you might know the cause of the holdup."

"No, sir, I'm afraid I don't." Quinn held up his chin, refusing to look away. It occurred to him he had an adversary — one much more powerful and malicious than Mayor Posey. One who thrived on the shame of believers.

The mayor pursed his lips, staring Quinn down. After a moment he stood up, rapping his knuckles against the table. "Mr. Baldwin, I would appreciate any influence you can wield in this unfortunate situation. Have a good afternoon."

Quinn slowly got to his feet; all joy in the day dimmed. Skeet was right. There was no use worrying about what was out of his control.

When Elva Kay returned that afternoon from a day of volunteering at the hospital, Susannah was playing Frisbee in the backyard with Monty. She flung the disk over the clothesline and burst into laughter as the dog galloped halfway across the yard and spied the cat lying in a flower bed ready to pounce. Monty came to a screeching halt.

"You'd think he'd realize by now Belshazzar has no claws." Elva Kay stood in the back door with her hands on her bony hips. Dressed in a copper pants outfit with a sheer patterned scarf pinned at the throat, she looked more like a business executive than a retiree.

Susannah fished the Frisbee out of the birdbath and shook the water off. "Let's don't tell him. I think he enjoys the suspense."

"Okay, dearie, but don't ask me to pay for his trauma counseling." Elva Kay grinned. "Would you like to come in for a potato salad lesson?"

"Can I?" Susannah had already learned to make banana pudding and fried chicken and a number of other high-calorie southern dishes she couldn't wait to try out on her dad when she got back home.

"Come on in and wash your hands." Elva Kay held out an apron. "The secret is red potatoes and homemade sweet pickles."

An hour or so later, the two of them sat down in the beautiful jewel-toned dining room. Susannah enjoyed the experience of regular meals taken at a leisurely pace on fine dishes—she'd smiled at the information that every well-bred southern lady had a designated potato salad dish—and lingering afterward for dessert and conversation.

To her disappointment, her cell phone rang just as she was pouring her third glass of iced tea. She looked at the ID and grimaced. "Rats! Sorry, I have to take this. Leave the dishes and I'll get them in a minute."

Elva Kay shook her head and rose. "I'll do it. You go on, love."

Susannah headed for her room as she opened the phone. She didn't want to talk to Simon Webster in front of Elva Kay. "Hello?"

"Miss Tait! Simon Webster with Independent Mutual."

How, Susannah wondered, could a company be both independent and mutual? Talk about oxymorons. And speaking of morons, why did this guy always call when she was either asleep or eating dinner?

"How are you, Mr. Webster?"

"I'm frankly a little perturbed I haven't heard from you all week. How about filling me in on your progress?"

"Sure. So far I have no evidence Baldwin set the explosion on purpose."

"What do you mean? Your job is to prove he did."

"No." Susannah sat down on the rocker. "My job is to find out the truth, and the truth is I think somebody's setting him up."

"But—"

"Mr. Webster, Baldwin's a nice guy. He's diligent, responsible, and generous with his time and money. He's actively pursuing new contracts. Why would he blow up half his equipment and ruin his reputation on purpose?" There was a long silence. "Mr. Webster?"

"Miss Tait, have you been fraternizing with the subject?"

"Fraternizing?" Susannah set the rocker into agitated motion. "That's ridiculous. I've had to spend time with him. He's the main subject of the investigation."

"Just make sure you don't step over the line, or I'll have to find somebody else to take your place. I should have known you were too young and—and—"

"Female?" she said sweetly. "Don't worry, Mr. Webster, the line is very clear in my mind. I'll have a report for you by Monday. Look for my email."

She slapped the phone shut without saying goodbye. Steaming, she took a deep calming breath.

Forget Simon Webster. She was doing her job the best she knew how.

Her glance fell on the Bible on the nightstand. After their conversation Sunday night, Quinn hadn't mentioned it, and neither had she. It was as if the subject were taboo. Too many things between them were taboo. Frustrating to meet a guy who intrigued her on so many levels, but was so off-limits.

This is a no flirting zone, she told herself as she leaned over to grab her running shoes. *Just do your job, get paid, and go home to Arizona where you belong.*

"I've never been to the mountains," Quinn gasped as he and Susannah pounded around the track together for the last quarter mile of their workout. "I bet you could run circles around me in thin dry air."

"I could run circles around you right now, if I wanted to." Giving him a saucy grin, she increased her pace and pulled ahead of him.

He bumped up his pace until they were both running full out, laughing.

It was good to let go and blow off some restless energy. It had been a horrendous day. After the time-consuming call to the insurance company and the mayor's harangue at the Kiwanis luncheon, he'd arrived back at the office to confront a surprise ATF visit. He'd passed, but the agent sent for the inspection—not Beverly O'Neal—had issued warnings in a couple of minor areas. Tried and found wanting. His worst nightmare.

"Give," Susannah panted on another burst of speed.

He looked at her and grinned. Even under the halogen track lights, her face was flaming red. Most of her hair had fallen out of its rubber band and blew around her head in coils of living gold.

"I will if you will."

"Okay. On three. One. Two—"

They both squeezed out an extra bit of speed until they were laughing so hard they staggered to a halt at the same time, bent double and gasping for breath.

"You are insane," said Quinn, heaving in air. "A person could die of a heart attack exercising with you."

"I'll write it on your tombstone. 'He let a girl beat him.'"

Quinn groaned and fell over into the grass, spreading his arms wide. "You're just like Tacy and Toni."

"The little girls on your team?" Susannah plopped down beside him, forearms on her knees.

"Yeah. I never coached girls before, but they keep up pretty well. Tacy may even make all-stars."

"Good for her. I've never had any problem keeping up with the guys in—" Susannah bit off her sentence. "In track or anything else."

Quinn frowned. She did that a lot—starting to say something and changing her mind.

"Hey, I've been reading that Bible," she said before he could pursue the subject of competition. "I'm nearly finished with the gospel of John."

"Are you?" He accepted the new topic, bone lazy now that they'd stopped running. "What do you think about it?"

"It's not as dry as I expected, for one thing. But some of it I don't understand at all."

"What, for example?"

"Okay. Take Jesus and his buddy Lazarus." Susannah yanked handfuls of grass as she talked. She sat in a puddle of light, her hair gilded, nearly turned to fire. He'd never seen anything so beautiful. "Lazarus is sick, right? His sisters come to tell Jesus about it, beg him to come make the guy well."

"Yeah." Quinn waited. So far she had a pretty good understanding of the passage.

"Then why does he wait around and let the guy die?" Susannah threw up her hands, tossing grass everywhere. "It makes no sense!"

"I think there's something in there about demonstrating his power over death. So Mary and Martha would know without a doubt he was God."

"I can get that, but he *cried* before he did it. So was he God or was he a man?"

Quinn sat up. "I guess it is kind of confusing. The answer is both. He and Lazarus were good friends. We talked about this the other night. It hurts when you lose someone's companionship." He lifted his T-shirt to wipe his sweaty face, glanced at Susannah and found her with her head in her hands. "Susannah? What's the matter?"

She shoved her hair out of her face with her fingers. "It's just that I'm an analytical person. Ambiguities make me nuts."

"Somebody told me one time—I think it was Clint, my friend from church—there's enough in the Bible that's clearly understandable, to keep you busy for a lifetime. The rest of it is faith. Maybe God left it like that on purpose. He wants us to choose him with our minds, but trust him with our hearts."

"I'm not sure I can."

"Why not?"

She fell back, elbows to the ground, and looked up at the moon sailing full-blown overhead. "The things I've seen ..."

Quinn waited, but she didn't elaborate. He took a deep breath. "There are terrible things all around. You remember what I said in church Sunday night ... that's not my whole story." He wondered if it was wise to open a door he'd shut a long time ago. The situation seemed to call for it.

Susannah stared at him. "What do you mean? Wasn't it true?"

"Oh, yeah, but I didn't tell about the way I grew up." He licked his lips. "My dad drank and knocked us around—me and Jana and my mom. My grandparents wouldn't intervene."

"Quinn ... that's awful," Susannah whispered.

He nodded. "I got away when the scholarship to State came through. But about a month after Jana left home, I went back one weekend—don't ask me why, I hated it there—and caught my dad roughing up my mother. Over money. So I took a baseball bat out of my car and—and tried to—" He jerked to a halt. He never let himself think about that afternoon anymore. Why was he bringing it up now?

Susannah sat upright, lips parted. Horror darkened her eyes.

"He'd been cleaning his gun and told me if I didn't get out, he was going to shoot my mother. I didn't believe him."

There was a moment's frozen silence.

"He ... He did it? Right in front of you?"

Quinn nodded. "He made it as far as Florida before they caught him. He's in prison now."

Susannah jumped to her feet, distress puckering her face. "Quinn, how can you trust a God who would let something like that happen to you? To your mother? If Jesus is God, where is he when people need him? How do you know his whole story isn't just some elaborate myth?"

Pure terror gripped Quinn when he realized what he'd said, and how Susannah had reacted. He *never* talked about the things in his past, for good reason.

Father, help me straighten this out!

Quinn got up on his knees and opened his hands. "It's *not* a myth, Susannah. Every word of it's true. The thing is, God loves us enough to give us free will, even people like my dad. I'm still working through everything that means, but this much I know. Jesus died for *my* sin, and if he can forgive me, he can forgive anybody."

"Maybe that's true." Susannah clutched her hands together. "I'm so, so sorry all this happened to you, but I've got to think through it some more. Skeet told me to make sure I'm deciding for myself."

Quinn rose, frowning. "When did you talk to Skeet about it?"

She blinked and looked away. "The other day when I went by his school." A grumble of thunder rolled in the distance, and a bank of clouds scudded across the moon. Looking up, Susannah backed toward the gate. "We'd better go before we get wet."

Quinn stood there a moment before following. He wanted Susannah's salvation more than he'd ever wanted anything. He prayed he hadn't messed everything up.

chapter 15

Susannah woke in the night to a thunderstorm shaking the rafters. Her only window, a dormer with a stained-glass panel, allowed lightning to flash in weird pink and yellow streaks against the mirror, reflecting into her face. She lay tossing and turning, watching the digital clock on the desk blink, one numeral at a time, toward four o'clock. Monty cowered under the covers, shuddering against the back of her knees.

The noisy light show would have kept her awake anyway, but she couldn't stop thinking about Quinn. How could a person go through such enormous loss and emerge a man of integrity and courage and faith?

And after thirteen days she was sure beyond doubt he was all of these things. How could this be? She was not an impulsive person. She'd agonized over the decision to leave ATF. She did not easily bestow her trust.

But Quinn had weakened her defenses with his shy smile, his slow, gentle way of talking, and a protective manner that awakened every feminine chromosome in her body.

Susie, Susie, she thought, watching the lightning flicker across the ceiling, *you are so in trouble.*

The thing was, if Quinn was everything he seemed to be, then her mission here in Mobile was about to be turned on its head. There had to be something screwy with that letter in the file on her desk. The more she thought about it, the more imperative it became to figure out who had written it—and why.

Fingerprint analysis of the original document had revealed nothing more than faint traces of chemicals common to fireworks construction: nitrate, carbon, and the perchlorate used for a binding agent. Which meant it had most likely been printed in Quinn's own warehouse by one of his employees, or by someone in a rival company.

She'd stayed up late last night scouring the Internet for competing pyrotechnics companies. She'd narrowed the list down to five. The closest to SkyPainters in terms of distance was Xtravaganza Events, located just across the Mississippi state line in Biloxi.

She could call, but the place was less than an hour away. No reason she couldn't just drive over. Amazing how much more you could get from a face-to-face interview.

Plan of action made, she threw back the sheet. "This is ridiculous," she muttered, wide awake. Might as well get up and read or something. She'd started keeping a stash of soda in Elva Kay's refrigerator for just such emergencies.

She padded barefoot toward the stairs, and the dog picked his head up, eyes at sleepy half-mast. "Stay, Monty. I'll be right back." She grabbed Dana's Bible off the dresser as she went by. Maybe she'd take it out onto the screen porch and watch the rain come down.

With every fresh boom and crack of thunder, the house rocked and rolled on its hundred-year-old foundation. She could hear the sump pump chugging away in the basement. No way it was going to keep up with this downpour. *Water, water everywhere.*

Yawning, she rummaged in the fridge for her six-pack of Cokes, ripped one out of the plastic collar, and took it back into the living room. Thank goodness Belshazzar preferred to spend the night on a heating pad between Elva Kay's feet. That was one spoiled cat, and Susannah had no desire to encounter his hair-raising hiss in the dark.

She was about to turn the old-fashioned key left in the screen-porch door, when she realized it was already ajar. She poked her head through the opening. The porch was dark and damp with an almost palpable mist, and all she could hear was the rain drumming on the roof and sloughing off into the flower beds.

"Elva Kay?"

"Come on out, dearie. I'm over here on the swing."

Susannah waited until her eyes adjusted to the darkness, then joined Elva Kay on the swing. "The storm woke you up too, huh?"

"It probably would have, but I'm up this time of day most every morning." At Susannah's incredulous silence, Elva Kay chuckled. "Us old folks don't sleep too well, so I always have a nice talk with the Lord while it's quiet and dark."

A jag of lightning lit the porch for a second, followed by an ear-splitting clap of thunder, and Susannah laughed. "Not so quiet."

"Sometimes I get the full symphony," Elva Kay said, chuckling.

They sat quietly as the rain poured down.

After a minute or so, Susannah couldn't stand it. "Did you know about Quinn's father?"

Elva Kay sighed. "He's in prison in the Mississippi State Penitentiary."

"So it's true. I can't believe Quinn had to watch —" Susannah shuddered. "If that had happened to me, I'd be lying in a mental hospital somewhere."

"Quinn is a remarkable young man. The Lord has his hand on him in a mighty way."

Sighing, Susannah slid down to rest her head on the back of the swing. "I can't quit thinking about it. Why does God pick some people and leave others alone?"

"Oh, honey," said Elva Kay with a smile in her voice, "the Lord wants us all to come to him, but he'll use those who listen to him in an extraordinary way."

Susannah felt something take root in her heart. Something that grew out of her brother's loving persistence, Elva Kay's gentle wisdom, and Quinn's kindness. Suddenly all her questions and excuses seemed like weeds in an otherwise lovely garden. "I want that. I want to learn how to listen, and I want to be useful." She sat up. "Will you tell me what to do?"

Elva Kay chuckled. "I have a feeling this is the first time you've ever said such a thing."

"If you only knew."

"All right, my dear, the Bible makes it pretty simple. If you'll believe in your heart Christ was raised from the dead and confess with your mouth Jesus is Lord, you'll be saved." Elva Kay took the Bible from Susannah and brushed her hand across its cover. "Making him Lord means confessing you've been going your own way. Turning toward him and agreeing to do things his way in the future."

"Is that all?" Susannah sat there dumbfounded.

"Yes, but be sure you mean it before you say the words. There won't be any going back."

"There's no doubt I've gone my own way, my whole life. And I'm tired of it. It's too hard. I want what Quinn has—and what you have. I want Jesus in my life too."

"Then just tell him so."

"Now?"

Elva Kay laughed. "Why not?"

"I thought I had to be, like, in church or something."

"Right here's fine."

Feeling shy, Susannah opened her hands as she'd seen Quinn do while praying. She closed her eyes. "Okay, God, here I am. Remember me? You know I don't understand everything about you; in fact I don't understand *anything* except I'm tired of running around in circles." A sudden enormous peal of thunder made her laugh. "Good one. Anyway, you and I both know I haven't done such a great job of running my life. So if you want it, I'm handing it over to you. Jesus, I want you to be my boss from now on. Is that all?" She peeked at Elva Kay, who nodded, smiling. "Oh, and thanks. Thanks very much." Susannah gulped as tears began to pour down her cheeks. "Oh, no!" she groaned, bending over with her face in her hands. "What am I crying for?"

Elva Kay pulled her close, wrapping frail arms around her and making a comforting sort of clucking sound. She smelled of peppermint and roses, a wonderful old-fashioned scent that reminded Susannah of her mother.

She sat stiffly for a moment, then gradually relaxed against the soft folds of Elva Kay's chenille robe. She felt Elva Kay's chin on top of her head.

Blessed. She'd heard the word before. Now she knew what it meant.

Susannah spent Thursday morning in Elva Kay's basement, knee deep in muddy water.

The storm had passed before daylight, but it had overpowered the valiant efforts of the sump pump. When Monty took an ecstatic flying leap off the stairs into the impromptu swimming pool, soaking both her and Elva Kay, the only option was to laugh and help bail.

Four or five times she pulled out her cell phone to call Quinn, but something stopped her every time. It would be fun to see the look on his face when she told him about last night.

After she'd cleaned up and eaten lunch, she decided she might as well use the afternoon to drive over to Biloxi and meet with Adam Brown of Xtravaganza Events. About to grab her keys and backpack off the top of the armoire, she caught a glimpse of herself in the full-length mirror. In deference to the climate, she'd traded the Birkenstocks for flip-flops, and the jeans for cutoffs. Other than that, she still looked like the Arizona nature-girl she was.

Hair every which way, tank T-shirt, no makeup.

Ooh.

By now she had a pretty good idea of what impressed southern businessmen, especially the older ones. Even Rebecca, toiling in the Dickensian obscurity of an industrial warehouse, went to work dressed like the latest Trump bride.

She looked at Monty, who had followed her upstairs and waited by the door, tennis ball in mouth. "Monty, it may be time for a makeover. What do you think?"

The dog let out a bored sigh, padded over to the rug, and lay down, his expression plain: *Wake me when this is over.*

Susannah scraped her hair back with her fingers, turned her face and lifted her chin. At least she had good skin, thanks to careful use of sunscreen.

She yanked open her door and went pelting down the stairs. "Elva Kay! Hey, Miss Elva Kay! Want to go shopping?"

Susannah's idea of shopping was a trip to the thrift store for a new T-shirt. Or a ten-minute foray through the *Land's End* catalog.

Elva Kay, however, insisted on dragging her through every department store in two malls, plus five different discount outlets located up and down Airport Boulevard, Mobile's main shopping drag. By three o'clock there was no hope of making it all the way to Biloxi to visit the Xtravaganza office. She gave in to the tidal wave of her fashionista's single-minded zeal.

Eventually she stood in front of a dressing room mirror at a tiny boutique in Spring Hill with her mouth hanging open.

"My purse has to match my shoes? What's wrong with my backpack?"

Elva Kay folded her hands on top of a stack of silky tops and cotton skirts. She sat on a stool in a corner of the big dressing room, giving a thumbs-up or thumbs-down to outfits provided by the saleslady—who, in Susannah's opinion, was having way too good a time spending somebody else's money.

"Don't worry about a purse right now. We'll take care of that and your jewelry down at Steinmart."

"You mean there's a store in this town we haven't been to yet?" Susannah tugged at the bronze-striped skirt fitting snugly around her hips. She liked her clothes loose and comfy. "Would you look at these shoes?" she fretted. "I'm gonna have to announce myself with 'ho-ho-ho' when I walk into a room."

"You've got to get over this self-consciousness about your height. Three-inch heels are perfectly manageable." Elva Kay batted her eyelashes. "Besides, the person who matters is plenty tall enough to handle a statuesque companion."

Susannah put her hand against the wall to keep from teetering. "I'm not trying to impress Quinn."

"Of course you're not. He likes you just like you are."

"Do you think so?" Maybe this was a big mistake, trying to be something she wasn't. She'd never felt so disoriented, so *skinned*. All her emotions felt tender and raw.

"I'm sure of it." Elva Kay stood up and gave her a gentle hug—around the waist.

Heartened, Susannah kicked off the high-heeled sandals. "Okay, I bow to your greater wisdom. I'll take this outfit. But don't ask me to get my ears pierced. I don't do pain."

An hour later she stared in horrified fascination at a lifelike hairy scalp pinned atop a Styrofoam mannequin head. Perched on a stack of magazines on the beauty salon counter, it looked for all the world like a prop from a Stephen King movie.

The hairdresser, a vivacious blonde named Tricia, seemed to be equally appalled. She took one look at the spectacle in her chair and put both hands to her mouth. "Oh, my. I bet you have a time with all them curls, don't you, darlin'?"

Susannah slumped in the swivel chair. "I told Elva Kay this was hopeless," she muttered.

Tricia pulled herself together and picked up her scissors. "I've never lost a patient yet. Now you got a couple of choices here. I can show you how to straighten it—"

"How long will that take?"

"Not long. Twenty minutes or so every time you do it."

Susannah gaped. "Twenty *minutes*? On my hair? No way!"

Tricia gave her a cherubic grin. "Then we'll have to tame the beast. Do you trust me?"

Susannah couldn't help another surreptitious glance at the mannequin's rug. "Looks like you're a pretty accomplished taxidermist." She shut her eyes, resigned. "Okay. I'm at your mercy."

This could be bad. She'd seen those makeover shows where women came out looking like ten-dollar hookers who'd fallen face-first in a bucket of paint. *Please, God,* she tried out a shaky prayer, *don't let me look like that. I couldn't take it.*

Thirty minutes later, Tricia whirled her around to face the mirror. "Come on. Tell me you don't like it."

Susannah opened her eyes and blinked. "Wow." What she saw when she looked in the mirror was a flattering layered shoulder-length cut that made her look ... controlled. And yet still herself.

She met Elva Kay's eyes in the mirror. The older woman had taken off her glasses to dab at her eyes with a lace-edged handkerchief.

"You look lovely, dearie." Briskly Elva Kay tucked the hankie into her purse. "Thanks, Tricia. You're a gem. Now all we need is a trip by the Clinique counter."

Susannah shook her newly coifed head. Was this trip down the rabbit hole ever going to end?

"What are you doing?"

Startled, Quinn took off his headphones and looked over his shoulder. Rebecca stood behind him, peering at his computer screen.

"Nothing." He flicked off the window.

"You've been staring at that site for ten minutes. I thought you were working on the Bellingrath Gardens show."

"I am. It's coming together." Quinn pulled up the design. "See?"

Rebecca slammed the file drawer she'd been fishing in and propped her arms on top of the cabinet. "Quinn, you've gotten really weird in the last couple of weeks. Is something bothering you?"

"Weird? *I'm* acting weird?" He cast a pointed look at the stack of bridal magazines on Rebecca's credenza. "I'm not the one obsessing over somebody else's wedding."

"Sheree is my favorite cousin and I'm *directing* the wedding, and don't avoid the subject. Why are you looking at gemstones in an Internet jewelry store?"

"I'm deciding on colors I want to use." Which was true. Thinking of Susannah's eyes, he'd been googling blues and ran across the word *lapis*. Curious, he'd looked it up and there it was. Lapis lazuli, a luminous blue with golden pyrite inclusions that reminded him of the center of a flame.

Rebecca stared at him for a moment as if she didn't believe a word of it. "You're acting like you're in love."

"Like I'm *what*?"

"You heard me. I've never seen you this spacey. If it's Susannah Tait, you better watch your back. I told you there's something funny about her."

"I'm not in love! And if I were, it wouldn't be with ..." As irritating as she could be, Rebecca had an uncanny ability to judge character. "What's 'funny' about her?"

She perched on the stool beside Quinn. "I've been thinking about the day she came over here. The way she walked around and looked at things." Rebecca took off her glasses and polished them on the tail of her blouse. "The look on her face when I showed her that design."

"What do you mean? What look?"

Rebecca jammed her glasses back onto her nose. "Like she wished I would go away."

Quinn snorted. "You've been reading too many Grisham novels."

She scowled. "You're not taking this seriously, are you? I think she came by *because* she knew you weren't here."

"Rebecca—"

"I was at your church last Sunday, remember? I saw the way you looked at her when she came out of the counseling room. That's why I invited her over to supper the other night. Mom's got great character judgment. She thinks Susannah's hiding something."

Now that gave him pause. Years ago Alice had recognized his own readiness to leave behind his driftwood life. She saw people with clear spiritual eyes.

Rebecca didn't give him time to respond. "You are headed for a big fall, Buddy-Roe. I wouldn't tell you this if I didn't care about you."

"We've already had this discussion. I'm not dating a woman who has no relationship with Christ. Period."

The conversation with Susannah last night had dragged him back to a rock-bottom period of his life with no apparent redeeming result. Even an email from Elva Kay asking him to come by after work for a surprise hadn't kept him from worrying about it. A plate of brownies would be nice, but it wouldn't fix the deep ache that had lodged itself somewhere under his rib cage.

Skeet had warned him. Even Rebecca had warned him. Repeatedly.

Shutting her up with a look he rarely used anymore, he closed the lid of the laptop and started collecting his stuff to go home for the day. "I talked to Phillip yesterday. He promised he'd go by and see your mom this weekend."

"He did?" Rebecca gave him one of her rare smiles. "Oh, thank you! She'll be so happy."

"And we also discussed using his share of the next show to pay your mom back for the phone."

"You're the best!" Rebecca hopped off the stool and gave him an awkward hug. "Mom has such high hopes for him, and I hate it when he throws away everything we give him—"

"I know, I know." Quinn held up a hand. "But he'll be a lot more likely to appreciate it if you don't try to micromanage everything he does. Let him fall on his face a time or two. He'll wake up."

Rebecca put her hands on her hips. "Whose side are you on?"

"I'm just telling you what I've learned from experience." He picked up his briefcase. "Come on, let's leave early today. I've got to get to the pet store before practice. It's Bob's dinner day."

Rebecca huffed. "Sometimes you treat that snake better than your employees."

chapter 16

Driving past Elva Kay's house on his way home, Quinn saw his elderly neighbor out in the yard refilling her hummingbird feeder.

Oops, I was supposed to stop by. He made a quick U-turn at the next intersection and parked in front of the house.

He could feel his tension fade as he entered the deep shade of the oak tree arching across the sidewalk. The grass was a dark jewel green, and the tulips he'd helped plant during the winter were showing hints of crimson, yellow, and pink in the beds near the house. Elva Kay had a gift for growing things and generously shared her knowledge and experience. He'd learned so much from her.

At the corner of the house he stopped to watch her hang the feeder, a red cut-glass bottle with a fanciful flower-shaped spout, on its iron hook beside the screen-porch door. She'd have tiny, jewel-toned birds fighting over sugar water all summer. She looked a little like a hummingbird herself, with silver hair tied back in a turquoise scarf that matched her belt and sandals, and red pants with a patterned blouse. Her movements were quick, economical, hardly reflecting her advanced age.

Whistling to announce his presence, he rounded the corner, then laughed at a deep welcoming bark from behind the fence. Monty, the fearless guard dog.

Elva Kay greeted him with a hug and a delighted smile. "I'd about decided you wouldn't have time to stop by. How was your day?"

"It was okay." He brushed his foot across the top of the greening grass. "Looks like I need to get the mower out after all. Spring has sprung."

"Yes sir, it sure has." Hands on hips, she surveyed her flower beds with satisfaction. "My caladiums are coming back. But I can run the mower myself. I know you've got better things to do."

"Shoot, this little two-by-four postage stamp doesn't take me five minutes. No reason I can't do it when I do mine."

Elva Kay snorted. "Your concept of time is a little off, but you're a sweetie. Why don't you go pet that miserable hound dog before he wags himself into the next county, and I'll get us a glass of iced tea."

"Deal." He walked over to the chain-link fence, where Monty was digging a hole under the gate. Abandoning his project, the dog leaped with joy, nearly making it over the fence. "Hey, sport, quit that! Down!" Quinn brushed at the muddy paw prints on the front of his shirt. Oh, well, it was laundry night.

Opening the gate, he laughed as Monty bounded out and tackled him. Ten minutes of hand-to-paw wrestling with the dog left him lying in the soft grass tired, relaxed, and more than ready for the tea Elva Kay brought out on a tray.

"I'm sorry you missed Susannah." Elva Kay served Quinn as he sat up, then seated herself on the porch step where the cat lolled in a patch of sunlight. "We got back from shopping, but she left again. Said she might not be back until late."

"That's okay." Suppressing a stab of disappointment, he stroked the thick ebony coat of the dog, who lay panting across his knees. He laughed when Monty slurped his ear. "Would you don't?" He shoved the dog away and peered up at Elva Kay. "Not that I'm greedy or anything, but what's my surprise?"

Elva Kay looked cagey. "I think I'll wait and let Susannah tell you herself."

"What's she got to do with it?"

"Did you think it was something to eat?" Elva Kay laughed. "Just like a man, always thinking with his stomach. Never mind, I'm not stealing Susannah's thunder. I'll get her to call you when she gets back."

"Where, uh—" He cleared his throat. "Where is she, anyway?"

"I believe she was going to meet that sweet little Carter girl for supper."

Susannah was having supper with *Dana*? The mind boggled. "Are you sure you don't want to tell me what's going on?"

"Quite sure." Elva Kay stroked the cat, which had crept into her lap. "I'm more interested in what's on *your* mind."

Quinn drank the last of his tea, relishing the tang of lemon and mint against his tongue. He rolled the icy glass between his hands. "I guess I *could* use some advice."

"That's what old ladies are good for." Elva Kay sipped her tea, eyes bright.

"That and hummingbird cake." He grinned, then sobered, ruffling the dog's ears. "I've been thinking about my family today."

"Have you?"

He nodded. "Susannah asked about it, and I couldn't lie about my parents. It occurred to me ..." He sighed. "My father's been in prison for nearly ten years, and I've never been to see him. I just shut him out of my mind completely."

"Do you ever pray for him?"

"Sometimes. Do you think I have to go see him?"

Elva Kay's eyes were compassionate. "I don't know that you *have* to. But I have a feeling that's not the real issue. Have you forgiven him?"

He frowned. "How can I forgive somebody who's never asked for forgiveness?"

"Quinn." She leaned toward him, clasping her knees with knobby, arthritic fingers. The big diamond cluster on her left hand sparkled in the last ray of afternoon sun. "Jesus said he forgives us as we forgive those who are indebted to us. They aren't required to ask first."

"But what he did was criminal!" Quinn struggled against the anger that lingered like a thorn beneath his skin. The pain throbbed every time something touched it. "If it was just me, maybe I could—but he took my *mother* away. He destroyed our family, out of pure meanness and selfishness." He bent down to Monty, who snuffled close, licking Quinn's face.

Elva Kay sighed. "I didn't say it was easy, darlin'. Trust me, in sixty years of walking with the Lord, I've had lots of experience with different levels of forgiveness. The offenses that hurt the most—the ones that are hardest to get over—are the ones committed by the people we love."

"I did not love my father!" The words burst out before he could stop them.

"I'm sure at one time you did." Her voice was gentle. "Love and trust aren't uprooted overnight. And they aren't rebuilt so quick either."

He looked down, unable to answer. He wanted to do the right thing, but his feelings wouldn't catch up.

"Listen to me, sweetheart. Forgiveness is not saying what the other person did is okay. It's letting go of your rage, and extending grace even where it's undeserved. Because God cannot heal you if you hold on to bitterness."

After a minute, he gave a shaky laugh. "I didn't know I was going to get into this when I came over here. I thought I was coming for a plate of brownies."

"You can have a brownie too," Elva Kay said promptly, then smiled. "If you eat your dinner first."

"Uh-oh." He sat up. "Speaking of dinner, I've got a dead mouse in the front seat of my truck. I need to get home and feed Bob before baseball practice."

"All right." Elva Kay dumped the cat off her lap. "Wait right there for a second while I get the brownies." She pushed to her feet and smiled down at him. "You're going to be just fine, Quinn. Never doubt the good plans of the Lord."

"He-Brews is a book in the Bible," Dana confided to Susannah as they pulled into the nearly full parking lot. "Isn't that a cute name for a coffeehouse?"

Susannah surveyed the brick building and landscaped grounds. With its steeply pitched central roof, wide double front doors, and covered porte cochere, the place bore an uncanny resemblance to a funeral home. She pictured herself driving up in a hearse and ordering a double latte.

"Very clever." She smothered a grin.

Having survived the shopping trip and Elva Kay's beautician with dignity more or less intact, Susannah was ready to sport her new look to the natives. She'd called Dana on the way home. Still, she found herself apprehensive about walking into such a blatantly Christian establishment.

Prying herself out of the small car, she followed Dana into the coffee shop. They bought drinks—fortunately soft drinks were available, as well as that nasty coffee—then found a table near the stage where the band would be performing. Susannah looked around, impressed with the trendy and inviting décor. The artwork featured local artists, as well as framed historic photographs of the city. The effect was warm and charming. She relaxed.

Dana tipped her head to survey Susannah. "I like your haircut."

Susannah put a hand to her head. "I didn't know being a girl could be so much fun."

Dana dimpled. "You just needed to get in touch with your inner Barbie."

Susannah grinned. At first, Dana's artless—okay, *airheaded* —pronouncements had gotten on her nerves a little. But there wasn't a mean bone in the girl's size 2 body, and it was impossible not to like her. "When I first met you, you kind of scared me," she confessed.

"You're kidding! Why?"

"Because ... I don't know. My mother died when I was small, and I never had anybody to teach me how to primp and cross my legs and stuff like that." She shrugged. "Girls like you make me feel like a big clunk."

Dana's eyes were wide. "But that's so silly. You're tall and elegant and ... and commanding. I never met anybody so sure of herself."

Susannah fingered her hair. Maybe because she'd always operated in technical fields dominated by men, she'd *had* to adopt that in-your-face attitude, at least on the surface. But she didn't *feel* confident on the inside, especially when it came to negotiating the physical and emotional dynamics between men and women.

This was the perfect opportunity to learn from somebody who knew the ropes.

"I have a feeling most men would take little and cute over tall and commanding. Is there somebody in particular you're interested in?"

Dana's eyes crinkled. "Maybe. But I'm not in any hurry. I just keep busy doing what the Lord puts in front of me until the guy wises up."

"You mean, like your kindergarten job?"

"Yes, that and stuff at church. Like the water table at the Azalea Trail Run. And I'm getting ready for a mission trip to Japan this summer."

"What are you going to do there? My dad was stationed in Japan one time."

"We'll be teaching English to university students in Tokyo, and taking every opportunity to share Christ with them."

It dawned on Susannah her decision to accept Christ might have some unforeseen ripple effects. She made a face. "I didn't much like it there."

"Why not?"

"For one thing, I felt like a freak." Susannah smiled. "I was only in the sixth grade and already hitting five foot eight. But you should fit right in."

"I can't wait! Skeet and I have been learning a little Japanese."

"Skeet's going too?"

"Yes, we're taking a musical team. The Japanese people love American music."

"They also love eating raw eel." Susannah shuddered. "My brothers and I lived at McDonald's when we were stationed there."

Dana laughed. "That's so funny. You strike me as being the adventurous sort."

"There's adventure, and then there's food. I don't mix the two." Susannah suspected she had just embarked on a different kind of adventure. She hadn't yet gotten up the nerve to tell Dana about her decision. Was she expected to go around preaching on street corners now?

There was a guy back in Tucson, at the agency. All the other guys made fun of him, calling him Deacon and Holy Roller. He'd been a little obnoxious maybe, but she'd secretly admired his stand against barhopping and cheating on wives and girlfriends. She'd somehow known she could trust him to shoot straight with her.

And there was her brother, of course. Jeremy had his faults, but of her three siblings he was the only one who called to check up on her. Even if he did nag, she knew it was out of love.

That was the thing. Instinctively she'd known love should characterize a Christ-follower, and she'd recognized it in Elva Kay and Quinn, then Skeet and Dana. Rebecca not so much, but what did Susannah know? Maybe Christianity came in different sizes.

"I enjoyed living overseas for the most part, but I was always ready to get back to the States." She smiled at Dana. "Did you always want to be a missionary?"

Dana's eyes widened. "Oh, I'm not a missionary! At least not a career one. This is just a short-term trip. *Anybody* can do this kind of thing."

"Is it, um, required? You know, to belong to your church?"

Dana gave her an unexpectedly shrewd look. "No, silly. But you've been thinking about it, haven't you?"

Susannah nodded and looked away. "I thought about it enough to decide to go for it. I ... sort of prayed this morning."

Dana's mouth fell open. "You prayed? You mean you gave your life to Jesus?"

"Whatever you want to call it. I've been reading all week, and—yikes!" Dana had hopped off her café chair and nearly strangled Susannah in a hug.

"Oh, I'm so happy, happy, happy!" Dana let go of Susannah long enough to jump up and down like a kid on a trampoline. "Yea!

I knew there was something different, but I thought it was just the hair. Oh, wait until Quinn hears this!" She turned around and waved at Skeet, who had just come in with an armload of equipment. "Skeet! Come here! What's Quinn doing tonight?"

Skeet dumped the guitar and amplifier on the platform. "I think he had baseball practice. Why?"

"Tell him, Susannah!" Dana beamed.

Mounting excitement overrode Susannah's reserve. "I gave my life to Jesus." Dana's words seemed to fit. She felt as if she *had* given away something, but then received something of incalculable value in return.

Skeet let out a loud whoop and grabbed Susannah.

Great. Now she had *two* people pogo-ing around the table, attracting all kinds of attention. She pressed her hands to her cheeks. She couldn't leave; she didn't have a car.

Embarrassed and thrilled, she stood smiling, tears starting in her eyes, as her new friends celebrated. For her! Amazing. When Skeet grabbed a guitar and a microphone and started playing the "Happy Birthday" song, hip-hop style, Susannah had to laugh. Everyone in the place sang along, and music rang off the brick walls.

"Thank you," she whispered to her new Lord, who'd given her a birthday like none other she'd ever experienced.

The only thing missing was Quinn.

Quinn was on the pitcher's mound, trying to convince Alden Makin's mother a fishing trip with his father was more important than taking up space in right field, when his cell phone rang.

"Hey, man, are you coming to He-Brews tonight?" It was Skeet, beginning a conversation as usual without identifying himself.

Quinn almost hadn't answered the phone. Cindy Makin folded her arms, impatient with the interruption. Alden was chasing one of the other boys around the dugout, tongue out, fingers in his ears.

"I forgot about it." Quinn stifled a sigh. He'd like nothing better than to veg out in a coffee shop listening to some good music, but he had laundry piled to the ceiling and he *really* needed a good night's sleep. The storm — and praying for Susannah — had kept him up most of the night. "Sorry, I don't think I can —"

"Okay, dude, it's not optional this time," Skeet interrupted. "There's something you gotta see."

"Hold on just a minute." Quinn lowered the phone. Cindy had charged over to corral her son. "Cindy, I'm sorry," he called. "You do whatever you think is best and I'll back you. Okay?" He took a deep breath when she scowled at him over her shoulder. "I know you resent your husband — I mean ex-husband — interfering with your schedule, but in the long run Alden needs time with his dad."

She snagged Alden by the elbow and yanked him toward her car. "Yeah, whatever. Thanks, Quinn. I'll let you know."

Quinn watched her peel out of the parking lot and put the phone to his ear. "Sorry, Skeet. Sort of a crisis situation going on here."

"Everything okay?"

"Hunky-dory." Sounded like a party going on at Skeet's end. "What are you doing? Isn't the band playing tonight?"

"Taking a break. First chance I've had to call. Look, man, this is an emergency. Get your keister over here."

Quinn rubbed his eyes with red-clay-stained fingers. The field was empty now; even Phillip had gone to have supper with his mom and Rebecca. At least he had packed all the equipment before he left.

"All right. I need to go home and change clothes —"

"Just come as you are. I don't want you to miss this."

Quinn sighed. "Okay, okay. I can be there in—" he glanced at his watch—"maybe ten minutes if traffic is good."

"Cool. Hurry."

Skeet was gone, and Quinn jammed the phone into his pocket.

The things he did for friendship.

"Quinn's on his way over here?" Susannah shouted to be heard over the CD blaring above the noise of conversation and laughter.

"Yep." Skeet downed half the bottle of water he'd left on their table while he'd played the first set with the band. He grinned. "I knew he'd want to get in on the party. But I didn't spill the beans."

Susannah's stomach flipped. The music had almost taken her mind off Quinn. Lively, fresh, and now the lyrics meant something to her. She'd found herself singing along, with a strange urgency to learn everything there was to know about her newfound faith.

Why hadn't Jeremy ever told her how clean and whole she would feel? Actually, she thought, he had. She just hadn't been listening.

Skeet charged back onto the stage to grab a microphone and crank up the guitars and drums again. Susannah sat in the audience, smiling at his antics onstage and helplessly looking forward to seeing Quinn. He was the rock-solid center of this circle of friends, like the nucleus of an atom, with particles spinning and bouncing and connecting on some invisible level.

Three quarks for Muster Mark, she thought, remembering her favorite James Joyce poem. *Sure he hasn't got much of a bark, and any he has is all beside the mark.*

That about nailed Quinn. Gentle and kind and dependable. Too good to be true?

Or too good for me?

Some of the things she had said to him had been flat-out lies. And gradually during the day it had begun to sink in that she had grievously taken advantage of his emotions. Playing the male-female card to open him up. Well, she wouldn't do that anymore.

She felt her cell phone vibrating against her hip. When she checked the ID screen, her eyes widened. She got Dana's attention, mouthed "Excuse me," and headed for the nearest exit.

On a lamp-lit patio at the rear of the building, she sat down on a concrete bench and flipped open the phone. "Susannah Tait here."

"Ms. Tait, this is Beverly O'Neal with the Mobile ATF. Sorry to call so late, but it's been a crazy day."

"No problem." She gulped. *Why now?* "What can I do for you?"

"More in the nature of what I can do for you," said O'Neal. "I thought you'd like to know your request for information on the SkyPainters case has been processed. You can come look at the debris tomorrow morning."

chapter 17

With the windows of his truck down, Quinn could hear the music from He-Brews a block away. Good thing there were no residential areas close by. He had to drive through the parking lot three times before he saw someone leaving, and managed to squeeze the big Suburban between a midsize sedan and a sports car. The place was rocking tonight.

Looking down at himself as he got out of the truck, he grimaced. *Brother.* Clay stains on his khakis, large muddy paw prints on the front of his shirt, and grime clogging his baseball cleats. He'd find out what Skeet wanted, then get home to start the laundry.

And eat. He hadn't had anything since the brownie at Elva Kay's house and his stomach hurt. Or maybe *that* had something to do with the conflict with Cindy Makin over Alden's fishing trip.

How could a guy walk out on his family — leave a pretty wife and a great kid like Alden — then expect everything to work out okay? Quinn knew he shouldn't stand as judge and jury, but half the time the world just didn't make sense. He had a lot of questions to ask God when he got to heaven.

Elva Kay's counsel from that afternoon came to mind as he walked into the coffee shop and looked around for Skeet. *Grace.*

Forgiveness and healing. Nice thoughts in theory, but awfully hard to apply to real life.

There was Skeet onstage with the band, rockin' out. He wasn't the best singer of the group, but he could play the mess out of that guitar. What would it feel like to have creative talent like that? God sure gave good gifts.

He was about to lean against the wall at the back of the room and wait for Skeet's next break, when he spotted Dana Carter sitting at a table near the front. *Whoa.* Did that mean Susannah was here too?

He dodged through the crowded room, keeping an eye out for Susannah. He didn't see her. *Shoot.* He dropped into a vacant chair at Dana's table.

"Quinn!" she squealed, as usual making three syllables out of his name. "You made it!" Her eyes widened at the state of his clothes. "Did you fall in a hole?"

"Baseball practice in a former swamp. What's going on?"

Dana grabbed his arm. "She went outside! Go find her!"

"Who?"

"Susannah! And I'm not saying another word!" She mimed zipping her lip.

"Has everybody lost their mind?" First Elva Kay, then Skeet, now Dana. His head was starting to ache.

Dana shook his wrist with both her tiny hands. "Go out on the patio right now, before I have to hurt you!"

Quinn laughed. "All right, already! Tell Skeet I'll be back." He ran into several friends from church as he crossed the room. By the time he pushed open the patio door his head was pounding.

The fresh night air on his face, not to mention the sight of Susannah sitting on a bench under an antique lamp, made him feel a lot better. She was on the phone, involved in a serious conversation, judging by the pucker between her brows.

She gasped when she saw him. Ending her call, she stood up and stuffed the phone in her skirt pocket.

"Susannah?" She looked different somehow, but he couldn't put his finger on it. Wait a minute. A skirt? He'd never seen her in heels, either. They stood nearly nose to nose. "What's the matter? Skeet said there was an emergency, and Dana's been acting like Julia Child."

"Julia *Child*?" She frowned in confusion. "Wasn't she a chef?"

"She was also a spy during World War—" He grimaced. "Never mind. What's the problem?"

"I don't know of any …" She gave him a self-conscious little grin. "Oh. It's nothing bad. They just wanted me to tell you what happened this morning."

"Does it have anything to do with Elva Kay's surprise? She emailed, asking me to come over this afternoon, but when you weren't there, she wouldn't say what it was about." He peered at Susannah. She had crossed her arms, and he'd swear she was blushing.

"We … we had this major flood in her basement this morning. Did you know her plumber is related to the former president?"

"Of the United States?" Quinn shook his head. "Surely *that's* not the big mystery."

"No. It's not, really." Susannah gave a nervous laugh. "But that's how it started. The storm woke me up in the middle of the night, and I was thinking about what you and I talked about, and what I've been reading in Dana's Bible this week."

"Wait a sec." Quinn held up a hand. "Can we sit down?"

"I guess so." Looking like a bottle rocket ready to go off, Susannah perched on the bench.

He sat beside her, resting his forearms on his knees. The bench was small, and he could feel her tension. "What time was this?"

"About three. Why?"

He shrugged. "I was awake then, praying for you."

"You were praying for *me*?" Her voice came out in a husky whisper that went right through him.

He nodded. "That God would speak to you."

"I guess he did." She gave him a nervous look. "Not in an audible voice, though."

Quinn smiled. "He doesn't usually. What did he say?"

"When I couldn't go back to sleep, I decided I was thirsty, so I got up to get a Coke." Susannah's lips curled upward. "I was going to read Dana's Bible on the screen porch, but Elva Kay was already out there. We started talking about ... about—" she gave him a self-conscious look—"about stuff, and all of a sudden I could see some things I hadn't understood before. I felt loved like I've never felt love—by Elva Kay and by God. I knew I wanted to have a better purpose for my life, like you said that night you were talking in church. Before I knew it I was praying, and I asked Jesus to come into my life."

Quinn stared at her. The glowing lapis lazuli eyes told him it was true. Something had changed her, inside out. He put his head down, clasping his hands behind his neck. He'd planted a seed, Dana had watered it, and Elva Kay got to be in on the harvest. Humility and gratitude nearly drove him to his knees.

He didn't want to scare her, though, so he sat up and smiled at her. "I bet Skeet went bananas when he found out."

"Pretty much." Susannah laughed. "He made the band play the 'Birthday Song' for me. I thought Dana was going to have a kitten."

"You know, to all of us ... it's a very, very big deal."

Her expression turned serious. "It's a very, very big deal to me too. I have to tell you something, Quinn, okay? Please don't take this the wrong way, but I'm so grateful you went to all the trouble of picking me up for church and treating me with such respect and care." She swallowed, twisting her fingers together. "Would it be appropriate for me to hug you and tell you thanks?"

His eyes stung. "I didn't do anything except be in the right place at the right time." He grabbed her, felt her arms go around his waist and that soft curly hair tuck under his chin. He felt her sigh as she relaxed against him. They sat that way for some time, comfortable, until Susannah tilted her head to smile up at him.

Suddenly he wasn't so comfortable anymore. His gaze dropped to her mouth. She had some kind of polish on her lips that made him want to find out what it tasted like.

"Dana's already trying to get me to go to Japan on a mission trip," she said, jerking him out of insanity.

He took a breath. "There's no reason you can't."

"Yeah, except for I have a job." Her smile died. She pulled away from him and stood up. "I mean, I have to finish my thesis."

"Susannah ..."

"Hey, look how late it is! I need to get home, and don't you have to work tomorrow? Thanks again, Quinn, I'll see you later." She backed toward the door and disappeared into the coffee shop.

Quinn sat there for a whole minute, trying to figure out what he'd said to send her charging off like Wile E. Coyote after the Road Runner. Had she sensed his shift in concentration, the moment when he'd almost blown it by kissing that movie-star mouth? Praying she hadn't, he went inside the coffee shop, only to find Susannah and Dana had already left. He listened to one more song and decided to call it a night.

He would never in a million years figure out what made women operate. But boy, what a great night it had turned out to be.

Susannah rolled over and groaned when the alarm went off Friday morning. For the second night in a row she hadn't slept well, but this time her insomnia had nothing to do with the weather and everything to do with the sense of impending doom that had gripped her since that phone call last night.

Going to the ATF office to examine the debris was the only thing to do, but it could start an uncontrollable chain of events. Depended on what she found.

She had no illusions. Quinn might be physically attracted to her—oh, yeah, there was no doubt he'd wanted to kiss her last night on that moonlit patio. But he was fighting it with every ounce of an uncommonly strong willpower. One minute he'd been holding her close, making her feel small and feminine and, yes, even cherished. She'd looked up at him and seen that flame of awareness in his eyes any woman over the age of twelve could recognize. Then he'd deliberately doused it.

Which was just as well, because he was going to hate her guts when he found out why she was in Mobile. Sooner or later he was going to find out she'd been lying to him for two solid weeks.

Insanity to feel this way about a man she'd known for such a short period of time.

Falling in love with Quinn felt exactly like the time she'd gone tumbling down a trailhead on Tucson's Mount Lemmon. No stopping. Cactus and rocks along the way. Crash at the bottom inevitable.

The worst thing was, she had nobody she could talk to. Everybody here in Mobile thought she was some egghead doctoral student. The idea of talking about her love life to her crusty, military-minded father or any of her three brothers made her cringe.

She looked at the clock and realized she'd spent thirty minutes revolving an impossible problem around in her mind. Her eye fell on the Bible. She had read it before going to bed, soaking it up like a thirsty desert plant.

Last night when she and Dana had parted ways, Dana had given her a verse to learn, calling it "God's phone number." Goofy to think you could talk to God anytime like that, but it had stuck in her mind. Jeremiah 33:3.

What the heck, let's look it up.

She climbed over Monty, grabbed the Bible, and settled in the rocking chair. After fumbling through the New Testament, she finally found the book of Jeremiah with a bunch of other weird-sounding names in the middle of the Bible.

Okay, here it was. "Call to me and I will answer you and tell you great and unsearchable things you do not know."

Intrigued, she shut the Bible on her finger. Maybe there *was* somebody she could talk to any time of day or night and receive undivided attention. Another lightbulb went on. God would answer. About what? Little things? Small things?

Things you do not know.

Boy, that covered just about all the bases. She couldn't even find the books of the Bible without looking them up in the table of contents.

Tucking the Bible against her chest, she wrapped her arms around her legs. This was about all she felt ready to handle right now. A monster-sized bite of spiritual truth to chew on all day.

But what good would it do to read it without doing something about it?

Call to me. Okay.

She looked around—stupid, since there was nobody there with her except Monty—and got down on her knees in front of the chair. She cleared her throat. "Hey, it's me, Susannah. Remember, from yesterday?"

Instantly she was crying, as if the waterworks came from an untapped oasis spring.

"Oh, man, I hope this isn't going to happen every time," she gulped. She found a T-shirt under the bed, wiped her face, and took a breath. Then she poured out her heart to her new best friend.

The ATF evidence vault was nearly as cold and bare as the former railroad station's marble atrium lobby, but completely lacking its ambience. Seated at a metal folding table in the tiny insulated room, Susannah had on one of her new outfits, a jeans skirt and novelty top with flirty little flat sandals. She was longing for the down-lined parka and hiking boots she'd left in Tucson.

Agent Peabo Fontaine had checked her bag and her person, then escorted her to the vault. He'd dropped his massive frame into a metal chair just outside the open door, leaning against the wall with gravity-defying proficiency. He left her alone to sift through the debris from Quinn's late departed company truck.

She pulled on latex gloves and picked up the pieces one at a time. With a strong magnifying lens she examined each bagged item, comparing it to the list on the lab report. Hunks of charred metal and shards of glass. Twisted wires and stinking burned rubber gaskets. Just as you'd expect. Very little remained of the papier-mâché shell casings, but what was there seemed normal. She had the pictures too, taken by the on-scene investigators. So far everything matched.

For nearly an hour she hunched over the table. Once Peabo asked her if she wanted a bottle of water, but she shook her head and went back to work. Engrossed in the task, she just wanted to finish. This was probably a pointless exercise, but she had to make sure.

She knew the guys at the ATF forensics lab in Georgia, knew how good they were. She could understand why they'd determined the cause of premature ignition to be inconclusive. Nothing in the debris looked like a detonating device, or even a piece of one. The shells had been wired with squibs, of course, but none of them had yet been connected to the cables and computer.

She'd been through every bag twice. Checked and rechecked the contents. There was nothing here to connect Quinn or anybody else with arson. Nothing.

Picking up the lab report again, she straightened, arching her back. One more look at this thing and she'd call it quits. *Go home and have a brownie or something else productive.* She scanned the list of chemicals on the printout, and halfway down the third page something stopped her.

Her instincts jumped. Instincts she wanted with her whole heart to ignore. There were taggants in that debris—chemical traces that should not have been in a simple fireworks show. Faint, so faint they could be overlooked or explained away by agents overwhelmed with more pressing cases.

Explosives. A new combination of combustible chemicals. In use for less than six months, still little-known and controversial.

She'd missed it the first two times she'd looked at it. Easy to see why the agents processing the report had missed it too. But as sure as the goose bumps on her arms—it was there. Somebody *had* set off those fireworks early, with a device timed to cause the most damage.

But without retesting the materials herself—or finding an actual piece of the device—she'd never prove anything.

What should I do?

She dropped the report as if it might blow up in her hands. Yanked off the gloves and gripped them as she processed her thoughts.

Of course, she would have to talk to O'Neal about this. The agent was an intelligent officer, and would take Susannah seriously. But something didn't feel right. She had to get away and think about this first. Shaking, she returned the bags to their fiberglass container.

She stood up. "Agent Fontaine," she called, "I'm done."

She heard the chair crash to the floor, and the burly agent appeared in the doorway. "Ma'am?"

"I'm finished. I'd like to sign the debris back over to you. O'Neal said I could take this copy of the lab report with me."

"All-righty. Just put your John Hancock on this line right here, and I'll take you back to the front."

"Thanks."

Susannah signed out on the visitor's log, stuffed the printout into her backpack, and left the ATF office. She blindly passed the elevator and took the stairs, her steps echoing on the marble. At the bottom of the stairs she stood irresolute. Quinn was not a criminal. She'd stake her life on that truth. But somebody was, somebody who'd had access to the fireworks truck.

Somebody with a motive to destroy either Quinn, his company, his reputation, or all three. But when, and who?

Wandering out the back way toward the parking lot, she slid into her Jeep. She sat there listening to the seagulls calling in poignant countermelody to the deep, guttural blast of a train whistle as it rattled along the river. A cool breeze whipped across the parking lot, teasing her hair as she laid her head back against the seat.

Sooner or later she was going to have to tell Quinn who she was. It used to seem clever to be able to pretend to be somebody else. Lately it had begun to feel wrong. She dreaded the look of betrayal she'd surely see in his eyes. For just a little longer she wanted to imagine he was falling in love with her. She wanted to know what it would feel like to be part of his world.

Quinn was safety and goodness.

She shut her eyes against the sun burning under her sunglasses and felt tears sliding down her cheeks.

Lord, is it too soon to ask you for something that big? That you would help me straighten out this whole thing? Is it too much to ask for him to love me no matter what I've done?

Man, what a crybaby she was getting to be. She sat up and sniffed, wiped her nose on a McDonald's napkin stuck under the seat. Good thing nobody could see her.

She started the Jeep and pulled out of the parking lot. She still hadn't talked to Adam Brown at Xtravaganza Events. Maybe she could catch him this afternoon.

chapter 18

Caught by a traffic light, Quinn stopped at the junction of I-165 and Water Street, where the old train station sat on one corner and the huge new office of the *Mobile Register* occupied the other. He was on the way home from rural Chickasaw, where he stored his fireworks in compliance with ATF code. He'd gotten up early for one of his regular inventory inspections. After that surprise ATF visit the other day, he was doubly cautious about regs.

He finished the inspection in record time because inventory was embarrassingly low, and headed for Battleship Park, site of the Bar Association's May Day gig. He always walked around a proposed venue well ahead of time, making notes and getting a creative feel for the place. Every site had its own sense of ambience and history, and he often got ideas from the geometry of surrounding buildings and the canvas of the skyline.

Traffic was brisk on this beautiful spring morning. A train rumbled along the waterfront, and he could see a couple of enormous international ships hulking out in the bay. A fresh breeze whipped through the open windows, bringing in the unique noise and scent of the waterfront. He loved being part of this city.

He'd reached over to turn up the radio when an open-top Jeep driven by a curly-haired blonde came out of the old train depot parking lot and turned onto Water Street. Susannah. Quinn's day suddenly got brighter.

The light changed, and he took off after her. Catching up to her at the next light, he hit the horn.

Her head jerked around, eyes widening as she realized who was behind her. A luminous smile lit her face.

Quinn leaned out his open window. "Hey!" he yelled. "Pull into the next parking lot. I want to talk to you."

She waved agreement, and less than a minute later he'd pulled in beside her, just past the Convention Center at Riverside Park.

"What were you doing down at the GM&O building?" He rested his hands on her open door. "You're mighty dressed up today." She wore a knee-length denim skirt and bright green cotton top.

Dark purple sunglasses hid her eyes, but a sudden blush stained her cheeks. "Oh, I—you know, I'm looking at all the historic sites in town. The GM&O is a really cool building." She tipped her head toward the river. "Want to go sit in the park for a minute?"

"Good idea."

He opened the door for her and they walked across the tracks, by tacit consent heading for the riverside railing. The breeze blew Susannah's hair away from her face, and he noticed a faint sprinkle of freckles across her nose and collarbone. Caught by admiration, he tried not to stare. It seemed like she got prettier every time he saw her.

She released a deep contented sigh as she leaned out toward the river. "I really like it here."

"Why don't you stay?" The words were out before he could censor them. He waited, holding his breath.

"The bums might not want to give up a bench." She smiled.

"I meant—"

"I know what you meant." She slid her bottom lip through her teeth. "I can't stay in Mobile indefinitely. I have to go back to Tucson."

"I know you have to finish up your doctoral work. But you could always move back here later. We have two universities here, plus a couple of smaller colleges—"

"I don't want to teach." She turned to face him, clasping her arms with a shiver. He could see goose bumps on her upper arms. "I thought I had my life all planned out, but now everything's gotten weird, and I can't make decisions like I used to." She ripped off her sunglasses, and he could see her eyes, red-rimmed as if she'd been crying. "Is that what being a Christian means? Feeling like you're all out of control?"

"Maybe." He shook his head. "Sometimes I feel that way too. But remember God's always working behind the scenes, and he's in control of everything." Ironic to hear himself borrowing Elva Kay's words. He caught a lock of hair that blew across her cheek, rubbing its satiny texture between his fingers. "Susannah, what's the matter?"

She replaced her shades, then fumbled at her skirt. "Rats, this thing doesn't have any pockets." She sniffed, then exhaled deeply. "I'm okay. Like I said, it's nothing I can do anything about, so it's pointless to dwell on it."

"Maybe if you talked about it—"

"No. I can't." She gave him a determined smile to soften the clipped response. "So what's going on with you?"

"You mean besides my insurance company giving me the shaft? Inventory so low I have to grovel to a major competitor to buy enough shells for next week's show?" He ticked off his fingers. "Let's see. A thousand fireworks shells to wire by a week from Saturday, with about half my usual crew. A baseball team who needs my attention." He shrugged. "Like the Word says, I press on."

He thought she wasn't going to answer. Resting her elbows on the rail, she looked at him for a moment. "I can help you wire squibs."

Startled, he laughed. It was the last thing he'd expected her to say. "Thanks, that's nice of you to offer, but I have to have people certified to ATF standards. There isn't time to send you to a training session."

She hesitated again. "I've helped with fireworks shows in Arizona. I'm certified."

He stared at her, incredulous. "Why on earth didn't you tell me this before?"

She shrugged. "It's a boring, tedious job. But I'll be glad to help you anyway."

"No, I mean, you know what I do for a living, and this is the first time you've mentioned having some experience with fireworks." He backed away from her. "It just seems like you'd have said something before now."

Just how little he knew about Susannah hit him between the eyes. What else had she not told him about? Like maybe a boyfriend stashed somewhere. Or even a husband.

"It just didn't seem that big a deal to me." She smiled, batting long eyelashes. "Come on, Quinn, just because *you* have an obsession, it doesn't mean the rest of the world does too." When he continued to stare at her, troubled, her smile faded. She sighed. "I can have my paperwork faxed over, if you need it for your permits. The least I can do is help you out. Christians are supposed to share the load, right?"

He stared at her, wishing she'd take the sunglasses off again. What was this sickness in his personality that he was so attracted to a young woman who would share so little about her life? "Of course I need the help, but . . ." He shook his head. "I'm beginning to realize you never talk about anything important to you."

She pressed her beautiful lips together, then allowed them to turn up in a whimsical smile. "Maybe it takes us westerners a little longer to open up than you do down here in the South. Call it caution. Come on, Quinn, don't be mad at me. We'll have lots of time to talk while we're wiring."

His emotions seesawed, but he needed the help.

"All right. We'll be working in the warehouse starting Wednesday. Whenever you're free to come by, we'll be glad to have you." He hesitated. "I'm headed over to the battleship now. Would you like to come? If you've helped with fireworks shows before, I wouldn't mind having your opinion about the show I'm gonna do there."

She shook her head, straightened, and backed toward the park entrance. "I have some work to do at the library. But maybe we could run later this afternoon?"

"Okay. Bring Monty."

"Sure. See you, Quinn."

He watched her hurry away, dodging across the tracks just before the warning bell sounded and the guardrails came down.

Great. He was going to be stuck here for the next ten minutes at least. Oh well, he needed time to pray and get his head straight. Susannah Tait had messed it up again. Bad.

Susannah hit the interstate headed for Biloxi at a speed well over the limit. At this point, however, she would almost consider it a blessing to be thrown in jail. At least she could get off this roller coaster of emotion.

Why couldn't she have just said, "Quinn, I'm an insurance investigator, and I think somebody blew up your truck on purpose"? Why couldn't she have told him she knew how to wire fireworks shells because she was a trained CES, a Certified Explosives

Specialist, with a string of other equally laudable endorsements trailing after her name?

Why? Because she was afraid. Not afraid in a physical sense. But afraid of losing Quinn's regard. In the park he'd *looked* at her again, with that soft, bemused tenderness that made her want to fly into a million pieces like a glitter palm firework. She was an unlit fuse waiting to go off.

And it was not going to be neat and tidy when she did.

She got to Biloxi in about an hour and found the offices of Xtravaganza Events according to the directions given over the phone by Brown's receptionist. The place was new prefab and brick, with lush landscaped grounds and blacktop parking lot. Prosperous. Susannah made mental notes as she went inside.

A lovely auburn-haired woman sat at the desk, talking to someone over a headset and flipping through a clothing catalog. She ended her call and smiled at Susannah. "Can I help you?"

"I called this morning for an appointment with Mr. Brown," Susannah said, borrowing as much southern drawl as she thought she could get away with. "I'm Jo Beth Connery," she added, giving the alias she sometimes used when she needed to conceal her identity. If Brown happened to be an acquaintance of Quinn, she didn't want him mentioning the blonde writer named Susannah Tait who had interviewed him.

"Oh, yes! Have a seat." The woman indicated a chair by the window. "I'll tell Adam you're here." She left and returned momentarily with another dimpled smile. "He says you should come on back. I'm Julie Brown, Adam's wife." She led the way toward a large corner office with big glass bank-style windows. "You're the writer, aren't you?"

"Yes." It was the most convenient story she had been able to come up with. "I'm writing a novel about a fireworks designer, and I just don't know enough about it."

"I'm sure Adam will be thrilled to help you." Julie stuck her head into her husband's office. "Here's Miss Connery, honey. Don't forget you have a lunch appointment at one."

Brown stood up to shake hands and then indicated a chair for Susannah. After the introductory pleasantries, Susannah got to the point.

"Mr. Brown, I know you don't have much time for me, but I'm hoping you can tell me a little about the explosion over in Mobile a couple of months ago. I saw it in the papers and on the news, and it just struck my imagination like you wouldn't believe."

"You mean the SkyPainters disaster that messed up the Convention Center?" Brown's thick brows twitched together. "Why don't you just talk to Quinn Baldwin about it? I'm sure he's got time on his hands after the explosion."

Susannah gave him a sweet smile. *You are such a pompous turkey.*

"Of course, I *could* talk to Mr. Baldwin, and I still might, but I wanted to talk to somebody who knows what they're doing."

"Baldwin's a competent pyrotechnician. In fact, I trained him myself nearly ten years ago and gave him his first job. Early on I even had some money invested in his company until SkyPainters was strong enough that he could buy me out." Baldwin smiled. "Looks like I funded my future competition, huh? Look, honey, accidents occur—that one just happened to be fairly dramatic."

Susannah stared, astonished he would divulge such private business details. Then she realized he was bragging. And he had called her "honey." Her lip curled. "I was just thinking what a good story it would make if a pyrotechnician decided to sabotage his own company if it were tanking. Wouldn't it be hard to determine if an explosion like that were an accident or not?"

"I can see why you wouldn't want to look as if you were accusing Quinn of such a crime." Brown looked severe. "He's a most upstanding young businessman and would be embarrassed at the very suggestion."

"Oh, sure, sure," said Susannah, almost forgetting her southern accent. She retrieved it. "I mean, you don't think there's even a remote possibility?"

Brown's frown deepened. "As you said, it would be next to impossible to prove. If this is the story you're going for, I think you'd better forget it."

"If you say so," Susannah sighed. "When did you find out Baldwin had blown up the Convention Center?"

"Not until two weeks later. I was in Tokyo for the whole month of January."

On Saturday morning, dressed in shorts, sandals, and Azalea Trail Run T-shirts, Susannah and Dana drove downtown early and parked at the Civic Center before the police closed the area for the race.

"Come on," Dana said, "let's go check out the starting point before we go to the water tables. We've got plenty of time, and it's something to see."

Dana filled Susannah in on the details of the race as they walked. Considered the premier 10K race for pros as well as amateurs, the Azalea Trail Run drew runners from as far away as Africa and New Zealand and all over the United States. Nearly ten thousand were expected to participate, including senior adults and families with children who would do the two-mile run/walk.

"Ten *thousand*?" Susannah echoed. "How will they get that many people on one race route?"

Dana laughed. "Wait and see. You'll be amazed at how orderly everybody is."

As they turned onto Government Street, lined with police barricades and people in lawn chairs, Susannah saw what Dana meant. The sidewalks hosted booths for refreshments and souvenirs. Reporters swarmed the place, as did cameras on trucks and motorcycles.

"Where's Quinn?" Susannah tried to look as if it were a casual question.

Dana cut her a look, not fooled. "Warming up. He gets to line up on the front with the elites."

"He's that good?"

"Oh, yeah. He's placed in the top thirty of the Open division twice."

"Holy guacamole." The *Chariots of Fire* comparison hadn't been so far off, then. "When we run together, he always paces himself with me."

"That's Quinn." Dana smiled. "He's not a show-off."

They passed a sprawling white three-story building with marble columns, massive concrete steps, and a central dome. It was a bit mildewed, but still impressive. Susannah looked up, shading her eyes. "What's that?"

"Barton Academy, the public school system administrative offices. It's been here since before the Civil War."

"Cool." Susannah chuckled as a teenage girl in an enormous ruffled hooped skirt walked past. "Looks like *she's* been here awhile too."

Dana giggled. "I have one of those. My mother has it on a mannequin in the guest room."

"You've got to be kidding. Why?"

Dana dipped a curtsy. "Azalea Trail Maids are a fine Mobile tradition. It's an honor to be chosen."

"I'm sure." Susannah grinned as the girl in the swaying lemon yellow dress stopped to be interviewed by a reporter from FOX news. Besides the dress and parasol, she wore a ruffled hat with the dimensions of a Chinese gong.

"As a former Trail Maid, I can tell you anything you want to know about Mobile history." Dana struck a simpering pose. "Established in 1701 on 27-Mile Bluff as the capital of French Louisiana, Mobile came under British rule in 1763 and became a major trade center. Captured by the Americans during the War of 1812—"

"Okay, okay." Susannah laughed. "I get the picture." Dana's unexpected ability to poke fun at herself made Susannah like her even more. Loudspeakers were barking polite instructions, making it difficult to carry on a conversation. "Hey, aren't we supposed to be at the water table?"

"Yikes!" Dana looked at her watch. "The race starts at eight. We'd better go."

Susannah couldn't help searching the crowd for Quinn as they went back the way they'd come. She hoped he'd run well today. He deserved something wonderful to happen.

After his warm-up miles, Quinn went by the water station manned by the Fellowship group, where he changed into his racing flats and stashed his training shoes under a table. Ten long tables had been set up end to end along the curb, about half a mile from the finish line.

People lined the streets waiting for the start of the race, and the electric atmosphere pumped adrenaline through Quinn's veins. Taking a couple of deep breaths, he called the volunteers together to pray before he took off for the starting line. He found Susannah standing behind Dana. Though it had to be killing her not to run, she gave him a thumbs-up along with her bright smile. She understood his excitement and nerves. For some reason the knowledge calmed him down.

"Thanks for coming, everybody." He scanned his rather motley crew as he gave them brief instructions. Besides Susannah and Dana, he had Skeet and the rest of the praise band, Clint and Julianne Harrison, and Pastor Martin's family. He finished and smiled as Clint lifted a hand. The big man had covered his bald head with a camouflage fishing hat strapped under his bearded chin. Quite a sight. "What is it, Clint?"

"I helped with this thing last year, and I just wanted to remind everybody to stay out of the way when the elite runners come by. They'll mow you down and not look back."

"Is that experience talking?" Pastor Martin teased.

Clint just grinned. "I think I still got a tread mark on my back."

Quinn laughed. "Good point, Clint. But the amateurs coming after them will be looking for you. And remember what Jesus said about giving a cup of cold water in his name."

He caught Susannah's eyes again. They were filled with an attractive new softness that made him feel suddenly light-headed.

Gotta get out of here.

But Susannah ducked around the group of volunteers and caught him as he turned to jog toward the starting line. "I'll be praying for you." She tucked her hands into the pockets of her shorts. "I just wanted you to know."

"Thanks." He restrained an urge to pick her up and hug her. "If you'll do that, I should have a pretty good chance."

She grinned and backed toward the table.

He made himself turn away. *The race. Focus on the race.*

During the lull before the first wave of runners passed in front of the table, Susannah helped fill what seemed like half a million four-ounce paper cups with water. She found herself enjoying the camaraderie with the rest of the volunteers, especially the young pastor and his wife. They'd brought their oldest son, who was about eleven and reminded Susannah of the kids on Quinn's baseball team. When she asked him if he played ball, he lit up and they were soon fast friends.

By twenty minutes past eight, nothing more exciting than a malfunctioning water tank had occurred. Susannah stood across the street from the water station as the first wave of runners tore by. Hard-boiled, rail thin, and focused, not a single person in the men's elite division even glanced at the volunteers.

Stepping back, Susannah waited a couple of minutes before the next group came down Broad Street—the elite women mixed with a few local men. Her heart took a wild leap when she realized Quinn was right on the heels of the woman in the lead. She'd been looking for him, but the sight of that all-out Eric Liddell stride made the blood pound in her veins.

Please don't let him look at me, don't let me distract him. She wanted him to win so badly she could taste it. She even withdrew the cup of water in her hand and stepped back from the curb, knowing serious runners wouldn't hesitate for anything. She would wait until he'd passed before holding out the water.

"Go, Quinn!" screamed Dana, who stood beside her, jumping up and down.

Quinn glanced toward them, and for an instant his eyes met Susannah's. His stride faltered just enough that the man behind him caught up. "Go on!" Susannah shouted, waving him on.

Quinn jerked up his chin and bore down again. He and his competitor made the turn onto Canal Street and headed for the finish line out of Susannah's sight.

Dana grabbed her in a hug. "Quinn's winning!"

Susannah shook her head, unable to answer because of the noise from a motorcycle-camera that passed, filming the runners behind the pack of elite women and local champions. She concentrated on her job of offering water and pictured the look in Quinn's eyes as he'd passed her.

Please, God, let him win.

chapter 19

Quinn ran toward the roped-off finish line chutes. Blake McCoy, his primary rival in the race, had edged past him at the curve. Less than a quarter mile to catch up.

Serious mistake, looking for Susannah and taking his eyes off the goal. Not her fault. Waving her arms like a wild woman, she'd been screaming at him to run.

Suck it up, Baldwin, and recover.

Pushing himself, he ran harder.

Forgetting what is behind ...

He was on McCoy's heels.

Straining toward what is ahead ...

Shoulder to shoulder with McCoy.

I press on toward the goal ...

Gasping, he passed McCoy to catch the woman in third place.

To win the prize ...

He and McCoy split off from the women to enter the race chute for Men's Masters Division.

For which God has called me heavenward in Christ Jesus.

Lungs bursting, he found another ounce of strength and shot past the finish line ahead of McCoy and everyone else.

He threw his hands high.

Susannah heard the crowd roar, and knew the men's division winners had crossed the finish line. How could she stay here, dashing back and forth across the street to hand out water, not knowing whether Quinn had won?

But she'd made a commitment. She stayed.

And then, like a rumor, word came down the line that Quinn Baldwin had come in first, Men's Masters Division.

Susannah wanted to believe it, didn't trust it, until she saw him jogging around the corner. His face was lit from within, dark hair plastered against his head, body gleaming with sweat, every muscle still pumped from massive exertion.

"You won, didn't you?" She laughed as he grabbed her and swung her around. Flinging her arms around his neck, she hung on for dear life as water showered in all directions.

And then he was kissing her, focusing all the intensity and joy that was Quinn, straight from his lips to hers. Held off the ground, explosions of sweetness going off in her chest like sparklers, she closed her eyes and kissed him back.

Then, a minute later he dropped her, jerking his mouth away. She opened her eyes and stared at him for a frozen moment. He looked like he'd just slammed head-on into a wall.

She grabbed his forearms as her knees buckled. "Hel–lo ..."

"I've got to change my shoes," he muttered, as if that had anything to do with the kiss of the century. "Gotta cool down."

"Okay." Cooling down was a very good idea.

She let go of him and watched him reach under the table for his duffle bag. Collapsing into somebody's abandoned lawn chair, he replaced his racing flats with training shoes. After shoving the duffel bag back under the table, he took off down the street as if the hounds of hell were after him.

Susannah watched Quinn disappear around the corner. If her lips hadn't been on fire, she wouldn't have believed what had just happened.

"Susannah!" Dana squealed. "Quinn just kissed you! In front of God and everybody! Yea!"

Incapable of speech, she blinked down at Dana.

"I knew it!" Dana flung her hands up. "I *knew* he was in love with you, but he just wouldn't admit it. Ha! Just wait till Sheree hears about this."

"What? No!" Susannah shook her head. "No, don't tell anybody else." She looked around. It appeared the rest of the team had been busy serving water and had missed the spectacle.

Holy guacamole, I am so dead. What if her boss found out about this? *Fraternizing …*

"But, Susannah—"

"I mean it, Dana." Susannah brushed her hands down the front of her T-shirt, damp from Quinn's sweaty embrace. She felt like she might spontaneously combust. "Let's—let's just keep this between us girls."

"But—" Dana was looking at something over her shoulder.

Susannah was too flustered to care. She grabbed two cups of water to replace the ones she'd flung to the four winds and raced across the street when she saw a break between runners.

For the next hour and a half she was so busy she barely had time to think, much less dwell on whether or not Quinn had lost his mind or she had—or more likely both.

Pick up cups. Race across the street. Hold out water. Repeat. Over and over she did it until her arms were so tired she wanted to lie down in the street. Maybe somebody would run over her and put her out of her misery.

Finally the last walker had staggered past on the way to the finish line, allowing the water team to close shop. The plan was to join everybody else—participants, volunteers, and spectators—in the Civic Center for red beans and rice, ice cream, and soft drinks. In Susannah's mind, it was a strange combination of "health foods" for an athletic awards ceremony celebration, but she locked arms with Dana and Skeet, and the three of them managed to achieve a fairly creditable monkey walk down the middle of Canal Street. By the time they reached the Civic Center, they were laughing so hard she was afraid people would think they'd drained one of the beer cases in abundant supply.

Even a week ago Susannah might have been tempted by the free-flowing alcohol, but she was having such a good time keeping up with Skeet's puns and corny jokes it never occurred to her to do more than walk past with a vague sense of relief. Relief she was with people who cared about her enough to include her in *good* things, things that mattered. Things that would last, as Quinn had said, forever.

He kissed me, she thought in wonder. Watching Skeet give Dana a bite of his ice cream sandwich, Susannah touched her lips. Where was he? How could he have done that, then disappeared like a puff of smoke?

The tension had been there between them, almost from the beginning. She felt like the pressure cooker Elva Kay used to cook butter beans. Like the little gizmo on its lid, their attraction had wobbled and whistled for two weeks, steam building up inside until today—when the whole thing had blown up.

She'd been kissed before. Casually and, she realized with shame, indiscreetly. By men who wanted nothing but immediate pleasure. Her feelings for Quinn made those previous encounters seem blasphemous.

Oh, Lord, can I really start over?

Blindly she sank into an empty chair beside the ice cream booth. Sound bites of things Quinn had told her about himself flashed through her mind. He had recovered from rocky beginnings too. It *was* possible to come to life after death.

Suddenly she was grateful to have fallen in love with a man who could understand and forgive her doubts and confusion. All she had to do was find a time and place to confess what she'd done.

"Where'd you go after the race?" asked McCoy as he and Quinn found seats in the section reserved for the local top ten, near the awards platform. "Reporters were all over me, looking for you."

Quinn pressed his lips together.

I was making an idiot out of myself by kissing a woman I've known exactly two weeks.

He forced a laugh. "Changed my shoes, did a couple of cool-down miles. Went back to check on my water table crew."

Yeah, he'd approached the table, but hung back watching Susannah run back and forth across the street, laughing and cutting up with Skeet and Dana. Looked like the kiss hadn't affected her much at all. So he'd turned around and walked straight to the Civic Center, where he'd made the rounds of the food and soft drink booths. Drooling over sports equipment he could only dream of being able to afford, he'd dodged the reporters. He wasn't sure he could put together a coherent sentence.

Just went to show you what happened when you'd shut off your emotions for eons and then suddenly fell in love. *Whacked your brain out, man.* Whacked *out.* He needed to get alone with the Lord, figure this thing out.

You can't love a woman you've got so little in common with, he told himself. *You can't love someone you barely know. You can't love someone who's been a Christian for less than forty-eight hours.*

The problem was, he *should* love her, at least in the spiritual sense. And he *definitely* loved her in the physical sense—he loved everything about Susannah Tait.

But the romantic, agape kind of love you needed for the woman you wanted to marry ... Didn't that take time? Weren't you supposed to court her, get to know her family, make sure she didn't have any communicable diseases?

Quinn's brain skidded into a tailspin. As Skeet would say, *Dude, you are freaking.*

Apparently McCoy could tell he was out to lunch. He gave Quinn a sardonic look, then turned his attention to the president of the Port City Pacers, who had stepped onto the platform to start the awards ceremony.

Right now Quinn couldn't have cared less about another plaque to hang on his wall.

A little peace of mind, however, would have been welcome.

The SkyPainter Braves took on the AAA Auto Salvage Astros that afternoon, forcing Quinn to leave the after-race celebration early. Alden didn't show up, and Quinn assumed he was somewhere on the Chickasabogue River fishing with his dad. Which was great, but it left the team without a catcher. Substituting Kenny Pettway behind the plate turned out to be a serious mistake. In the third inning the kid ripped his face mask off too soon—just in time for the Astros' best hitter to catch him in the mouth with a mighty backswing. Quinn wound up spending most of the afternoon in the emergency room, while Kenny heroically allowed an intern to sew his top lip back together.

Dog-tired and looking a bit like a gunshot victim himself, Quinn put Kenny and his mother into her beat-up Chevy before heading home. He called Phillip on the way.

"Hey, man. Did we win?"

"Believe it or not, we did." Phillip laughed. "I put Tacy Stevenson behind the plate and she threw a kid out at third in the last inning. Girl's got an arm like an assault rifle."

"Well, that's something." Quinn stifled a yawn.

"How's Kenny?"

"He'll have a battle scar for life. Anyway, thanks for taking over when I left. I owe you one." Quinn turned into his driveway. "Which reminds me, can you work next week, starting on Wednesday? We've got about a thousand shells to wire for your cousin Sheree's wedding."

"Sure, I guess so. But I've got a car show Saturday I'd like to go to. Can you fire it without me?"

"You're not going to the wedding?"

"Sheree and Rebecca locked me in the attic when I was four. She can get married without me."

Quinn laughed. "Okay. Just help me wire, and I'll let you off the hook."

"Deal."

Quinn ended the call and staggered out of the truck. He'd have to hurry to get showered and changed before the water table group arrived. Everybody had wanted to watch the five o'clock news and celebrate his Azalea Trail win. Quinn owned the biggest flat-screen television, so his house would be party central.

He'd hardly gotten the door open when his cell phone rang again. "Hey, Rebecca." He flopped into the recliner.

"Quinn, I need to talk to you. Can you come over to the house?"

Quinn looked down at the front of his bloody T-shirt. It was beginning to smell. "Can't you just tell me whatever it is over the phone?"

"No. I cannot."

He sat up. "Is it your mom?"

"No, I just have to tell you something, and no, it can't wait until Monday. Please, Quinn."

"All right," he sighed, "but I have to be home by five. I have company coming."

"Is it Susannah?"

"It's a whole bunch of people." He rubbed his forehead. "I'll be there in about thirty minutes."

He took a shower, put on clean clothes, and was out the door in record time. Knocking on the Mansfields' door, he tried to imagine what could have Rebecca in such a snit if it didn't have anything to do with her mother's health. Maybe Phillip had pulled some lame-brained stunt. He'd just talked to Phillip, though. Maybe—

Rebecca yanked open the apartment door. "Hey." She pulled him inside and surveyed his still-damp hair. "You didn't have to dress up."

"I told you, I've got company coming over tonight." He ran a hand around the back of his neck. "What's the matter?"

"I found out something today. Sit down." She shoved him at the sofa.

"Okay, okay, good grief. Where's your mom?" He dropped onto the sofa and laid his head back. Man, he felt like a cooked spaghetti noodle.

Rebecca stood over him, twisting her hands. "She's resting. I couldn't leave her, that's why—"

"I know you can't leave her. That's why I'm here." Rebecca never acted nervous. What was going on? He softened his voice. "Look, sit down, you're making me jumpy."

"That'll be the day." But she perched on the edge of the nearby love seat. "Okay, I know you don't have much time, but I've got to tell you this right now. Susannah Tait is not who you think she is."

Quinn looked at the ceiling. "Here we go again. Conspiracy theory number two hundred eighty-four."

"Don't you dare tease me," she said, teeth clenched. "I knew it all along, but now I can prove it to you."

"Prove *what*? What's so scary about a sociology doctoral student?"

"She is not a student. She's an insurance investigator for Independent Mutual. That's our company."

Quinn sat up. "I *know* that's our company. But what makes you think—"

"I don't *think*. I *know* it. I googled her name yesterday afternoon and found her cited in a couple of other insurance fraud cases. She's an explosives expert for an outfit called Stryker Investigations, and contracts out to insurance companies. She used to be an ATF agent in Tucson."

Quinn gripped his thighs with both hands. He felt like someone had just punched him in the stomach.

This explained how and why she was certified to wire fireworks.

But it didn't explain much else.

Why would Susannah tell such a big whopping lie, unless ...

"Do you think she's investigating *me*?"

Rebecca's dark brown eyes were filled with an odd combination of anger and sympathy. "Why else would she go to so much trouble to worm her way into friendship with you? To inspect our office? She asked me a lot of questions, Skeet and Phillip too, and I bet she's even talked to Clint and Julianne and the pastor. Everybody who knows you."

Quinn put his fingers to his temple. He felt like somebody had just slammed *him* in the head with a bat. "I can't believe it."

"You better believe it. She's not enrolled at the University of Arizona, at least not now. She did graduate from there about six years ago with a masters in chemistry." Rebecca released a breath. "Quinn, I'm so sorry, but I had to tell you. There's no telling what she's getting ready to pull on us. If she's trying to prove insurance fraud, you may have a legal battle that will go on for years and cost you everything."

"But ... that explosion was an accident! There's no way she can prove I set it on purpose." Quinn jumped to his feet, paced to the door, and wheeled. "Can she? Because you know I didn't!"

Rebecca leaned back, looking disgusted. "I don't think so. The fire marshal and local ATF determined it to be an accident. But Susannah's apparently a very smart woman, and she's won the last two cases she was involved in."

Quinn turned to face the door. He didn't want Rebecca to see his face. Confusion and hurt shook him. As an athlete he'd always loathed cheaters. Deception like this was the worst kind of cheating.

What made it worse was the fact he liked Susannah. A lot. To think he'd been falling in love with this girl.

The thought made him nauseated.

How could he have been such a gullible idiot? She'd had him on the hook since the first time she'd caught up to him on the track at Murphy. What an easy mark he'd been. Tongue practically falling out of his head every time he looked at her.

Which was what the Bible warned against.

Stupid stupid stupid.

He took a deep breath and looked over his shoulder at Rebecca. Her eyes were dark with distress. This wasn't her fault. She'd just been trying to protect him.

"Okay, Rebecca." His tongue felt thick as the words came out. "Thank you for going to the trouble of finding all this out. I'm not sure what I'm going to do right now, but I'll figure it out."

"Quinn, I'm so sorry," she repeated. "I'll do whatever I can to help. Right now I think—" she hesitated—"I think you'd better avoid Susannah."

"I'm not sure I can." He put a hand on the doorknob. "Besides, knowledge is power. Now that I know who she is, I can protect myself."

"I guess that's true." She stood up, wringing her hands as if she didn't know what to do with them. "Do you want to say hi to Mama while you're here?"

He opened the door. "Can you just tell her I came by? I'll see her next time, okay?"

"All right." Rebecca got up and walked over to put a hand on his arm. "Be careful, Quinn."

"I will." He went out to his truck and sat there unmoving. After a while he cranked it and drove home. This was a time to pray, but he had no idea what to say to God.

How could you pull the rug out from under me like this again? Why? I'm not perfect, but I've served you, I've loved you, I've obeyed as best I know how.

He sat in his driveway, looking at his house and dreading his friends coming over to celebrate the race. His friends—and Susannah.

She'd been claiming to be a Christian. Was that even real, or had she pretended to believe in Jesus so they'd accept her into the group? So he'd open himself up to her?

God, is it okay if I'm really angry with you right now?

chapter 20

Susannah followed Quinn into his little kitchen, both of them carrying a towering stack of pizzas. They'd left Dana in the living room, Monty sprawled across her lap like a huge rug. Susannah had asked Quinn if she could bring the dog, and he'd just shrugged. "As long as he doesn't upset Bob."

"Oh, please," she muttered, eyeing the big glass tank on the breakfast table as Quinn adjusted the oven to warm. "Let's not disturb the snake."

One end of the terrarium contained an overturned flowerpot, a big gray rock, and a broken tree branch. At the other end, a bowl of water sat on an elevated shelf under a heat lamp. Nice digs for a serpent.

"Hey, Quinn."

"What?" He took the pizzas from her without meeting her eyes. He'd barely looked at her since she and Dana had arrived.

"Where's your buddy Bob?"

He glanced over his shoulder as he stuck the pizzas in the oven. "Probably hiding under the flowerpot. He likes the dark."

She peered at the hole in the pot. No beady eyes or forked tongue in sight. "Does that not tell you something about his character?"

"He's just shy. Like owner like snake."

Folding her arms, she leaned against the sink. "I think you let people think you're shy to avoid confrontation."

"Is that right?" He looked at her, and her stomach flipped as he walked toward her. "So are you provoking one? A confrontation?"

She had to tilt her head to look up at him. Her mouth went dry at the sudden heat in the storm-gray eyes. "No, of course not, I—" she gave a little huff—"what if I am?"

"Okay, then let's have one." He pressed his lips together. "I jumped the gun in a major way this morning. It won't happen again."

"You mean when you kissed me?" She searched his eyes, trying to decipher his feelings. He wasn't letting her in. "In case you didn't notice, I didn't exactly resist. Although maybe I should play a little harder to get, huh?" She'd expected him to laugh, but he just looked at her. She swallowed. "So ... why did you, Quinn? I know you well enough to know you don't go around k–kissing every woman you meet."

"You don't know me at all," he shot back. He studied her for a moment, then shrugged. "I guess I was just hyped up after winning the race."

"So I just happened to be in the right place at the right time?" She felt the backs of her eyelids prickle. "I don't think I believe that."

"I guess I'm not as convincing a liar as you are."

Susannah felt all the breath leave her lungs. "What did you say?"

"Come on, Susannah, did you think the stupid Alabama redneck was never going to figure out what you're up to?" Quinn's eyes had turned to ice. He was still physically close, but the emotional retreat was clear.

"You're not a s–stupid anything! I don't know what you think, but—"

"Cut it out!" He straightened so that he towered over her. "Rebecca found out you're working for the insurance company. They don't want to pay off my claim, so they sent you to snoop around, trying to prove I blew up my equipment and truck on purpose."

The truth sounded so baldly evil Susannah wanted to hide under the flowerpot with the other snake in the room. She put her hands to her face.

"And don't try to cry your way out of it. I won't fall for anything else you pretend to do."

"I'm not crying," Susannah whispered, whipping her hands behind her back. "I'm humiliated you found out this way, but—" She jerked her chin up. "How *did* you find out?"

"Mr. Google is an amazing guy."

"I should have changed my name," she said wretchedly, "but I never thought I'd be able to keep you from making me for more than a day or two. Everything just snowballed."

He just looked at her, and for the first time she saw the hurt behind the anger in his eyes.

"Quinn, I'm so sorry, I don't know what to say." She blinked to keep the tears back. "At first I was just doing my job. It was the only way to get an unbiased and clear picture of who you are. But the more I got to know you, the more ridiculous that letter began to sound—"

"Letter? What letter?" He backed across the kitchen until he was leaning on the refrigerator.

Susannah felt the coldness of the distance. "There was an anonymous letter sent to Mr. Webster, claiming you'd set the explosion because your business was in trouble and you wanted to collect. They had to investigate."

His eyes were narrow slits of slate. "I don't see why you couldn't tell me the truth once you started to believe I didn't do it. You *do* believe that, don't you?"

"Of course I do!" Susannah clutched her fingers together. "But once I'd laid my cover, it was impossible to back out of it. Quinn, I've only been a Christian for a few days! I don't know everything there is to know about handling—"

"I'm sorry, but I'm having a hard time believing even that was real, Susannah. How do I know you didn't just invent that story to make me trust you and let you hang out with my friends?"

The accusation pierced her like an arrow. Mouth trembling, she closed her eyes. After a thick, heavy silence, she dragged in a breath. He simply waited, hands pressed flat against the refrigerator, mouth clipped together.

"I would never pretend something like that. You can ask anybody who knows me."

"Who does know you, Susannah?" The words were laced with irony, but she took them at face value.

She shook her head. "I used to think I was a pretty simple, straightforward person. But I never let anybody into the softer part of me until I met you."

He frowned and opened his mouth, but she lifted a hand and stepped toward him.

"Listen," she said softly. "In my whole *life* I've never met anybody like you. I don't know how you can always do the right thing, the kind thing. Maybe I didn't tell you who I was because I didn't want to be your enemy. I wanted to be someone you'd talk to and listen to and enjoy being with. I did *not* make my decision for Christ just to impress you, but you sure had an influence on me. And that, Quinn Baldwin, is the truth."

"Let me tell *you* something," he fired back. "I *did* like talking to you and listening to you. I loved running with you, and that kiss was real. But can I trust you just because you say 'Oh sorry' and bat those blue eyes at me?" He closed his eyes.

Suddenly the dog started barking. Susannah and Quinn both jumped.

Quinn frowned. "What's the matter with him?"

"You're doorbell's about to ring."

Sure enough, a minute later Quinn's house was filled with laughter and teasing and the noise of the television as the rest of the team arrived with soft drinks, ice, and dessert.

Susannah covered her distress and frustration as best she could. Helplessly, she watched Quinn acting the perfect host. He made sure the women had the best seats on the couch and recliner, showed the pastor's two boys where the bathroom was, hauled Monty out of Julianne's face when the dog jumped on her. He smiled and refilled drinks and ran to the convenience store when the ice ran out.

But he never once looked at her again.

Quinn shut the door on the last of his guests and wandered into the kitchen with a couple of empty paper plates full of pizza crusts. He dumped them into the trash under the sink, then stood there staring into Bob's terrarium.

He felt like he might explode if somebody touched him. Holding himself together for two hours with Susannah in the room had been almost more than he could handle.

But by the grace of God he did.

"Yo, Bob." He tapped the top of the flowerpot. Snakes didn't like to be disturbed when they were hiding. But this was an emergency. A scaly head poked out of the hole. "There you are. Come on out, counselor." Of course, he should be talking with God, but he was still seriously hacked off. He sat down on a kitchen chair and propped his head in his hands. "She said she's sorry. What do you think about that?"

Bob stuck out his tongue.

"It's not dinnertime, so you can put your tongue back in your mouth. Did you hear all those nice things she said about me? You think she meant it? Not that it matters, I mean. She's a liar, right? Once a liar, always a liar."

Something didn't sound quite right about that, but he was too tired and too frustrated to straighten it out in his mind.

"She should definitely have to suffer awhile. God will punish her, that's what the Bible says."

That didn't feel as good as it should have either, and he made a face at Bob, who ducked back into his hiding place.

"I've got to go to bed too. It's nearly eleven, and there's church tomorrow." He stood up and turned off the light over the terrarium. "Thanks for your support, dude. Sweet dreams."

He trudged off to bed, looking forward to some messed-up dreams of his own. Thanks to a certain blue-eyed blonde. *Yee hah.*

Most days Elva Kay had already read the newspaper cover to cover and started on her daily Bible reading by the time Susannah got up. But this morning she gave up on sleep when the clock blinked 5:00 a.m. Dressed in shorts and T-shirt, she stumbled barefoot down the stairs. Letting Monty out, she tiptoed to the driveway to pick up the paper.

She put the tea kettle on to boil and leaned against the counter, staring at a Bible verse sampler over the window. "The steadfast love of the Lord never ceases, His mercies never come to an end; they are new every morning; great is thy faithfulness."

Boy, God, I could use some of that mercy, love, and faithfulness right now.

Monty woofed at the back door; she let him in and filled his dish, then sat down at the table with her tea. What was she going to do about Quinn? Clearly he wasn't going to volunteer any more information about his business dealings. Or any other kind of dealings. She would have to go ahead with the investigation without him and Rebecca—probably Skeet too.

He'd kept his mouth shut last night after that nasty confrontation in the kitchen, but she could hardly believe he would keep his knowledge of her identity to himself forever. What were people at church going to think when they found out what a deceiver she'd been? Were they going to kick her out of the church?

She needed to talk to somebody who'd been a Christian longer than she had, somebody she could be honest with. Somebody who would love her no matter what she'd done.

Elva Kay would fill the bill—and Susannah knew she'd have to confess to her mentor eventually—but the older woman was still in bed.

Susannah set her mug down with a clatter. Jeremy. How could she have forgotten? Her brother *loved* to tell her what to do.

Leaving the unopened newspaper outside Elva Kay's bedroom door, she ran upstairs and dug her cell phone out of the pocket of the shorts she'd had on last night. Hitting her brother's speed-dial number, she crawled back in the bed. He answered sleepily.

"Jeremy, it's me." She burst into tears.

"Susannah? What's wrong?"

"I have so screwed up."

He laughed. Yesterday she might have been tempted to hang up on him, but this morning it was a comforting sound.

"You forgot Dad's birthday, didn't you?"

"Dad's birthday! Oh, no! That was Friday, wasn't it?" She'd been so focused on herself she hadn't even sent her father a card.

"Trust me, he probably didn't even notice." Jeremy paused. "That wasn't what you called about?"

"No." It dawned on her she'd never told him about her conversion. "I have to tell you something. Are you sitting down?"

"Susie, you woke me up. I'm flat on my back in the bed."

"Oh, yeah. Right. Well, first I have to make sure you're not going to say 'I told you so.'" She paused. "Do you swear?"

"I'm making no rash promises. Susannah, what have you done?"

She pulled the covers over her head. "I did the thing where you trust in Jesus and pray and get to start over. You know, with God."

Dead silence hummed through the phone. "Okay. Cherry, call the paramedics. I'm hallucinating."

"Hallucinating is visual."

"Okay, then I'm hearing imaginary voices." Suddenly Susannah was deafened by a cowboy yell in her ear. She could hear Cherry laughing in the background and demanding to know what was going on. "Susannah's a believer! How? When?"

Her brother's joy almost overcame her utter misery. "A few days ago, here with my landlady, Mrs. Shue."

"And you're just now telling me? Didn't you realize I'd want to know?"

"I've been ... pretty busy down here. I'm sorry."

"I guess I have to forgive you. But why were you crying? What's the matter?"

She swallowed hard. "There's this guy—"

"I'll kill him. Who is he?"

"No, Jeremy!" She let out a cry that was half laugh, half sob. *I'm* the one who messed up. You remember me telling you about the guy I'm investigating?"

"The pyro?"

"Yeah. Well, he's innocent. I'm sure of it. Only I lied to him from the start—about who I am, I mean. I thought I could get more out of him if he were off guard around me."

"Sounds like smart undercover work to me."

"It was, until I—until I fell in love with him."

Her brother began to sing. "Oh, Susannah, oh don't you cry for—"

She interrupted him with an inarticulate shriek. "This is not *funny*!"

"I beg to differ. Just let me get it over with, then we'll move on." Susannah gritted her teeth as Jeremy howled with laughter. Finally he gasped, "Now. Where were we? Oh, yeah. First of all, you've known this guy—what, two weeks?"

"Fifteen days."

"Okay. I stand corrected. How can you possibly be in love with a guy after fifteen days?"

"You'd just have to meet him."

"Oh, trust me. I will. I presume he's in love with you too."

"I think he was getting there, until he found out what a liar I am. You'd be pretty ticked off too, wouldn't you?"

Jeremy snickered. "I guess I would be. You never do anything the easy way."

"Don't you have some advice?" She was beginning to doubt the wisdom of this phone call. His laughter stung.

"Let me ask you something first. Is this guy a Christian?"

"Jeremy, I'll never catch up to him in a million years. He's, like, super Christian."

"Wow. Okay, then, if he's mature, he'll realize you made a mistake and forgive you for doing your job the best way you knew how. If he's not—then you're better off without him."

Susannah absorbed that. "Maybe so. But this case isn't over. I still can't *prove* he's innocent."

Jeremy sighed. "Look, I can't fix this situation for you instantly. But I can pray with you if you want."

"Would you?" She clutched the phone, drawing her knees to her chest. Confusion seemed to have her whole body in a twist.

"Absolutely. Dear Lord, I thank you so much for bringing Susannah into the family. That she's my sister in Christ as well as my blood sister. I pray you'll cover her right now with your peace and wisdom. That you'll help her actions reflect her faith. And that—what's his name, Susie?"

"Quinn," she whispered, aching at the sound of his name.

"—that Quinn will be able to know your will too. That he'll treat Susannah with mercy and forgiveness, just like you've done for him. Amen."

"Thanks, Jer."

"Welcome." He cleared his throat. "Now a couple of things you need to do."

"What's that?" A plan of action always made her feel better.

"Confess to anybody you've hurt, and ask for forgiveness."

"I've already done that. But he wouldn't listen to me."

"Well, give him time. Sounds like you really stepped on his toes."

"Yeah. What else?"

"Just be as honest as possible in the future. And keep praying. God will show you what to do if you read his Word."

"I can do that. But keep praying for me. It's really a mess." For one thing, Simon Webster was not going to like it that she refused to make Quinn look guilty if he wasn't. By the same token, she knew she could not ignore any evidence that might turn up proving he *was*.

She said goodbye to Jeremy—and Cherry, who was listening on an extension—and lay under the covers for several minutes. Calling him had been the right thing to do. The situation hadn't changed, but she had a clearer idea of what God wanted her to do.

The first thing was to face the people at church. Including Quinn.

Turning over, she put her face in the pillow. Maybe he wouldn't be there. Maybe he'd be sick and stay home.

She sat up. *Susannah Tait, you are not a coward. Get your tush out of this bed and get dressed. Mercy, love, and faithfulness. Help me hang onto that, Lord.*

Quinn stripped the plastic wrap off the newspaper and settled in the recliner. He had a cup of coffee on the lamp table and a bowl of oatmeal cooking in the microwave. Sunday morning was his favorite time of the week. He always spent a relaxed hour reading the paper and looking forward to worship and Bible study and fellowship.

Today not so much. Would Susannah be there? Had he frozen her enough last night she'd take the hint and stay home?

A twinge of guilt snuck in under his guard as he flipped to the sports section. She'd pulled a dirty underhanded trick, but she'd looked miserable, ignoring the pizza while everybody else pigged out. Amazing she'd stuck it out, but hanging close to Dana the whole time, sending painful looks his way when she thought he wasn't looking.

Well, too bad. She deserved to feel guilty.

He grabbed the coffee mug and burned the roof of his mouth when he saw the picture in the middle of the front page. The caption read, "Quinn Baldwin, winner of men's local open division, receives warm congratulations from water table volunteer Susannah Tait."

Some enterprising photographer had caught their kiss in close-up living color. The banner advertising the church was clear as day in the background. He groaned.

How much worse can it get?

chapter 21

After her talk with her brother, Susannah headed downstairs, feeling much more prepared to deal with the complicated situation she faced. Heaving a deep regretful sigh that she'd gotten herself involved in this mess, she walked into the kitchen and stopped in her tracks.

Her landlady sat at the breakfast table with her hand over her mouth. Her twinkling eyes were wide as saucers behind the rhinestone glasses. She dropped the newspaper onto the table and crooked a finger at Susannah. "I think you'd better look at this, dearie."

The sports section? Why would she be interested in baseball or golf scores when her world was falling apart?

Wait. Quinn's Azalea Trail Run win would be in today's news. She leaned over Elva Kay's shoulder.

She gasped. "Oh, no!" Her knees gave. Clutching the paper, she sank into a chair. "Quinn's going to *die*."

"Is there something you haven't been telling me?" Elva Kay's beautifully arched brows climbed nearly to her hairline.

"No, I—it was a mistake. He didn't mean it."

"Looks to me like he was very serious about it." Elva Kay tweaked the paper out of Susannah's hands and brought it close to her face. "Definitely serious."

Susannah laid her forehead against the brocade place mat. All her tenuous confidence after praying with Jeremy evaporated like water in a Tucson arroyo. "He is so easily embarrassed. I hate this for him."

She felt Elva Kay's hand on her head. "What a sweetheart you are, thinking about his feelings."

"I should've been thinking about his feelings a long time ago," she mumbled. "Now it's too late."

"But ..." Elva Kay patted Susannah's head. "Baby girl, don't you know he's falling in love with you? He won't mind a silly picture in the paper!"

Susannah dragged herself erect. "I've got to tell you something." Jeremy had said she needed to confess. She'd wronged Elva Kay too. *Liar, liar*. "I'm not who you think I am."

Elva Kay's eyes widened.

"I'm not a criminal or anything," Susannah rushed to assure her. "But I'm not a doctoral student, either. I'm an insurance investigator. The company sent me here because they think Quinn committed insurance fraud. I was supposed to catch him and turn him in."

"But Quinn would never—"

"I know that, of course! Now I do, anyway. But he found out what I was doing before I could get up the nerve to tell him. I don't know if he's ever going to ... Miss Elva Kay, will you forgive me for telling you so many lies? I'm so sorry if I've hurt you." Susannah slipped out of her chair and knelt at Elva Kay's feet.

The older woman cupped her face. "Oh, honey. Of course I forgive you." She bit her lip. "But I'm afraid you're going to have a harder time with Quinn."

Susannah felt hot tears drip down her cheeks. "He's the first man I've ever loved. The only man I've ever—" She wiped her face. "Oh, what am I going to do?"

"We've heard so much about you." Julianne Harrison stood on tiptoe to press her cheek to Susannah's. "I don't know how we've missed each other in church."

Barefoot and dressed in shorts and T-shirt, Susannah had joined the rest of the Fellowship congregation on the beach at Fairhope Point, a lovely city park just over the bay from Mobile. Pastor Martin had asked her this morning if she wanted to participate in the baptismal service today or wait for the next one. Since she had no idea where she'd be next month, she'd eagerly accepted the invitation. It would have been nice to have Jeremy and Cherry here—and the rest of her family, for that matter. But somebody had set up a video camera just out of reach of the waves lapping onto the beach. She could always send a copy of the DVD back home.

Smiling at small, red-haired Julianne, Susannah rescued Elva Kay's beach umbrella, which was about to blow away in the ocean breeze. "I'm glad to finally meet you and Clint too."

She couldn't imagine what Quinn had said about her to the Harrisons. If it had been within the last day or so, it couldn't have been good. She hadn't seen him since church this morning. He'd sat on the other side of the worship center, then ducked out right after the service. Surely he'd seen the picture. The whole *city* had seen the picture. People at church she didn't know well had teased her, and she'd endured it, trying to smile, not knowing what else to do.

How could a person's emotions swing so wildly between humiliation and exhilaration? All day she'd looked forward to being baptized. Dreaded running into Quinn, hoped she would. Wondered what she'd say.

And now he wasn't here. Well, so be it.

She swallowed a lump in her throat. "Elva Kay, let's get you settled. Looks like Martin's trying to gather everybody up." She and Dana shook out the beach blanket they'd brought from the house and planted the umbrella in the sand. Kneeling beside Elva Kay, Susannah took the older woman's hands. "They want me to tell my testimony. What should I say?"

Elva Kay smiled. "Just tell how you came to know Christ and what he means to you. The Holy Spirit will give you the words."

The Holy Spirit? Something else she knew little about. "Will you pray for me?"

"You know I will, darlin'." Elva Kay squeezed her hands.

"So will I." Dana's big brown eyes were soft with affection. "Go get 'em, girl!"

Susannah smiled and got to her feet.

"Come on, people, let's get this show on the road." Martin was waving all the new converts toward the edge of the water.

Feet in cool, wet sugar sand, she stood listening as the others spoke one by one. Spread across the sky was a glorious smear of orange and pink and aqua that burned streaks of color across the water and washed up into the encroaching dusk. Peace descended on her in spite of everything. She missed Quinn, but he hadn't saved her soul. Jesus had.

Finally it was her turn.

"Speak up." Martin grinned and patted her on the shoulder.

She smiled at Elva Kay, her stomach doing backflips. "A few days ago I gave my heart to Jesus. I knew about him for a long time because of my brother, but I didn't want to commit to believing God had anything to do with the way I live my life. I guess I thought the Bible was old-fashioned and contradictory and intolerant."

She paused and caught Dana's eyes—then started. There was Quinn at the back of the crowd with Skeet. Unsmiling, he stood with his hands in his shorts pockets, shoulders hunched.

He'd come after all.

Susannah lifted her chin. "Then I met people who lived as if Jesus was real. They weren't perfect, but they seemed strong and joyful and full of peace. I started to read the Bible for myself. I wanted to be loved like that and to have a purpose for my life, so I asked my friend Miss Elva Kay how to do it." She swallowed. "So I did, and ... and got to start over. I wasn't a bad person, but I know I did some things that hurt other people as much as they hurt God. I've got a long way to go, so I need all the help I can get from you guys."

She blinked hard, drawing her toes in a line across the sand. She looked at Martin, not sure what to do now.

To her surprise, a chorus of "amens" sifted from the congregation gathered on the beach, and Martin squeezed her shoulders. "Good job, Susie," he whispered as he led the whole group of new believers into the water.

Susannah stood in the hip-high waves, hands clasped. She watched as one by one the others were put under the water, to rise, gasping as the fresh breeze hit wet clothing. When it was her turn she stood quietly as Martin prayed over her, blessed her, and committed her to Christ. She let him put her under, abandoning herself to a new life. It felt odd and right.

She came up to the sound of cheers and whistles. The first person she saw was Skeet, jumping up and down, arms high. Even Quinn had a big grin on his face. Laughing, she waded onto the sand.

"I'm so happy, happy, happy!" She ran for Dana, who wrapped a beach towel around her and handed her another one for her hair.

Dana was openly blubbering. "That was the sweetest thing I've ever seen!"

For the first time Susannah understood some of Dana's bubbly enthusiasm. *Washed clean to start over. Incredible.* She couldn't see Quinn, but for now it didn't matter. She had an advocate on her side now. Someone bigger and wiser than all the dumb things she'd ever done.

She plopped down on the blanket. Elva Kay enfolded her, sand and all. "See, I told you it would be fine."

"Yes, ma'am. It's fine."

She stayed for nearly half an hour after Martin concluded the service. Shivering in her damp towel, she was content in a way that couldn't be explained by her circumstances.

She just was.

Clint Harrison came by to give her a big bear hug, followed by his wife. "Bless you, sweetie," said Julianne. "We'll keep praying for you."

"You've been praying for me?" Susannah was still getting used to this gentle invasion of privacy.

"Quinn asked us to."

Susannah couldn't help it. Her gaze shot to the spot where he'd been standing. He was gone.

She blinked, some of her joy dimmed. Of all the people in this church, he was probably the only person who hadn't given her a hug and blessing.

Oh, my Jesus, it hurts.

Of course. Quinn should have known. Not only *could* things get worse, they did.

A lot worse.

Sitting in IHOP on Monday morning drowning his sorrows in blueberry syrup, his contact with the Bar Association called to tell him they'd decided to find another company to produce the fireworks for their May Day festivities. Rubbing salt into the wound, the woman asked if he had any recommendations.

"Recommendations?" He shoved his plate out of the way. "SkyPainters is the best fireworks company in the south. Why would you cancel the contract?"

"Mr. Baldwin, you do have a reputation for putting on a spectacular show, which is what we wanted to cap off the naturalization ceremony on the battleship. But in light of the article in the paper this morning—"

"You mean yesterday? The picture?" Embarrassing as it was, Quinn couldn't see how a public kiss should affect his business dealings.

"There was something yesterday too?" There was an awkward pause. "I'm referring to an article on this morning's front page, an interview with local ATF and your insurance company. Have you not seen it?"

Quinn swallowed hard. He'd left the house before the newspaper arrived. "No, ma'am, I haven't. But would you please hold off on this until I have a chance to find out what's going on?"

"It's pretty clear you're about to be charged with arson and insurance fraud. You can understand why we don't want the association."

"Yes, ma'am. I suppose so, but I promise you it's not true!" Arguing fruitlessly for a few more minutes, Quinn ended the call and pinched the bridge of his nose.

Susannah. How could she have given this story to the press? She'd seemed contrite when he confronted her. And last night at her baptism he'd begun to wonder, to hope, her conversion might be real. The radiance of her face when she came up out of the water made his eyes sting.

He had to leave, to keep from pushing through the crowd to pick her up and squeeze her tight.

Lord, I'm so confused.

He couldn't quite trust her. There was no way a reporter could have known about the investigation unless Susannah had spilled it. None of his friends would betray him.

He left money on the table to pay for his breakfast, then bought a copy of the paper from one of the machines outside the restaurant and read it in the truck. The article, along with a photograph of the burning Convention Center, occupied the whole right-hand column. Outlining the known facts of the accident, the article added Quinn's insurance company now had reason to suspect arson. The fact that SkyPainters was touted as an "award-winning local success story" did nothing to mitigate the scorching chagrin that ripped through him as he realized what was going to happen to the reputation of his company now. Things had just started to calm down.

SkyPainters might never recover from this public relations nightmare.

Thank you, Susannah Tait.

Nauseated, he tossed the paper onto the seat and cranked the truck. He might as well go to the office and start fielding phone calls.

He was on hold with the travel agency when Rebecca burst through the door.

"Quinn! Did you see the—Oh. You did." She dropped her purse onto her desk and stared at him, her round face wrinkled in distress. "What are you going to do?"

"I don't know what I *can* do." Putting down the phone he pushed a weary hand through his hair. Sleep had eluded him, and his eyes felt like they'd been washed in acid. His stomach felt the same way.

Rebecca stomped her foot. "You have to tell those people you didn't do it!"

"The story's already in the news. People are going to believe what they want to."

"Susannah Tait needs to be thrown in jail. She lied to us and tricked us and—"

"Rebecca." He uttered a halfhearted laugh. "That's a little over the top. She was just doing her job. Everybody involved will check out the evidence again. They'll have to come to the same conclusion the fire marshal did back in January. We're just going to have to weather this."

"But aren't you mad at her?" Rebecca clenched her fists. "Susannah totally acted like she was gaga over you, and you were falling in love with—"

"Rebecca, stop it!" Quinn lurched to his feet. He'd had enough of this. Needed to get away, even if he had no place in particular to go. He took a calming breath. "Listen, if nothing else, we've got Sheree's wedding to get ready for. I'm going out to Bellingrath to look around. Don't worry if I don't answer the phone. Just leave me a voice mail if anything comes up, and I'll check in later. Okay?"

Rebecca stared at him for a moment, looking perplexed. "All right. But if that woman calls here, I'm not responsible for what I say to her."

Quinn gave her a straight look. "Yes, you are, Rebecca. We're all responsible for what we say."

Susannah carefully laid her phone on the kitchen table and took a bite of grits. The nasty bland cereal stuck to the roof of her mouth.

"What's the matter, honey?" Elva Kay laid a concerned hand on Susannah's trembling fingers.

"I've just been fired. For fraternizing." She swallowed and nearly gagged on the grits.

"Oh my. The picture in yesterday's paper."

Susannah nodded, miserable. "Mr. Webster told me not to —but Quinn grabbed me before I could—and there were reporters everywhere ..."

Elva Kay's eyes were sympathetic but amused. "I get the feeling you didn't want that job anymore anyway."

"Elva Kay, the money's already spent." She dropped her fork onto her plate with a clatter. "They gave me an advance for expenses, and I gave it to my dad to help him with the earnest money on a hotel he's buying in Tucson. He's signed the papers, and he'll lose his entire savings if I back out on him. We were going to be partners."

"Oh, dear." Elva Kay's button-bright eyes darkened with distress. "You *are* in a pickle, aren't you?"

"I sure am. But that's not the worst of it. If they don't let me finish out the case, somebody's going to come in here who doesn't give a flip about Quinn, and they may convict him of something he didn't do."

"But, honey, if *you're* sure he didn't, why won't they believe you? You're the expert."

"Because," Susannah's voice broke, "I found an anomaly in the lab report indicating something other than fireworks chemicals. I don't know why they missed it the first time, but it's there, and it looks bad for Quinn."

Elva Kay frowned. "But you were going to tell the authorities what you found?"

"Of course I was." Susannah gulped back tears. "I've learned my lesson about lying. But I was also going to do my—my best to prove it wasn't Quinn who set the explosion."

Elva Kay linked her elegant fingers together on the table. "Is there any reason you can't *still* prove it? Even though you're no longer working for the insurance company?"

"Maybe. But I won't have the authority to get hold of certain kinds of information." Susannah sighed and laid her head in her hand. "This is all just so *discouraging*."

"I'm sure it is. But I've noticed you're a very ... determined young woman. I'm sure if we pray about it, God will give you the direction and wisdom you need."

"Determined." Susannah had to smile. "That's what Dana said about me. I'm beginning to think it's not a very attractive quality." She sobered. "And it sure got me in trouble with Quinn."

"Believe it or not, it's the way God made you. You don't have to let it be a negative characteristic." Elva Kay canted her head to study Susannah. "Once you learn to let the Lord buff off the rough edges, it can turn you into quite a strong leader in his kingdom."

"Really?" Susannah blinked. "Me?"

"I'm sure of it." Elva Kay squeezed Susannah's hand. "How about we pray about this right now and see what God does?"

Susannah bowed her head. She supposed she had little to lose.

Bellingrath was quiet this early on a Monday morning, though the parking lot would later be full of RVs, town cars, and minivans. Quinn headed straight for Mirror Lake. As he walked, he pulled out his PDA to make notes. Choreographing fireworks for the wedding of a Mobile debutante might be old hat, but he was determined that this one showcase his best work. Unique. Spectacular. Making the audience hold its collective breath, gasping with pleasure every time an explosion of color and sound went off. And yeah, in spite of everything, he wanted to be part of the celebration of the marriage.

He climbed a slight rise to one of several lookout points. The sun sparkled like jewels on the water, and in the distance massive oaks draped with Spanish moss and delicate willows leaned over for a drink. All around him lush green and bold color soothed his bruised spirit. The only sound came from birds singing and insects dipping into the water.

He dropped onto a bench, leaning forward to hold the PDA loosely between his knees. What were you supposed to do when your life plans came to a screeching halt? Let them go? Fight back?

Lord, I don't want to quit growing. If I have to give up something I love, to gain something you think is more valuable, please show me.

What did he love, after all? He loved his job. He had affection for his friends. But besides God himself, was there one person in the world he allowed to know him inside out—to peer inside the murky confusion and insecurity that was Quinn Baldwin and trust they wouldn't walk away in disgust?

If he had to be honest, there probably wasn't. Even Clint and Julianne, Skeet and Elva Kay saw only to a point. They thought he was strong. Together. That was what he wanted them to think. He thought of a line from a C. S. Lewis essay he'd read recently. *To love at all is to be vulnerable.* It had stuck in his mind like a burr he couldn't shake loose.

He didn't want to be vulnerable. If he forgave his father, he might have to love him too, with his comfortable shell of self-righteousness broken. Susannah's offense had brought the whole thing to a head. *God, I know you want me to forgive her too.*

Until he did, there was no promise of blessing or joy.

So which do I want more, Lord? Comfort and self-righteousness or blessing and joy?

He closed his eyes to the physical beauty of his surroundings and took a difficult look inside. "I believe you love me, God—in spite of the circumstances—but it scares me to make myself open to hurt again." He swallowed hard, remembering how he'd felt the day he'd walked into church the first time with Clint. Unworthy and ashamed and dirty. But God had reached down and rescued him from those days. Why was it so hard to accept others' imperfections? "You want me to go to the prison to talk to Dad, don't you? I don't know if I can do that. Please help me."

Hot tears leaked from his eyes, his nose ran, and he felt like flattening himself against the ground. But loneliness drained away as courage came in.

"Please, please help both Susannah and me."

chapter 22

Susannah took Monty with her to Riverside Park.

It was a glorious spring day, the sun reflecting in blinding radiance off the glass of the Convention Center and the surface of the river. Puffs of breeze cooled and dried the sweat as fast as it collected on her skin. Except for the worry clouding her mind, she would have been content.

Okay, so she was no longer employed by Stryker Investigations or Independent Mutual. She'd get another job. Dad could get a business loan. And Elva Kay had pointed out she could still finish the investigation of Quinn's explosion.

Think, Susannah. Think. There had to be something she'd overlooked, something she could still do about this situation.

ATF agents would have swept the blast site, adding a distance of 50 percent outside the debris radius. There would be little point in searching it again, especially after all this time, and taking into account the amount of rainfall in this below-sea-level area.

Interviews. One of the chief arts of an investigator. And Susannah might not be the best undercover agent in the world, but she knew how to conduct an open interview. She had already talked to all of Quinn's employees except Russell, Phillip's roommate. Maybe she could get something out of him. Who else?

Rounding the path onto the river side of the park, she slowed, pulling Monty in to trot beside her. She stopped and looked out across the river. The dry docks on the other side were clearly visible, and the field where the accident had occurred. Monty sat down, patient as always, and leaned against her bare legs. Reaching down to ruffle his ears, she murmured, "Wish you could tell me what to do, buddy. What do you think, huh? Is my career down the toilet, not to mention my love life?"

Elva Kay and Dana had given her credit for determination and self-assurance, but she felt as weak and confused as she'd ever been. Just three days ago she'd stood in this very spot with Quinn. Realizing she was in love with him, knowing what she was doing could tear his company to shreds, fearing what he'd think when he found out she'd lied to him. Ashamed.

Now the whole thing had exploded right in her face.

Oh, if she could somehow prove his innocence.

Lord, as sure as I know you're in my life now, I know he's innocent. But I need one of those miracles I've heard about.

Her eyes blurred, turning the hard edges of the industrial complexes and construction equipment on the opposite shore into a dreamlike vision.

As she wiped the tears away with her fingers, the dry docks warehouse and office came into focus. She wondered what the Clancy brothers had thought about all the uproar taking place practically on their property. For some reason, there had been minimal damage to their facility, even though it had been right next door to the blast site.

Susannah frowned. She couldn't remember reading any reports from Douglas or Johnny Clancy, who were listed as owners of the operation. Surely the fire marshal or one of the ATF agents had interviewed them after the explosion. But had they?

And another question was surveillance video, an invaluable tool. She could beat herself up about letting that issue slip, but she hadn't even been here four weeks. There simply hadn't been time to get to everything yet.

Straightening her shoulders, she looked down at Monty, who whined softly as a pelican flapped by. "Want to go on a little field trip through the tunnel again?"

At the sound of her voice he looked up and barked, ears erect and tail flogging her ankles.

"Cool. Let's go." Recharged, she took off running down the path toward the entrance. Monty galloped after her.

Ten minutes later she sat in a no-frills office at Clancy Brothers Drydocks. Across the desk from her sat a beaming gray-bearded giant with a dome so slick she could have spun a dime on it.

"Miss Susannah!" boomed Clint Harrison. "What are you doing over here on the wrong side of the river? I can't believe this."

She was pretty amazed herself. What were the odds of Quinn's friend being the manager of this place and just the person she needed to talk to? Since he was smiling at her and hadn't thrown her out on her ear, she assumed he hadn't seen the newspaper that morning.

"I wish I'd known you work here. I would have been in to talk to you a long time ago."

"That would've been a pleasure." His eyes twinkled under bushy gray eyebrows. "But now that you're here, what can I do for you?"

She rubbed her forehead. "It's kind of a long story, but I was hoping you might've been around the day that explosion with Quinn's truck happened out in the empty lot next door. Or maybe you know somebody who was."

"Darlin', I'm sorry, but it was so late in the day we'd already shut down. We can't get much done after dark." Clint rubbed a hand across his bare head. "That would've been some sight to see, I imagine."

"Yeah, I think so." She started to think up a tale designed to encourage him to talk, then remembered. *Truth, Susannah.* Deep breath. "Listen, Clint, you may not know how much trouble Quinn is in because of that explosion, but I—I have to confess I was working as an investigator for his insurance company. At least I was, until this morning."

The extravagant eyebrows rose. "Huh. That right?"

"Yes. But now I'm trying to prove he didn't have anything to do with setting it off on purpose." She gave him a hopeful look. "Do you know what I mean?"

"I think so." He shook his head. "But I don't know what good you think I can do."

"I was hoping you might have a security camera set up to guard your premises."

"Oh." Clint whistled through his teeth. "Yeah, I can see where that would be helpful. But I'm afraid you're out of luck, sweetheart. We don't need no camera way over here in the boonies."

Susannah stared at him, hope going down the drain. "Are you sure?"

He lifted his wide, hamlike hands. "Positive. I'm sorry, darlin'."

Susannah was about to ask about the construction crews working in the yard when a furious barking sounded from outside. She'd left Monty in the Jeep, not sure of his welcome in a busy warehouse. What on earth was the matter with him now?

"That your sidekick?" Clint grinned.

"Yes, I'm sorry," she sighed. "I hope he hasn't jumped out of my car. Let me go check on him. Thanks for your time, Clint."

"No problem. Let me know if I can do anything else to help."

"Sure thing." Susannah sprang out of the chair and took off for the door. Monty's noise had gotten louder and more strident. And the sound was moving.

Oh, no, please don't let him get into anything.

She stood in the doorway, the glaring sun blinding her until she slid her sunglasses off the top of her head onto her nose. The Jeep was empty.

"Montmorency! Where are you, you insubordinate stooge? Monty!" She could still hear his deep "woof," but he was nowhere in sight.

She saw his long tail sticking out from behind a Port-a-John outside the chain-link fence. The crazy mutt had a talent for discovering the most disgusting elements in any location. On the rare occasions she let him roam loose, he would proudly bring her moles, dead birds, snakes ... and then expect loud praise and adulation.

Great. I'll be riding home with him smelling like an outhouse.

Marching over to the opening in the fence, she realized Monty had been digging underneath the john. He already had a good-sized hole excavated, and his entire muzzle was coated in muck.

"Guh-*ross*!" She grabbed his collar. "*Why* didn't you stay in the Jeep where I—"

She stopped, eyeball to eyeball with the john. Just under the edge where Monty had been digging was a hunk of broken plastic that looked like part of a cell phone.

"Montmorency," she whispered, "what have you got?"

"Don't do it, man! You've got too much to live for."

Quinn, leaning over the rail around the deck in back of the Fish Shack restaurant, looked over his shoulder to find Will Fletcher heading toward him with an open grin.

He laughed and turned to shake hands with the lawyer-turned-political aide. "Don't worry, if I *were* idiot enough to jump off here, I'd land in about ten inches of water."

"You don't know how glad I am to hear that. Never did pass my Boy Scout lifeguard badge." Joining Quinn at the rail, Will heaved a contented sigh as they looked out on the bay spreading clear to the horizon. The restaurant was one of several seafood operations located on the causeway—also known as Battleship Parkway—that crossed the bay. Though nothing fancy, it was big on local ambience, and the food was outstanding.

Quinn eyed Will, trying to read his mood. A Christian entertainment lawyer and the grandson of a politician, Will was a good guy, but he had a talent for masking his intentions. "So what are you doing in this neck of the woods? Your message didn't tell me much."

Will moved his sunglasses to the top of his head and squinted at Quinn. "Zoë and I were on our way down to the Grand Hotel for our anniversary. I called Skeet when we came through. He told me what's been going on."

Quinn grimaced. "It's not that bad. You didn't have to interrupt your—"

"I read the article in the paper." Will's lean, clever face tightened with sympathy. "Seemed pretty serious to me, if ATF's involved. Do you need an attorney?"

"Not at the moment, but thanks for offering." Quinn shoved away his anxiety. He'd been struggling with his emotions since his prayer time at Bellingrath that morning. "I'm gonna ride it out and see what happens. I don't have anything to hide."

"I know that." Will gave him a searching look. "But Quinn ... I gotta tell you. Secret Service won't let you anywhere near a presidential candidate if you've got something like this hanging over your head. You'd better be figuring out what you can do to speed up the proceedings. Summer'll be here before you know it, and we'll be heavy into the campaign trail."

Quinn gripped the rail hard. Will was just putting voice to reality. "You got any suggestions?"

Will stroked his neat imperial beard in thought. "Do you have any reason to think somebody might be setting you up?"

"There was something about a letter the insurance company received, but it's got to be a crock." Quinn shrugged. "This is just so ... surreal."

"I know, man." Will grabbed Quinn's shoulder in sympathy. "Let's sit down and have lunch, and I'll help you talk through the possibilities. Fried oysters are brain food." When Quinn gave him a quizzical look, Will grinned. "Well, it's a theory."

Quinn found he just didn't have it in him to return to the office after lunch and listen to Drama Queen Rebecca rag on Susannah or Phillip or whoever happened to be her whipping boy du jour. So he shook hands with Will in the restaurant parking lot, sent regards to his friend's wife, and as Phillip would say, headed for the 'hood.

As he drove down Government Street, a vague sense of guilt dogged him until he asked himself who the CEO of SkyPainters was.

"You are, doofus," he muttered, turning up the radio. "Rebecca can't fire you."

On that moral victory he decided to treat himself to a visit to Pet-o-Rama. Bob wouldn't be in need of a mouse for another few days, but Quinn loved to go in every now and then to look at the puppies. People were always dropping off strays to be given away. One day he was going to cave in and take one home. *That* would give Bob a start.

The cowbell hanging in the doorway clanked as he walked in, and an elderly lady looking at cat toys turned around.

"Quinn!" exclaimed Miss Elva Kay. "What are you doing here this time of day?"

He smiled and gave her a hug. "I was out running around and decided to give myself the afternoon off. It's been kind of a ..." He hesitated, searching for a euphemism. "An interesting day."

She nodded, eyes soft. "I saw the paper this morning."

"Hey, dude!" Quinn and Elva Kay both looked around to find the teenage clerk leaning over the cash register, peering through a hank of orange-striped hair. "Dead or alive today?"

"*I'm* alive." Elva Kay looked up at Quinn with twinkling eyes. "How about you?"

Quinn chuckled. "Mostly alive, but I think he wants to know how I want my mouse." He shook his head at the boy. "I'll be back for snake food later this week. I'm just here to check out the puppies."

"Oh. Okay, no problem." The kid flashed a peace sign and went back to his comic book.

Quinn looked down to discover Elva Kay giving him a thoughtful stare.

She pursed her lips. "Puppies, huh? What's the matter, love?"

"Nothing." Squirming like a kid caught with his hand in his mom's purse, he wandered over to a wire cage near the front window. Two mixed-breed puppies, both the approximate size of lion cubs, were wrestling over a tube sock. They'd knocked over their food dish, scattering kibbles all over the bottom of the cage. Quinn reached in and picked up a puppy to cuddle it against his chest. A deep chocolate brown female with a white patch over one eye and ear, it started gnawing on his finger.

Elva Kay followed. "I've spent all morning praying for you and Susannah. She's very upset by all this media attention."

He clamped his jaw. He wasn't ready to talk about Susannah yet.

"She knows she hurt you badly."

He blew out a breath. "Well, she did. I remembered what you said about forgiveness, and I've prayed about it and tried to work it out in my mind." He shook his head. "Guess I'm not as far along as I thought I was. It's hard."

"Yes, it is, but it's not beyond you." Elva Kay reached over to stroke the puppy's head. With the sudden relaxation of the very young, she'd fallen asleep across Quinn's arm with her snub nose in his cupped palm.

"What kills me," he sighed, "is she's going to profit in a big way by ruining my business and my reputation. I don't think she should get away with that." When Elva Kay didn't respond, Quinn looked at her. Her gnarled hand was across her mouth. "What?"

"She didn't tell you she was fired?"

His mouth opened. "No. I've been out of pocket all day, and anyway I don't think she'd want to—" He looked down at the puppy's silky head. "Why would they fire her? Looks like she accomplished exactly what they were after. Making me look bad."

"Somebody apparently saw the picture from Saturday's paper."

"The one where we were ..." He felt himself blush. "Like I said, I guess that's what she deserves."

"Quinn." Elva Kay put her hands on her hips and gave him a look. "Sweet boy, do you know where Susannah's been all day?"

He shrugged. She was going to tell him whether he wanted to know or not.

"She's been retracing every step in her investigation, trying to prove you innocent. Quinn, that young lady loves you, and this misunderstanding is killing her. She wouldn't admit it, but I'm sure I heard her crying last night when you didn't speak to her after her baptism."

Crying? Susannah?

There were just some things a man would rather not know.

He put the puppy back into the crate, startling her awake, and she began to whine. He felt like joining her.

But he gave Miss Elva Kay as firm a look as he could manage. "I'm sorry I hurt Susannah's feelings, but a little healthy remorse might be good for her. After all, she *had* to be the one who leaked this story to the press."

A mighty scowl appeared above the rhinestone glasses. "How can you talk that way about the woman you love?"

"Love?" Quinn took a step toward the door. "I don't know where you got that from. Surely you don't think it's possible for me to fall in love after just a few weeks!"

"As I've told you more than once, it took me five days to fall in love with Dr. Shue." His miniature nemesis stared him down.

Unable to think of a single appropriate comeback, Quinn grabbed for emotional footing. "You just need to keep praying. I'm gonna need it after what Susannah stirred up."

Using gloved fingers, Susannah had removed the chunk of debris from its burial spot under the Port-a-John. She took it straight to ATF and asked for Agent O'Neal.

Frowning, Beverly O'Neal looked down at the sterile bag containing the small piece of plastic. "Where did you find this?"

"Under a Port-a-John at the construction site on the other side of the dry docks yard. I'm thinking this could be an IED." An Improvised Explosive Device. Susannah could hardly keep herself contained to O'Neal's extra chair.

The agent's frown deepened as she pulled on her lower lip. "You should have left it there."

Susannah leaned forward. "I told you, I'm a CES. I know how to process debris from an explosion. I had a camera and an evidence kit in my vehicle." Unzipping her backpack with shaking fingers, she withdrew her camera and set it on O'Neal's desk with a clunk. "Here are the pictures. We've got to get this to the lab and have it analyzed."

The agent had stone-faced impassivity down to a fine art. "Miss Tait, I hate to burst your pretty bubble, but it's unlikely our agents missed a piece of debris from the blast seat, especially as it was found so far away. And *under* a Port-a-John?" She shook her white-blonde head. "More likely somebody was just getting rid of a broken phone."

"Okay, look." Susannah took a deep breath to calm her voice. Nothing would come of antagonizing her only access to the best forensic lab in the country. "That piece of phone isn't just broken, and it isn't just charred by fireworks. It's been *blasted* apart by serious explosives. I've seen criminals use cell phones for detonation devices more times than I care to think about."

O'Neal's eyes narrowed. "There's still no way it could have gotten that far away."

"I've been thinking about that. Quinn said it stormed that night. He remembers looking up and worrying the rain would ruin the show."

O'Neal nodded. "It was coming down in buckets while we swept the place the next morning. I suppose theoretically the rain could have washed this piece away." She hefted the bag. "But where's the rest of it?"

Susannah lifted her hands. "I'm sure if you sweep the perimeter you'll find it. My dog is a retired explosives task force animal, which is what makes me so sure about this. Can't we go ahead and send this piece off to the lab?"

O'Neal's pale green eyes speared Susannah. "Have you got some kind of personal interest in this case?"

Susannah squirmed. "Um, I'm not working for the insurance company anymore."

"What?"

"They fired me because they think I got a little too close to Mr. Baldwin. And because I'm sure he's being framed for this explosion. They don't want to believe it."

"A little too close, huh?" O'Neal's wide mouth quirked. "You believe good-lookin' young Mr. Baldwin is innocent?"

Susannah stood up. "Agent O'Neal, you told me yourself you thought Quinn's a good guy. And I'd stake my career on it—what career I've got left anyway—but I can't just twiddle my thumbs and let somebody ruin his life!"

O'Neal grunted. "All right, I'll put a rush on it. We'll see if fingerprints or chemical traces show up. But it'll take a few days. You just hold your horses and don't do anything dumb, okay?"

"Yes, ma'am. Thank you for your help. Will you call me when you find something out?"

"You know I can't do that. But I'm sure if you're in touch with Mr. Baldwin you'll hear one way or the other."

"Okay." Susannah picked up her backpack and exited the building. Depressed, she got in the Jeep and headed for Elva Kay's.

Staying in touch with Quinn was not even on the radar screen. She'd seen neither hide nor snakeskin of him since her baptism last night. Maybe he'd forgive her if she could just straighten this whole thing out.

Quinn stood on his front sidewalk that evening doing a few warm-up stretches and trying to pretend he was going running because he needed the exercise. The truth was, he couldn't get Susannah out of his mind, and he knew he shouldn't put off talking to her any longer. For one thing, there was the forgiveness issue. He had to know why she'd given the story to the press. And he had to hear from her the truth about her feelings for him.

I wanted to be someone you'd talk to and listen to and enjoy being with. She hadn't said the "L" word, but she'd sure hinted she'd been heading that way.

He took off running.

Susannah Tait was something special. Bright and beautiful and funny. Tenderhearted and willing to admit when she was wrong. Willing to grow.

The perfect girl for me.

Except for the whole lying about being an insurance investigator thing.

He rounded the corner in front of the school, and as if he'd conjured them out of his thoughts, there were Susannah and Monty barreling around the track. After he'd cautioned her not to run by herself. Annoyance prickled along his skin. But then, when had she ever backed off from doing whatever she pleased? Taking a deep breath, he picked up his pace to catch her.

"Susannah! Susannah, wait."

She jerked to a halt, nearly strangling Monty with his collar. "Quinn! You scared the bejeebers out of me!"

He turned to face her, jogging in place. "Guess I'm lucky you didn't get me with pepper spray."

"You don't know how lucky. Pepper spray would be the least of your problems."

"Reckon you're a tae kwon do black belt or something."

"As a matter of fact, I am. Come on, Monty, sorry." She started running again, and Quinn hurried to catch up. Susannah glanced at him. "I thought you preferred running in the morning. And after what happened the other night, I sure didn't think you'd want to run with me."

"And I told *you* not to run at night by yourself," he countered.

"I don't have to do what you say."

See, Lord? She's making me crazy.

He jogged silently beside her for half a lap before she slowed to a walk, pulling Monty in. "Quinn," she sighed, "what do you want? You made it clear you don't—"

"I'm sorry, Susannah." He stopped her with a hand on her elbow, moved in front of her so that she bumped into him and stood so close he could have put his arms around her. If he'd wanted to. "For Saturday night, I mean. I was so hurt I don't know what I said, but I'm sure I didn't mean any of it."

"Oh, I'm positive you meant it." She stared at his chest. "And I deserved it."

"Yeah, well, I didn't have to be so cold. I just ... can't believe you'd blab everything to the press."

She looked up at that. "But I *didn't*! Quinn, I would never—"

"Then who did? How else would they know?"

They stared at one another at an impasse. "Maybe whoever is framing you for the explosion saw that picture and found out who I was."

"Maybe." There had to be an explanation. He could tell from the clarity of her gaze she had been telling the truth. She wouldn't betray him. His heart lightened. "I believe you." He squeezed her elbow gently.

She shrugged. "What bothers me is what *you* haven't said. Last night when I was baptized ..." She stopped on a hitching breath.

There was a moment's quiet, broken only by Monty's soft whining. Quinn felt his throat tighten. He slid his hand up to cup her shoulder, laid the other against her cheek and tilted her face up. "Elva Kay says the people you love the most are the ones who hurt you most."

Her eyes, shadowed lapis lazuli, lifted to his. "Don't say what you don't mean," she whispered.

"I wouldn't. Not right now." He rested his forehead against hers. "There's too much I have to straighten out. But I want you to know ... I'm sorry I accused you of playing with my faith and my feelings. I've never ..." He cleared his throat. "I've never been down this road before."

"Me either. I never had anybody talk to me like this, about such private things. It feels so weird ..." She nestled against his hand. "Will you pray with me, Quinn?"

He nodded. "Lord—" His voice broke. Embarrassed, he swallowed. "Thank you for Susannah's salvation. Thank you for helping her forgive me." She made a protesting little noise, which he stopped by brushing his thumb against her lips. "I needed forgiveness. Thank you for helping me forgive her. Please help us treat one another like you'd have us to."

His voice strengthened as he felt the Holy Spirit take away some of the guilt and anger that had paralyzed him for two days. "Father, I pray you'll give Susannah the wisdom she needs to resolve what she came to do. To do it with integrity and diligence. Please help me to be patient while I'm waiting to see what you do with me and my company. Help me set a good example for my employees." He took a deep breath as he confronted the hardest issue of all. "I know you want me to pray for whoever started this whole disaster. I admit I'm having a hard time with that one. Give me some time, and I'll get there.

"Most of all, thanks that this bad situation brought Susannah all the way down here to Lower Alabama, just so she could give me a hard time. It's been worth it, getting to know her. Amen." Smiling, he kissed her forehead. "I'm sorry you lost your job," he said against her ear.

"No, you're not. But that's a nice thing to say."

He laughed, and his lips might have traveled down her cheek to other territories, if Monty hadn't poked his cold wet nose against the back of Quinn's knee.

"Yow!" He jumped back, releasing Susannah.

She laughed. "What's the matter?"

"Your dog. I think he's jealous."

"Yeah, of me. He thinks you invented dog biscuits."

"Come on, I'll walk you home."

"But you haven't even run a whole lap!"

"I know. I just wanted to talk to you."

Together they walked to the gate. The night was quiet, still, filled with the sweet scents of wisteria and ligustrum. There were so many things Quinn wanted to say, he didn't know where to start. The natural thing was to pick up Susannah's hand and thread his fingers through hers. She looked up at him and gave him a troubled smile.

If his life hadn't been such a perfect mess at the moment, he'd have been happy. Paul's admonition to be content in every situation suddenly made sense. You could put up with a lot of junk, if you had at least one person you could be close to. He always had God. And God had sent this amazing, complicated woman—even if she *had* arrived under crazy circumstances.

After a moment he nudged Susannah's shoulder. "So are we going to start over?"

"Start over?"

"Yeah. Getting to know one another. I mean, me getting to know you. I bet you already know everything there is to know about me." He grimaced. "And some of it's not too pretty."

"Quinn." Susannah squeezed his palm. "Somebody told me we get to start over when we come to Christ. Isn't that true?"

"Yeah. Of course it's true. I guess forgiving yourself is just as hard as forgiving someone else." He sighed. "Anyway, how much of your cover story was true? Are you really from Arizona?"

"I was with Tucson ATF for five years. About a year ago I left to work in private investigations. Now ..." She bit her lip. "How'd you know they fired me?"

"I ran into Miss Elva Kay in the pet store this afternoon. Don't worry, as smart as you are, you won't have any trouble getting another job."

"That's not what concerns me the most about it. Quinn, they're not going to quit the investigation. They'll just send somebody else. Somebody who doesn't lo—like you as much as me."

He smiled at her small stammer, but chose to overlook it. For now. "I've been thinking about this all day. This whole hoopla has messed me up, but it's not the end of the world. You and I both know I didn't do anything wrong, and the truth will come out."

When Susannah didn't answer, Quinn caught her hand to his chest. "What? What are you not telling me?"

They stood under a light at the corner where Quinn's street crossed Elva Kay's. Susannah was watching Monty sniff at a nearby bed of jasmine. Her shoulders were tense, her mouth clamped tight.

"Susannah?"

She released a hard little laugh. "Do I have to tell the truth even when it's going to hurt you?"

Something like fear settled in his chest, making his heart pound. "I'm a big boy, Susie. You'd better let me have it all in one bad dose."

"Okay. I didn't tell you about Monty."

"Really." What did the dog have to do with anything? He searched Susannah's face. She looked more uneasy than upset, so he chose to joke. "He's got an incurable disease and has two weeks to live."

"That's not funny, Quinn." She scowled.

"Okay, then he's really Superdog and he's been spying on me with his X-ray vision."

"You're getting warmer." She sighed. "He's a retired K-9 task force animal. He's trained to sniff out explosives."

"Then why didn't you take him out to the site immediately? You'd have found out right away there were no detonation devices."

"I did." Susannah lifted her shoulders. "I took him out there on the Sunday you gave your testimony in church. He didn't find anything."

"See? I told you—"

"But—" She held up a hand. "I was back over there this morning, talking to your buddy Clint at the dry docks building. Monty was outside in the Jeep, and I heard him barking like crazy. When I went out to check on him, he was digging under a Port-a-John in the construction site next door. Way outside the perimeter the fire marshal would have swept, but within the realm of possibility, considering the rainstorm that night."

"Are you telling me he found something?" His mouth unhinged.

Susannah nodded. "Pieces of a cell phone, which makes a perfect detonator. Of course, we won't know for sure until the lab report comes back. That can take quite a while."

"You turned it in to ATF? And you're just now telling me?" Quinn took an involuntary step back, dropping her hand.

"This is the first opportunity I've had to tell you. *You've* been avoiding *me*. Remember?"

He stared at her, pressing his fingers to his temples. The implications were overwhelming. What if somebody had been trying to kill him? Somebody he knew. Maybe somebody close to him, someone he trusted.

"Susannah." He took her by the shoulders. "I'm not goofing around anymore. What are we going to do?"

"Elva Kay, I don't know what I'm going to do." Susannah sighed as she settled on the floor at her mentor's feet. Quinn had walked her home, kissed her hand—which nearly sent her into a meltdown—then reluctantly backed away. She'd stood in the doorway watching him lope out of sight, then locked up. Monty had followed her into Elva Kay's prayer room, where she'd found the older woman in her favorite chair with her Bible open.

Elva Kay laid a gentle hand on Susannah's head. "There's a lot of talk in the Bible about walking by faith and not by sight."

"See, I don't get that. I'm used to looking at facts and putting together a puzzle. Obviously I've got a bunch of pieces missing. It's making me nuts!" Susannah bumped her forehead against Elva Kay's knee in frustration.

"When you moved here, would you have ever foreseen falling in love with your suspect?"

"Not in a million years."

Elva Kay smiled. "Do you want a suggestion?"

"You know I do. That's why I came in here."

"All right. The Bible says if any of you lacks wisdom, he should ask God."

"I just did that. Or rather, Quinn did. We prayed together before I came in."

"Good. Then just one more thing. Jesus said when two or more gather in his name, he's right there with them and promises to answer."

"So ... the more the merrier?"

Elva Kay smiled. "That's one way to put it."

chapter 24

On Tuesday night, Susannah knelt between Quinn and Elva Kay, holding hands in a manner that even a month ago would have seemed embarrassing or downright hokey. Skeet and Dana completed the circle—four people she knew she could trust. *Where two or three come together in my name ...*

Even Susannah, rank rookie that she was, knew they needed Christ's presence. She'd figured one other thing out too. Nobody could live the life alone. Relationships founded in the Lord were the key to survival. Praying with Quinn last night had been an intimate experience that started a tidal wave of emotion she had neither the power nor the desire to stop. It had changed her, strengthened her, drawn her to him.

Everybody else had already prayed. Quinn nudged her shoulder with his. It was her turn.

She cleared her throat. "Hey, God. It's me again. I don't know what to do here, but I need wisdom. We all do. Please help us help Quinn. Thanks. And oh, yeah. Amen."

She opened her eyes to find Dana crying and Elva Kay smiling like a proud mother. Quinn squeezed her hand hard before letting go.

"She's gonna leave us all in the dust." Skeet winked at Susannah and hopped to his feet. "I'm sure you're all wondering why I called this meeting. Oh wait. Susannah called this meeting." He gave her an exaggerated bow. "Carry on, O fearless leader."

Susannah let Quinn help her to her feet, then waited for the others to settle down.

"Okay, you guys, I've put together this little handout." She gave a sheet to each of them. "It's got everything I know about Quinn's employees, business connections, relatives, and friends."

She'd spent all day analyzing the information. But she'd functioned as an ATF agent long enough to understand the importance of teamwork. Most times it took several agents working together to break open a case. And each of the five people in the room came with unique life experience, knowledge, and gifts. Surely they'd be able to figure this thing out together.

"First, everybody take a look at this list and tell me if you see anybody missing, somebody I haven't thought of who might have an interest in Quinn's company."

After a moment's silence, Skeet cleared his throat. "What about Russell Wallace, Phillip's roommate? But I can't imagine him having anything against Quinn, and besides the guy's such a computer geek—" He shook his head. "Nah, it just doesn't fit."

Susannah frowned. "He's on the list—see, right there under Phillip. But I haven't had time to talk to him yet. Can we arrange that, Quinn?"

"Sure. He and Phillip will be in the warehouse tomorrow afternoon helping me get ready for the Bellingrath wedding show."

"Good." She made a note. "I'd already planned to be there to help. You can introduce me, and it'll be natural to ask questions."

"Susannah, I want to help, but I don't know what I can do." Dana peered at the handout, nose wrinkled. "I'm pretty clueless about this stuff."

There was an awkward pause. Everybody knew how giddy Dana was, but Susannah had no desire to hurt her friend. Her gaze clanged with Quinn's.

He gave Susannah a wink, then smiled at Dana. "You and Miss Elva Kay have got the most important part of all. Prayer."

Quinn supposed every art form had its periods of drudgery. Sitting hunched over a table in the warehouse for hours on end wiring fuses to shells was a tedious and thankless task. Because it was critical to both the quality of the show and the crew's safety, he had to make sure they didn't tire and grow careless. Early on he'd learned to make a party out of the wiring process.

On Wednesday afternoon he and Rebecca and Susannah were at work, expecting the others—Skeet, Phillip, and Russell—to arrive as soon as school ended for the day. Music from Quinn's office stereo system banged off the aluminum walls, and his desk groaned under the weight of Krispy Kreme boxes, bags of corn chips, and jars of salsa. An enormous Crock-Pot full of queso dip squatted on Rebecca's desk. Susannah had even experimented with a monkey bread recipe—in keeping with her animal-themed baking lessons—and triumphantly contributed her creation.

Quinn had to admit it wasn't half bad.

But what did his heart good was watching *her*. The facets of her personality that had made her so attractive to him when he'd first met her seemed to sparkle as if she'd stepped out from behind a foggy glass. Maybe it was the added dimension of spiritual wholeness; maybe it was because she no longer had anything to hide.

After working alongside her all day, he'd discovered she loved crossword puzzles and had an astounding vocabulary. A couple years of Latin in high school enabled her to decode scientific and technical terms as if they were schoolyard slang. And she'd majored in chemistry at Arizona, earning a masters degree and acceptance into the doctoral program at MIT.

"And you didn't go for it?" Quinn put down the shell he was working on—gently—to stare across the work table at Susannah. "Why not?"

She shrugged, eyes on the fuse in her hand. "I was ready for a real job with real people. Doing something that would make a difference. ATF sounded exciting."

"Yeah, if you like interviewing felons and picking through body parts at a bomb scene." Rebecca shuddered. She sat at the end of the table packing completed shells into insulated boxes. After her initial hostility toward Susannah, her attitude had settled into a sort of prickly tolerance. "I would have gone to MIT. All those rich engineers ..."

Susannah grinned. "Have you ever dated an engineer?" She made a face. "Not that any of them would ever look twice at me anyway."

Quinn frowned, experiencing a crazy stab of defensiveness on her behalf. "I don't see why not."

She gave him a wry look. "Science dweeb. 'Nuff said."

"Which means you two will be perfect for one another." Rebecca rolled her eyes. "If I ever saw two more socially challenged individuals ..."

Quinn nearly dropped the shell in his hand, juggled it, and caught it. "Rebecca—"

"Oh, stuff it," she said. "I know bridal wreath and moonbeams when I see it."

Quinn looked at Susannah, who had ducked her head so that her hair hid most of her face. But he could see flaming cheekbones.

Phillip's car could be heard rumbling into the parking lot, and a moment later he slouched in with Russell. Throwing their backpacks into a corner, both boys proceeded to load up on the goodies in the office.

"I salute whoever made the monkey bread," said Phillip with his mouth full as he came into the warehouse. "Oh, hey, Susannah, what've you been up to?" He picked up a stool and moved it next to her.

"Making monkey bread." She smiled at the kid with what Quinn considered unnecessary friendliness. "How were your classes today?"

"Brutal economics test." He grimaced. "Should've just gone to tech school and opened a garage or something."

Quinn caught Rebecca's narrowed gaze and headed her off at the pass. "I hear working on cars isn't as much fun when you have to do it ten hours a day, and you're messing with somebody else's problems. Russell, haven't seen you in a week or so. Where you been?"

Phillip's roommate had gone straight to the Coke machine and jammed a couple of quarters in. He looked over his shoulder at Quinn. "Fooling around with my new computer system." A canned drink rattled down the chute. Russell grabbed it, popped the top, and glugged it down. "I've got a project due Friday, so I can only stay a couple of hours today."

"I'll take what I can get." Quinn pulled up a chair for him at the table. "Have you met Susannah? She's on special assignment this week, giving us a hand."

Russell glanced at Susannah with minimal interest. Anything that didn't come with a monitor, keyboard, and mouse didn't raise his pulse. "Yo."

Meanwhile, Phillip was looking over Susannah's shoulder. "Hey, you're not bad at that. Thought you said you didn't know anything about fireworks."

"I'm a fast learner." She leaned aside. "Show me how it's done."

Phillip gave her his I-know-everything-just-ask-me grin. "Watch the master." He picked up an eight-inch gold dahlia shell and a fuse, twisting them together in about three seconds flat. Handing it to Susannah with a smug look, he dusted his hands and bowed. "Tips in the jar, please."

Susannah laughed. "How about a second helping of monkey bread?"

"Now you're talking."

"Not now, Phillip." Rebecca packed away the shell her brother had just wired. "We've got a thousand more shells to finish by Friday at five. Unless y'all want to stay late that night."

Phillip slung his hair out of his eyes. "Give me a break, Becky, I just got out of class." He produced a tiny camera phone and punched a series of numbers to check his messages.

There was nothing unusual in the action. In fact the phone was practically a permanent appendage to Phillip's head. But Quinn suddenly remembered the conversation he'd had with the boy a week ago in Whataburger.

A conversation about a new cell phone.

The bottom dropped out of Quinn's stomach. "Let me see that," he said, holding out a hand. "I'm thinking about replacing my old dinosaur. It doesn't have a camera."

Phillip gave him the phone and picked up a shell to wire. "This one's wicked. It came with an awesome plan, all the minutes I need, and Internet service out the wazoo."

"Cool." Quinn scanned the menu but kept an eye on Phillip's face. "How long have you had it?"

"I got it about a month ago, after I lost my other one." Phillip shot Quinn a look. "Remember, we talked about it last week?"

"Yeah, but I don't remember what happened to the other one."

"He *says* it fell out of his pocket at a Mardi Gras party," Rebecca butted in. "After I told him a hundred times how dangerous and stupid those frat parties are—"

"Just because you have no life—"

"I have no life because you throw money away on expensive cell phones when we—"

The argument between brother and sister continued as Quinn looked at Susannah. Catching onto the thread of his questions, she had listened wide-eyed. Tapping her chest she mouthed, "Good cop." She pointed at Quinn. "Bad cop."

He nodded. "Rebecca, leave him alone." In the startled silence, the CD completed its cycle and started over. "Russell, turn that racket off. I have to talk to you all."

Russell shrugged and obeyed. He returned to his chair and slid down onto his tailbone.

Quinn stood up, folded his arms, and scanned the group around the table. "Rebecca, when does Skeet get here?"

"Any minute now—there he is." Rebecca jerked her head toward the partition between office and workroom.

Skeet appeared, juggling two loaded plates. "Who made the monkey bread?" He stopped when he realized everyone was looking at him. "What? I promise I didn't get the last piece."

"Flylady's got us in a lockdown, dude," said Phillip. "Somebody must've turned the toilet paper roll the wrong way. You better call your lawyer." He lifted his hands when Quinn scowled at him. "I'm just kiddin', man."

"Look, this is serious, so I'd appreciate it if you all would listen up for a minute."

"Quinn, we've got all these shells to wire." Rebecca swept a hand indicating the boxes stacked near the table. "Can't we work while you talk?"

"No. We can't. Because after this show there may not *be* any more work."

"What do you mean?" yelped Phillip. "You promised I could have a job as long as I'm in college."

"Yeah, but I'll have to shut the place down if ATF yanks my license. My insurance company thinks I fouled up the Mardi Gras explosion to collect on my premium."

"That's insane." Skeet set both his plates on a shelf in order to wave his hands. "Why would they think that?"

"The insurance company got a letter telling them so." Susannah stood up as the rest of the group looked at her.

"You gotta be kiddin' me." Phillip laughed. "She *is* a corporate spy."

"Not exactly." Susannah gave him a straight look. "I don't believe Quinn committed arson any more than you guys do. But we found what looks like an IED—an Improvised Explosive Device—just outside the blast site two days ago. It's already been sent off to the ATF lab. Just a matter of time before they track down where it came from."

Phillip and Russ looked at one another, and Quinn's hackles rose.

Leaning an elbow on the table, Phillip regarded Susannah with rapt attention. "Cool. How do they do that? Fingerprints and stuff?"

"Yes," she said. "It was a cell phone. When they can track down who it belonged to, it'll be a simple matter of getting phone records and tracing calls."

"Looks like Rebecca's busted," he crowed. "I always knew there was something evil about her."

"Shut *up*, Phillip, this isn't a joke," Rebecca said between her teeth. "That's a new cell phone. When did you buy it?"

The boy's icy eyes widened beneath the shock of dark hair. "*Me?* I got no reason to mess with Quinn's fireworks. He signs my paychecks, remember?"

"When *did* you lose your old cell phone, Phillip?" Quinn pursued Rebecca's question. "I can get your mother to look up the records and find out."

"I don't remember exactly." His face had paled, leaving a few freckles standing out on his cheeks. "Man, I can't believe you think I'd—" He looked at Russell. "Tell 'em you were with me the whole time!"

"Sure I was." Russell hunched his bulky shoulders. "So what?"

Quinn exchanged glances with Susannah. With a lifted finger she cautioned him to stay quiet.

Phillip leaped off his stool, sending it clattering backward onto the concrete floor. His eyes glittered. "You're not gonna pin something on me I didn't do! Wouldn't *ever* do!" Panting, he looked at Susannah. "So how would the device work? I mean, what would set it off?"

"If the right kind of explosives were in it—and we'll find that out from the lab report—a call from another cell phone could detonate it." Susannah slid her hands into her pockets, cool as a cucumber. "Phillip, if you have anything to do with this, you better come clean now so we can help you."

"I don't know anything because it wasn't me!" The kid's pallor had been replaced by a furious rush of color. "I love Quinn. He's been like a brother to me." He looked at Quinn, eyes pleading. "Dude, you know I do."

Quinn wanted to believe him right then and there, but Susannah intervened.

She put up a hand to draw Phillip's attention. "Okay, so tell us exactly—step by step—what you did the day of the explosion. Don't leave anything out, because we can corroborate it."

"Okay, well—" He gulped. "It was a Saturday, so I slept late at the dorm. Till about eleven. Then I went home to wash my clothes." He looked at his sister. "Didn't I, Bec?"

Rebecca nodded, nose wrinkled in disgust. "He saves all his dirty clothes for the whole week then comes home and dumps them on Mom. But he wasn't there long. We both met Quinn here, to help load the fireworks on the truck."

"Who else helped?" asked Susannah.

"I met 'em here at noon." Skeet had pulled a coin out of his pocket. He was flipping it and following the confrontation in uncharacteristic silence.

"Quinn, where were you?" asked Susannah.

"I was at the truck supervising the loading. Everybody else carried the boxes out to me."

"Okay, so, Russell, where were you?"

Russ sat up a little. "Phillip picked me up, so I was with him."

Phillip was still on his feet, shifting from one foot to another. "Me and him rode out to the site together in my car. Quinn drove his Suburban and took Rebecca. Skeet drove the fireworks truck."

Skeet nodded. "That's right. I followed the Suburban through the Bankhead, but the boys got a little behind us."

"Okay, back up." Susannah held up a hand. "Quinn, was there any length of time you weren't watching the truck when you guys were still here at the warehouse?"

"Maybe." He tried to think. "I remember going inside to answer the phone one time. But I didn't think anything about it, because it was just *us* out here. People I trust, you know what I mean?" He scanned the faces of a group that had worked with him for at least a year, some longer. The thought that one of them had betrayed him was sickening. He met Susannah's sympathetic blue eyes.

"I know," she said. "So what happened to split the group up right before the blast went off?"

"Phillip and Russell asked me if they could go across the river to get supper," said Quinn. "I let them go, because we'd been working like dogs all afternoon. I knew we'd be at the site until at least two in the morning, cleaning up after the show."

"Skeet and I went to get a Coke out of the ice chest in Quinn's Suburban," Rebecca said. "Quinn stayed with the fireworks to double-check some fuses."

"Whose idea was it to get supper?" Susannah speared Phillip with a hard look.

"Hey, man, I've got to go." Russell shoved his chair back. "I forgot, that project's due tomorrow."

Quinn put a hand on his shoulder. "Sit tight, bud, you can leave when we're done."

Russell squirmed for a moment, then slumped when he realized Quinn wasn't letting up. He shot a resentful look over his shoulder. "Look, I didn't have nothing to do with this. You gotta let me go."

"Russell's the one who suggested the wings." Phillip was staring at his friend, a muscle jumping in his jaw. "He was all hyped because Quinn wouldn't let him bring his phone onto the site, so he kept going back to my car to check messages. He wanted to go back across the river where Flylady wouldn't hassle us."

Quinn increased the pressure on Russell's shoulder. "I hate that you have to work for your money."

"It wasn't like that," mumbled Russell. "I was just hungry."

Phillip turned to Susannah, face livid. "We went through the tunnel and got to Lafitte's. I went in to get the wings, and Russ waited in the car. We were almost back in the tunnel when we saw the explosions across the river. Wait a minute." Phillip looked at his roommate, fists clenched. "You'd just dialed your phone, right before we went under the Bankhead. That phone wasn't gonna work in the tunnel! Dude, you were gonna let me take the blame for this, weren't you?"

"No way! Are you crazy?" Russell looked up at Quinn, cringing as Phillip advanced. "He's lost it!"

Quinn managed to catch Phillip's eye. "Hold up, man." His heart was about to jump out of his chest. "If Russell did it, we'll find it in the phone logs." Phillip stopped, breathing hard, face scarlet, and Quinn bumped his rigid shoulder with the back of his hand. "Come on. Sit down. We'll take it from here."

"You can't look at my phone logs—that's illegal." Russell struggled to escape Quinn's grasp.

Phillip gave him a contemptuous look. "I'm so sorry—I can't believe he did this! I knew he got a big wad of money from somewhere all of a sudden, but he said he'd sold a computer."

"I know," Quinn said. "Look, back off for just a minute, okay? We'll figure it out."

Phillip picked up the stool he'd knocked over and sat down on it next to Skeet, who looped a casual arm around his neck.

Quinn turned his attention back to the sullen miscreant under his hand. "Like Susannah said, you can tell us what you know now, and we'll see what we can do for you. If not . . ." He shrugged. "You're looking at some serious time, my man."

chapter 25

If Susannah hadn't already been in love with Quinn—and she most definitely was—his unsuspected talents as an interrogation partner would have sealed the deal. Russell Wallace sat hunched over the table with his head in his arms, crying like a baby. Standing behind him, Quinn had a hand on the boy's back, waiting for the storm to subside.

Phillip stood next to Skeet, arms folded, patent disgust oozing from every pore. "I cannot believe y'all thought I'd do something like that," he muttered. "I mean, come on. I may be a little on the lazy side—"

"A *little*?" Rebecca glared.

Phillip scowled. "Anyway, I'm not an arsonist."

At that, Russell looked up. "I'm not either!" His square face was swollen and red, eyes puffy. "She promised nobody would get hurt, and Quinn would get the insurance money to make up for whatever he lost in the blast."

"She?" Susannah sat down next to Russell, though it would have been a lot more satisfying to put him in a headlock. "Who was it? Start over and tell me how you got into this mess, Russell."

"Okay." Mouth distorted, trembling, he picked up the tail of his T-shirt to wipe his face. "It's my scholarship. Last semester my grades tanked, and they put me on probation. I'm not gonna wind up in a dead-end job like this, so I had to figure out a way to stay in school."

Susannah looked up to find Quinn, white-faced and stiff, staring at the boy. She wanted to reassure him, but needed to keep the pressure on Russell.

Lord, please help us ...

"Okay, Russell, that makes sense. So what did you decide to do?"

"Once I realized how fast the technical end of this industry is growing, I started looking for computer tech work. Quinn didn't have the money to invest in new equipment, so I asked around with some of his competitors."

"You didn't tell me any of this." Phillip looked as if he might jump on his roommate, until Skeet discreetly thumped his ear.

"Big help you'd be. All you care about is cars and girls." Russell's contempt was clear. "At least I've got some initiative."

"Okay, okay," Quinn broke in. "Who'd you approach?"

Russell's face collapsed. "Xtravaganza. They're close by and doing well enough, I figured they'd be willing to take on an experienced tech."

"Adam Brown?" Quinn's face was a study in horror. "Adam wouldn't do this to me!"

Susannah shook her head. "He was in Tokyo the whole month of January. I checked."

"That's right." Russell put his head in his hands again. "I talked to his wife. She's the one who came up with the whole idea. She said if I'd sabotage Quinn's next show, she'd pay for the rest of my tuition and give me a job. I didn't think it was such a bad thing, because like I said, the insurance was supposed to cover Quinn's losses."

"Russell, your moral code is pretty messed up," Quinn sighed. "But we'll get to that later."

The kid's Adam's apple bobbed as he gulped. "At first I thought it was gonna work. Me and Phillip went on through the tunnel, and all of a sudden the shells started screaming across the river. Right at the Convention Center. Then all—well, you know, everything broke loose. There were fire trucks everywhere and people running out of the building."

Susannah gasped. "Do you understand fireworks shells can kill people? What kind of arrogant idiot thinks they can set off an explosion and everything'll be just hunky-dory?"

She felt Quinn's hand on her shoulder and looked around at him. His eyes held hers, full of anguish and something else she couldn't quite interpret. *He* could have been killed, along with Skeet and Rebecca. Not to mention all the people at the Mardi Gras ball.

Exhaling a breath, she made herself relax. "All right, I want to know how you set the detonator."

Russell's voice was a reedy thread, his arrogance deflated like a balloon with a hole in it. "That was the easy part. I took Phillip's phone off his chest of drawers one morning while he was sleeping in. I knew he'd think he laid it down somewhere."

"You took my phone?" Phillip said, incredulous. "You used it to set off an explosion? What kind of sicko are you?"

Russell shrugged. "I thought it would be incinerated with the explosion. I didn't think they'd ever find it."

"And we wouldn't have, without Monty." Susannah had never been more grateful for her pet. She was going to buy him a nice juicy steak all his own.

"I don't understand why they sent you snooping around here." Russell hunched his shoulders. "The fire marshal said it was an accident."

"Apparently your buddy Julie decided ruining the show wasn't enough," said Quinn. "She hedged her bets by implicating me with arson. Just goes to show what happens when you get greedy."

"So what's going to happen now?" Rebecca couldn't keep her mouth shut any longer. "Is this crook going to jail or what?"

Susannah met Quinn's eyes. He had let her take over Russell's interrogation, but she treasured his strength. "We've got to let ATF take it from here. I imagine what will happen is that, if Russell's willing to talk to them—maybe wear a wire to help nail Mrs. Brown—" She lifted her shoulders. "They'll go easier on him."

Russell, demoralized, slumped onto the table again. "I'll do whatever I have to. I want out of this."

Quinn laid a hand on the boy's head. "You're not getting out of it, but we'll help you through it however we can. Right now, you wait here while Susannah gets hold of the cops."

Susannah woke up Friday morning to find she'd once again made the morning news.

"Come here, sugar, take a look at this." Elva Kay crooked a finger as Susannah stumbled into the kitchen, seeking the source of the lovely cinnamon and yeast smell that had wafted up the stairs. "You've turned out to be quite the celebrity around here." She peered over the top of the paper. "Oh, and have a scone."

Helping herself to tea and one of Elva Kay's thick, sweet biscuits, Susannah sat down at the table. She was getting used to eating at daybreak now. She scanned the front-page story with little interest and handed it back.

"I guess they mostly got it right." Cradling her teacup, she closed her eyes to inhale the aroma of blackberry tea.

According to the reporter, Julie Brown—wife of Adam Brown of Xtravaganza Events in Biloxi—had been taken into custody by

ATF officials. She would be questioned, along with college student Russell Wallace, regarding the January SkyPainters explosion. As the investigation was still unfolding, details were sketchy, but it appeared that Wallace, as a first-time offender still under the age of twenty-one, would receive some leniency. As Susannah had predicted, his willingness to cooperate with officials would mitigate the charges against him.

"Aren't you happy to have the whole thing over?"

Susannah opened her eyes to find Elva Kay watching her, head tilted birdlike. "I suppose."

Elva Kay patted her wrist. "Feeling a little out of the loop?"

She shrugged. Because she now worked for neither ATF nor the insurance company and had completed her interview with Agent O'Neal yesterday, she would have very little to do with the rest of the proceedings. Maybe she did feel a bit of a letdown.

"I've got plenty to keep me busy before I go home to Tucson." She forced a smile. "I'm going to help Quinn wire the rest of his shells today, then I'll get to go to the wedding, to help him fire the show. That'll be fun."

"Has Quinn not spoken for you yet?"

Susannah squinted. "What do you mean?"

"Never mind. I can tell by looking at your face he hasn't." Elva Kay released an irritated sigh—for her, the equivalent of a full-blown temper tantrum. "What am I going to do with that boy?"

"If you mean, has he asked me out on a date, I can tell you right now that's not his style. And even if it were, I'm not his kind of girl. He needs somebody sweet and southern and ... and ... spiritual, like Dana."

"Dana *is* sweet, but she'd drive Quinn insane in the space of half an hour." Elva Kay tsked. "You may have to take the bull by the horns, love."

Susannah sat up, alarmed. "If you mean chasing him down, you can forget it. He made it very clear he doesn't like to be chased."

"Susannah. You don't *have* to chase him. Quinn loves you very much; he just doesn't know what to do about it. We're going to have to give him some ideas."

"Elva Kay—"

"What time do you have to be at the warehouse to help with the shells?"

"Just whenever I can get there."

"Good. Then we're going to run a little errand first."

"Hey, Coach Quinn!" Alden Makin tugged on the back of Quinn's shirt. His freckled face was contorted with curiosity. "I think your cell phone's ringing."

Sliding the ice chest into the back of his Suburban, Quinn stopped to listen. Not surprising that he'd left his phone in the front seat of the truck. For the last couple of days he'd had a hard time keeping his mind on anything.

His team had just won their second game of the season, and as a bonus, Alden's dad had shown up to watch. Inspired, the kid had knocked a triple to earn three runs. Quinn had awarded him the game ball.

"Okay, thanks, Alden. I'll get it." He teasingly pushed the kid's cap down over his eyes. "Tell your dad I said you played a great game today."

"Thanks, Coach." Alden gave him a gap-toothed grin and ran toward his father. "Dad! Dad! I got the game ball!"

Quinn shut the Suburban's back door and hurried to retrieve the phone. He caught it before it quit ringing. "Will!" he exclaimed when the lawyer identified himself. "Aren't you supposed to be building sand castles with your wife?"

"I am. Or rather, I have been. While we're waiting for dinner I thought I'd give you a buzz. I saw the paper this morning. Looks like you're in the clear."

"Yeah, big relief." Quinn got into the truck and turned on the air conditioner. The afternoon sun had just about cooked his brains. "Thanks for your prayers, man."

"No problem. That's what brothers are for." Will chuckled. "Thought you should know, I don't see any problem getting you cleared to work the convention."

Quinn let out a whoop. "Oh, man, that's awesome!"

"You'll do a great job." Quinn could hear the smile in Will's voice. "Also, there'll be some smaller venues this summer, leading up to the big one. So you'd better start hiring extra staff to make sure you can keep up."

"Don't worry." Quinn laughed. "I'm on it."

"Well, I just wanted to say congratulations. Take care, man."

"Thanks, Will."

Quinn closed the phone and plugged it into the charger. He was going to have to hire more crew. With Russell out of the equation, it had been a struggle to get enough shells wired to complete tomorrow's production at Bellingrath. Thank the Lord Susannah had pitched in to help today. Fortunately, she was almost as fast at wiring shells as Phillip, who'd suddenly developed an amazing work ethic. Apparently Wednesday's confrontation had shocked the kid into growing up a little.

In any case, the shells were ready for the wedding reception, and Susannah had agreed to help him set up and fire it, along with Rebecca and Skeet. They should make a great team.

He and Susannah would make a great team.

If he could figure out how to convince her to stick around.

"Elva Kay promised me this was a good idea." Standing on Quinn's front porch, Susannah looked down at Monty, who was whining against her legs. She shifted the heavy puppy in her arms. The orange-haired kid at the pet store said it already weighed forty pounds—and judging by the size of the paws, would probably grow to the size of a Shetland pony. "What do you think?"

Monty gave a soft woof and turned his head.

"I can't bear to look either. Quinn's going to kill me. If he'd wanted this dog, he would have already brought it home."

The puppy was a female, which meant she'd have to be spayed. And she had just peed all over the backseat of Susannah's Jeep. This was not a nice, tidy gift to give a man—like, say, a wallet. Susannah sighed. Elva Kay insisted Quinn was goo-goo eyed over this puppy.

So here she stood, waiting for him to open the door. Boy, was that a metaphor for her life.

The puppy woke up and started to squirm. She smelled like flea soap with a soupçon of wet dog, since she'd just had a bath in Elva Kay's tub. Susannah cuddled her closer and got a lick on the nose. She laughed. "You sweetie, maybe I should just keep you."

The door jerked open. "Susannah!" Quinn stared at her in shocked silence. "What are you doing here?"

At least he wasn't handling the snake—she'd braced herself not to scream this time. He wasn't smiling either. "I promise, I didn't walk over here by myself—I drove. Can I come in?"

"No! I mean—" He looked over his shoulder—nervously, she thought—then came out onto the porch, shutting the door behind him. "I have a policy not to have single women in the house alone. Doesn't look right, you know?"

She'd never heard of anything like that, but shrugged. "Okay." Now that he was staring down at her, arms folded, she felt stupid.

"Are you going to tell me what you're doing here with that puppy?"

She put up her chin. "Bob needs a sister."

"Bob needs a—" He put his hands in his hair. "Are you crazy?"

There was no doubt she'd lost her mind. "I was in the pet store this morning, and I just couldn't leave her there. She was the only one left—since Elva Kay had called and asked them to hold the puppy. I thought you'd like to have her. Here."

She shoved the puppy at Quinn. Looking completely bewildered, he gathered the brown bundle to his chest. He nuzzled the top of her head and got his chin washed with that pink tongue. *Definitely goo-goo eyed.* Susannah almost cried with relief.

"But if you really don't want her, I understand. I'll take her back, and maybe the Humane Society can figure out what to do with her. Elva Kay can't take on another animal, and I'm going back to Tucson soon ... can't have another pet in my apartment. So ..." She peeked up at him.

He didn't say a word for a long minute, just buried his face in the soft, thick fur at the puppy's neck. Finally he looked up. His eyes were wet. "Thanks, Susie. I wanted to go get her, but I've had a lot going on this week, and I figured somebody else had already taken her by now."

She felt like doing one of Skeet's hip-hop moves. Instead she grinned at him and patted Monty. "I put her crate over there by the steps. You'll have to get a collar and leash, though. She's had her shots, but you might want a vet to check her out anyway."

The dark gray eyes were bemused. "You were at the warehouse all afternoon, and you didn't say a word."

"I wanted it to be a surprise. I knew you had the ball game this afternoon—by the way, how did you guys do? Did you win?"

"Stomped 'em." He grinned. "And Will Fletcher called to say the presidential contract is a go. It's been a great day." He scratched the puppy behind her ears. "This makes it perfect."

Susannah waited for him to say "I've waited all day to see you alone." Or "How about coming in for a Coke?" Or *something* a little more sentimental than "Are you crazy?"

Clearly he liked the dog. But he glanced over his shoulder at the front door again, as if he had something more pressing waiting inside.

"Okay, then." She took a step backward. "Guess I should get home. Elva Kay said she'd puppy-sit him tomorrow while we're at the wedding. If you want."

"Tell her that'd be great. I need to go in and get a good night's sleep too. It's been a long day." He looked down at his new pet. "Does she have a name?"

"Not yet. That's for you to pick out."

"Okay, I'll think about it. The patch over her eye ought to give me some ideas." He backed toward the door. "'Night, Susannah. And thanks again."

"You're welcome. I'll be there in the morning to help you set up." She tugged Monty toward the Jeep. This was the guy who had kissed her brains out a few days ago. What was the matter with him now?

Or better question — what's the matter with me?

Baldwin, what is the matter with you?

Telling Susannah he was going to bed at eight o'clock, like he lived in a retirement home or something. Seeing her on his front porch with the puppy in her arms had blown his limited social skills all to pieces.

He put the puppy down on the rug in front of the door while he went to get the crate. She promptly made a puddle, which he had to clean up before he could take her inside and look for a Cool Whip bowl to put some water in. He hadn't had a puppy for so long he wasn't sure what to feed it. He'd have to make a trip to Pet-o-Rama in the morning.

Filling the bowl from the kitchen faucet, he smiled. Susannah was something else. It had been all he could do not to snatch her up and show her how crazy about her he was. He liked the puppy a lot. But mainly because she'd brought it. Caring for a baby like this would be a major headache, though he'd never let Susannah know that.

He hoped she wouldn't go back to Tucson, but if she did—at least he'd have this little squirt to remind him of her.

Squatting down to watch the puppy lap at the water, he tried to imagine his life without Susannah. "Lord, I'm counting on you to work this thing out. I'm gonna be one unhappy pyro if she leaves."

chapter 26

Awestruck, Susannah craned her neck to watch a fountain of fuchsia-colored shells explode in the black velvet sky over Bellingrath Gardens.

After a long day of dragging around racks of mortar tubes and hauling boxes of shells, she should be dead on her feet. But her nerve endings tingled with excitement at the culmination of four days' work.

Four days of being part of Quinn's world.

Now she knew why he was so good at his job. He had a way of lightening the hard physical work and repetitious tasks with camaraderie and fun. Though Phillip and Skeet had worked with Quinn so many times they hardly needed his instruction, his directions were clear and concise, leavened with humor and respect. Susannah appreciated being treated like a valued member of the team.

She was proud to have helped put together this spectacular experience.

All but deafened by the reports of the shells exploding in perfect synch with the music, thrilled by the bursts of color and light overhead, she couldn't contain her joy. Laughing, mouth open in amazement, she tipped her head back and spun in a circle as fusillade after fusillade broke, sending crackling purple stars and golden tourbillions cascading to earth.

Flinging her arms wide, she slowed until she teetered on the balls of her feet, dazzled by the colors and the music. "Oh, God, the heavens declare your glory," she murmured, repeating words she was hardly aware she knew. "How you thrill me! Thank you for letting me be a part of your design. I'm so, so glad you turned me in this new direction." She laughed again, eyes open so as not to miss one sparkling detail of the show.

The fireworks paused as the soundtrack, a swelling romantic ballad, amplified on a tide of strings, percussion, and horns. The finale was coming. Knowing the artistry of the man she loved, it would be incredible. Breath caught in her throat, skin electrified, she waited ... waited ...

Boom! A huge battery of Roman candles in a complex mixture of blue and purple and gold went up, followed in rapid succession by an artillery of crimson comets. Heart in her throat, Susannah watched as explosion after explosion burst for a solid two minutes, probably fifty or sixty shells.

Then it was over. Her ears rang, and smoke drifted like a dream in the heavy night air. Almost dizzy, she looked for Quinn. He'd been at the computer a few yards away, controlling the firing of the shells, but now he'd disappeared. Enraptured by the show, she hadn't noticed Skeet taking over.

Hoping Quinn hadn't gotten sick, she took off her hard hat and gloves, then removed the earplugs he had given her. She waved at Skeet. "Hey! Where's Quinn?"

Skeet grinned. "He left me in charge. You're supposed to stay right here and look up."

"What? The show's over, isn't it?"

"Not quite. Look up." Skeet pointed.

Susannah frowned. Come to think of it, music was playing again, the theme from *Chariots of Fire*. What was going on?

She looked up just as a blast of heart-shaped red shells went off. The pattern held for less than a second and disappeared in a glittering fall of stars. Susannah blinked. She could have sworn the pattern had spelled M-A-R-R-Y.

Then a second smaller explosion sent another pattern of bright red skyward.

M-E.

Her stomach clenched. Something very weird was going on here. The wedding ceremony had already taken place. Quinn had made a monumental mistake somehow.

She'd opened her mouth to express her dismay to Skeet, when she felt a pair of big warm hands grasp her shoulders. Quinn. She knew instinctively it was him.

"Look up," he said in her ear.

Shivering, she tipped her head back against his shoulder, and felt his arms slide around her waist, his cheek against hers.

A third burst of shells went off. Sapphire-colored flowers this time.

S-U-S-A-N.

She turned her head. "Who's Susan?"

Quinn started laughing. "Whoops, late break. Look again."

More blue flowers spelled N-A-H.

The music rose to a crescendo, burst into a timpani roll and exploded into a huge orchestral swell. Now she could hear, from across Fowl River Bayou, where the wedding reception was taking place, the faint sound of whistling, applause, car horns honking.

She had just received arguably the most public proposal of marriage in history. Spectacular, sweet, romantic. Totally Quinn.

There was only one thing missing.

She looked around to find Skeet and Phillip had both disappeared. She was alone in a smoky, shell-strewn, grassy river bottom with Quinn.

He cleared his throat. "So ... what do you think?"

She turned to face him, laying her hands on his chest. His denim work shirt reeked of black powder, his dark hair stuck to his forehead in sweaty jags, and his cheeks were streaked with dirt. He was the most beautiful thing she'd ever seen.

She blinked back tears. "I think Susan's going to be a very happy woman."

His face fell. "Susannah ..."

"I'm just *kidding*." She poked him in the chest. "How did you know *Chariots of Fire* is my favorite movie?"

He stared at her. "It's *my* favorite movie."

She smiled. "Really? What's your favorite book?"

"It's not *Three Men in a Boat*, that's for sure." He grinned. "We've got all the time in the world to talk about junk like that. I thought you were going to tell me what you think."

"About what?" She dipped her chin as she'd seen Dana do around Skeet, and looked up at Quinn from under her lashes. She wasn't going to be the first one to say *I love you*.

"About—about ..." Blushing, Quinn looked up at the sky, where the smoke was beginning to drift into wisps over the bayou. "About the fireworks going on here."

All *right*. Now they were getting somewhere. "I don't know." She looped her arms around his neck. "Fireworks are just a bunch of loud noise and pretty lights. I'm looking for something a little more substantial and long lasting." Plus, she really, really wanted Quinn to press that amazing mouth of his to hers. A repeat of what had happened after the race would be nice.

For a second she thought she was going to get her wish. His lips parted and he tilted his head, the beautiful eyes darkening to slate. "Oh, shoot," he muttered, "I knew I was going to mess this up." Catching her by the waist, he set her away from him.

Susannah stood overcome with emotion as Quinn dropped onto one knee and took her hands. Looking up at her, he took a deep breath and released it. "Susannah, I know we haven't known each other very long. But I have it on good authority it's possible to find the other half of yourself in a heartbeat. I've found that in you."

He paused as his voice roughened, but he didn't look away. "I love your passion for whatever comes your way, especially for the Lord. I love your humility and willingness to learn. I love your humor, and I even love your dog. Both our dogs." He heaved another breath, but this time his voice grew stronger. "And I'd consider myself the most blessed man on the planet if you'd forget about going back to Arizona, and stay here to love me and be my wife."

Incapable of speaking past the constriction of her throat, Susannah shook her head.

Quinn's eyes widened in alarm. "I can move to Arizona, that's no problem—"

"Quinn!" With a hysterical little laugh she tugged at his hands. "You don't want to live in Arizona. There aren't any trees there."

"Trees are highly overrated." He jumped to his feet. "Give me a good cactus any day."

Susannah laughed and flung her arms around his neck. "Just shut up and kiss me before I realize how insane this is. My brothers are going to have me committed."

To her immense satisfaction, that amazing mouth claimed hers and a fireworks explosion of a different kind rocked her world. A minute or so later Susannah rather drunkenly pulled away. "I forgot something."

"I think you covered it." Quinn set her on her feet, but lifted her hair to kiss the soft spot under her ear.

"No, I forgot ... I forgot ..." There was another long pause before Susannah could gather her thoughts enough to mutter, "I forgot to tell you I love you."

"I gathered that," Quinn said, a smile and just a touch of smugness in his voice. "Leia apparently loves you too. She cried for you all night."

"Leia?"

"*Star Wars* is my second favorite movie." He held her face in his hands and kissed her softly. "You forgot something else, Miss Arizona. I'm waiting."

"Oh yeah." She laughed. "The answer's yes."

Fair Game

COMING WINTER 2007!

Elizabeth White,
Author of Fireworks

Jana Cutrere's homecoming to Vancleave, Mississippi, is anything but dull. Before she's even reached town, the beautiful young widow hits a stray cow, loses her son in the woods, rescues an injured fawn, and comes face to face with Grant Gonzales, her first high school crush.

Grant recently returned to town himself amid hushed controversy. His only plan: leave the corporate world behind and open a hunting reserve. Seeing Jana again ignites old memories ... and a painful past. Tensions boil over when he learns exactly why she returned. Jana plans to convince her grandfather to develop a wildlife rescue center—dead center on the prime hunting property he promised to sell to Grant!

With deadlines drawing near for the sale of the property and no decision from her grandfather, can Jana trust God with her and Grant's future, or will explosive emotions and diametrically opposing views tear them apart?

Softcover: 0-310-26225-9

Pick up a copy today at your favorite bookstore!

ZONDERVAN™

GRAND RAPIDS, MICHIGAN 49530 USA

WWW.ZONDERVAN.COM

Read an excerpt from Elizabeth White's next novel, *Fair Game* ...

chapter 1

Jana Marie Baldwin Cutrere, DVM, had just run over a Black Angus cow in broad daylight. Maybe it wasn't the worst thing that could have happened on her first trip home in ten years. And technically speaking, she hadn't run *over* it. After all, she'd been going less than twenty miles per hour in a geriatric Subaru, not a Sherman tank.

The ink barely dry on her vet school diploma and already she'd committed bovine homicide.

Her eight-year-old son Ty was staring wide-eyed at the steam oozing out from under the crumpled hood of the car. "Look out, Mom, she's gonna blow."

Presumably he meant the radiator and not Mrs. Angus, who rolled over with a grunt, lurched to her feet, and lumbered off down the highway. Jana's relief was short-lived. Four-year-old LeeLee, buckled into her booster seat in back, chose that moment to start screaming her head off.

Jana scrambled out of the car, yanked open the rear door, and scooped her daughter into her arms. "It's okay, sweetie." She hugged LeeLee until the screams subsided into muffled hiccups. "You're not hurt, are you?"

LeeLee clamped her arms and legs around Jana. "I'm all shook up."

Jana laughed shakily. "You're a trouper, kiddo." She squeezed her preschool Elvis-freak tight and looked to the cloudless blue sky. "Thank you, Lord, we're all okay."

The front passenger door opened and Ty poked his head out. "It's hot in here, Mom. Can I get out?"

It was hot outside too. Sweat beaded under Jana's bangs and ran down her back. Barely into summer and the temperature was already over ninety degrees.

Welcome back to the Gulf Coast.

"Okay, but stay close. I don't need you to get run over too."

"I'm smarter than some old dumb cow." Ty tumbled out of the car and wandered over to inspect the roadside ditch, filled with water from a recent rain shower. No telling what wildlife she'd find in his pockets later.

With a final hiss the car fell silent. Maybe the cow had survived, but the bovine had sure done a number on Jana's transportation. Now what was she going to do? Even if she'd wanted to hitchhike, not a single car had passed in several minutes.

When LeeLee began to wriggle, Jana set her down and looked around to assess the situation. Dense woods stretched off to the right, and across the highway ran a rolling pasture that hosted the cow congregation. She should have been paying attention instead of rubbernecking with the children. Pointing out the cypress knees poking out of the swamps, she'd forgotten that something might appear around one of these dogleg bends.

"Mommy, this car is a mess!" LeeLee planted her fists on her hips, a ferocious gesture mitigated by the sticky blue ring around her mouth.

Jana sighed. "I know. We'll either have to walk or call Grandpa to come get us." Rats. This old car would be the first thing she replaced when she got her practice going.

She reached through the open window for her cell phone. At least Grandpa wouldn't have far to go. The Farm and Feed was only a couple of miles down the highway in Vancleave. Grabbing LeeLee's hand to keep her from running out into the road, she began a one-thumb search of the phone menu.

"Mommy ..." LeeLee tugged on her hand. "I'm not tattling, but where's Ty going?"

Frowning, Jana looked around. LeeLee had recently decided that what Mommy noticed for herself couldn't technically be called tattling. Ty had vanished.

She clutched LeeLee's hand. "Where did he go, baby?"

"He ran into the woods."

"The woods!" Jana jammed the phone into her pocket. "Which direction? Show me."

LeeLee pointed.

Jana swung her daughter across the ditch, then jumped over herself. When LeeLee couldn't keep up, Jana picked her up and walked faster. Tall switches of Bahia grass stung her bare legs and left black seeds clinging to her socks. All three of them were going to be miserably sweaty and itchy by the time they got to Grandpa's.

"Ty, where are you? Ty!" Jana stepped into the woods, a typical Mississippi forest of oak, sweetgum, and pine, overgrown with scrubby underbrush and briars. Pine needles and rotting leaves created a slippery foundation beneath her tennis shoes, and a sharp, whining drone buzzed in her ears and nose. Hopefully Ty wasn't in any real danger, but the mosquitoes would eat him alive. It wasn't like him to run off.

Jana slowed down to look and listen. If she hadn't been so irritated, she'd have enjoyed the clean scents that took her back to childhood. She would never forget the first bunny nest she'd found when she was about LeeLee's age. It had almost been worth the whipping she'd gotten when she came home with a tear in her shorts.

This would be the perfect place to put the wildlife refuge she'd dreamed of for so long. She'd been praying for a way to lend her gift back to God's creation that had in a sense saved her soul. This was it. The Twin Creek Refuge.

LeeLee leaned back and patted Jana's cheeks. "If Ty's lost, he's supposed to go to customer service, right?"

Jana blew her bangs out of her eyes. "This isn't Wal-Mart, baby. But we'll find him." *I hope. Please, Lord.* "Ty!"

She hadn't walked much farther before she realized they were following a path. Orange plastic ties marked a few skinny white oaks, and reflective tacks were stuck here and there at eye level. She stopped. "I thought we were on Grandpa's property, but it looks like somebody's been hunting it."

"Hunting's bad, Mommy."

"That's right." Deer season didn't open until October, so they should be safe. A thought came to her. "Poachers."

"Could I have a poacher egg? I'm hungry."

"Honey, poachers are bad people who kill animals. We'll eat as soon as we get to Grandpa's, but first we have to find your brother. Ty! If I find you hiding, that Game Boy is mine!" She waited, shushing LeeLee with a finger on her lips. Nothing.

A gunshot ricocheted through the woods.

"*Ty!*" Jana tore through the trees, hardly able to hear anything except the thudding of her heartbeat and her own gasping for breath.

A moment later a faint but clear boy-soprano drifted through the woods. "Mo-o-om!"

Relief nearly buckled her knees as she followed the direction of his voice. "Where are you? Are you okay?"

"Mom! C'mere!" Ty's voice came from the right, a few yards ahead. "Come see what I found!"

With LeeLee still clinging monkeylike to her neck and waist, Jana pushed through a brushy growth of oak and magnolia seedlings. She almost stepped on Ty, who sat cross-legged in a nest of pine needles with a tiny spotted fawn cradled in his lap.

"Ooh, look, Mommy." LeeLee leaned down. "It's Bambi."

Ty looked up, cheeks poppy red, sweaty blond cowlick standing at attention. A cut on the back of one hand bled freely, but otherwise he seemed healthy and whole. Jana closed her eyes in relief.

"I think his leg's broke, Mom. Can you fix him?"

"I don't know." Jana set LeeLee down and sank to the ground beside Ty. "He's so little. How in the world did you find him?"

Keeping an eye on the knifelike hooves, she examined the quivering animal as best she could. Its liquid brown eyes were wild with fear.

Ty looked up at Jana, absolute faith in her healing abilities shining in his dark blue eyes. "I saw him at the edge of the woods. I could tell there was something wrong with him, so I ran after him to see if I could help." He looked faintly guilty. "I didn't have time to call you 'cause he was running so fast. Then he sorta fell down, so I waited 'til you came."

The tenderness of her son's sturdy, sun-browned hand stroking the deer's back stayed the lecture poised on Jana's lips. "Sweetie, his mama will come after him. She probably just went looking for food. If we take him out of the woods she'll worry—just like I did when you ran off."

"But Mom!" Ty blinked back tears. "If we leave him here he'll die."

"Not necessarily—"

"Mommy!" LeeLee tapped Jana's shoulder. "There's G.I. Joe!"

Jana looked around to see what LeeLee's spectacular imagination had conjured up this time. A young man, perhaps in his early thirties, dressed in faded jeans and a maroon cap worn backward on his head, stepped through the woods behind her. A camouflage T-shirt stretched across shoulders wide as any action figure's, and he carried a bow-shaped contraption that looked like some kind of military weapon. He had a quiver full of neon-fletched arrows strapped on a belt at his waist.

"Did you folks know you're trespassing on private property?" His slow, pleasant baritone belied the threat of the weapon. He propped his arm against a tree. "If you're lost I'll be glad to show you the way out."

Jana was incapable of answering. The moment she'd jerked her gaze up from those shoulders to look at his face, a crazy mixture of humiliating memories nearly shut down her brain. Grant Gonzales had changed: the facial bones had sharpened and hardened with manhood, and his curling dark-blond hair was hidden under the cap. But those brown eyes—the only remnant of fourth-generation Hispanic descent—still had a lazy, deep-lidded droop that told you he knew more than he was letting on. More than you wanted him to know.

Of all people to run into when she wasn't prepared for confrontation. And here of all places.

She struggled to speak in an even tone. "I'm not trespassing. This land belongs to Alvin Goff."

"Not for long. I'm in the process of buying it from—wait a minute!" His gaze raked her, eyes alight with an appreciative gleam. "Jana Baldwin. I thought you looked familiar."

Jana's heart pounded in her throat. *He* was the one buying Grandpa's property? She'd come home not a moment too soon. The nebulous "really good offer" had turned into the person of her first high school crush.

"It's Jana Cutrere. Richie and I got married." She rose, silencing the children with a look at Ty and a hand on LeeLee's shoulder. "And we're not lost. After all, I grew up here." When Grant frowned, she felt compelled to explain their presence further. "Ty saw the fawn and followed him to make sure he was okay."

Grant's gaze homed in on Ty. The small space seemed to shrink even further as he stepped into the glade with them. Kneeling with a graceful fold of his body, he gave Ty a sharp look. "Did you see his mama?"

"No, sir."

Grant glanced at Jana, his expression awkward.

Ty's eyes widened. "You killed her, didn't you?"

"This time of year? Of course not!" Grant looked genuinely shocked. "I was out here marking trails for an archery shoot. Didn't you hear that gunshot? I'd just found the doe when I heard y'all hollering. I didn't want to move her until the game warden—" Apparently realizing he was still under accusation, he appealed to Jana. "I didn't know she had a fawn. Listen, the poacher may still be out here. You all better go back to your car."

Jana shook her head. "We can't leave the fawn—its leg's broken. It'll die without its mother."

"I'll tell the warden where it is." Grant stood and extended a hand to Ty. "Come on, I'll walk you out."

Jana wasn't about to leave an injured deer in the care of this man and his weapon. "Go on back to your scouting, Hawkeye. We'll take the fawn with us." She took the animal from Ty and stood up. It squealed and struggled, but she managed to calm it in spite of her own agitation. "Ty, hold your sister's hand." She headed for the road.

Ty jumped to his feet. "But, Mom—"

Jana resisted the urge to look over her shoulder to see if Grant followed. "My supplies are all packed up, but we'll take the fawn to the vet."

She might have known Grant wouldn't be gotten rid of so easily. He caught up in two strides. "At least let me carry him for you." He stalked beside her, pushing tree limbs out of the way before they could slap her in the face.

"I've got him. We don't want to upset him any more than he already is." She grudgingly gave the guy points for chivalry, though she wished he would go away.

Such wishful thinking came to an abrupt end when Jana emerged from the woods. Her disabled car still hunkered like roadkill in the middle of the highway. She had no way to get to a veterinary clinic—or anywhere else for that matter. "Oh, man."

"What happened to your car?" Grant's voice vibrated with amusement.

Seeing the pathetic, overloaded little wagon through his eyes, Jana could have died of mortification. "We had a minor confrontation with a cow."

"Looks like the cow won," he drawled. "The vet clinic's nearly five miles from here. You planning to walk?"

Jana gave him a pained look. "I was just about to call my grandpa." Carefully holding the fawn in one arm, she dug the phone out of her pocket. "If you'll excuse me ..."

"No, wait, now." Grant blew out an exasperated breath. "It's right at a hundred degrees out here, and Little Bit's liable to melt if you have to wait on Alvin." He grinned at LeeLee, who was all but turning herself wrong-side-out trying to reach a mosquito bite between her shoulder blades. "I'll take you wherever you need to go. And I'll call my brother-in-law to come tow your car. You remember Tommy Lucas?"

"Of course I do. We grew up in the same trailer park." Jana paused with Grandpa's number half-dialed, considering her options. "I guess it *would* be faster if you took us to the vet, so Grandpa wouldn't have to leave the store. Where's your vehicle?"

"Not far. Just around the next bend."

While Jana locked the Subaru—not that there was much in it worth stealing—and checked the padlock on the U-Haul, Grant handed his bow to Ty.

"Take care of that for me, would you, bud?" Without asking Jana's permission he reached down to hoist LeeLee onto his shoulders. "Come on, Sally, let's go for a ride." He set off down the side of the road.

"My name's not Sally!" LeeLee squealed, clutching his forehead.

"It's not?" Grant turned to walk backward and winked at Jana. "Then it must be Snigglefritz."

"No!"

"Pudd'n'tain?"

"No! It's LeeLee Annabelle Cutrere."

"Hey, I was close, wasn't I?"

"Yessir. Mommy, look at me, I'm tall!"

Jana swallowed. "I see you, honey." Grant was well over six feet. Even walking backward through clumps of weeds reaching to his knees, he moved with an athletic grace that attested to a life spent outdoors. Why didn't he turn around and quit looking at her? Did he remember the last time he'd driven her home—and what he'd said to her? She certainly hadn't forgotten.

"You better watch where you're going."

"Oh, backseat driver, huh?" He turned around with a sudden dip of the knees that made LeeLee giggle.

Another few steps and they rounded the bend in the road. An enormous dark-green pick-up was parked on a red-dirt track extending off the highway. A steel tool box took up a third of the truck bed, and through the back window she could see the inevitable gun rack. The undercarriage and wheels were coated with fresh mud, but the top half of the vehicle gleamed with a recent waxing.

Here was a man who cared for his possessions.

The thought gave Jana a funny pang, but before she had time to question it, Ty raced past her and clambered over the tailgate.

"Mom! Can I ride in the back?"

"No!" she exclaimed at the same moment Grant said, "Sure."

He held both of LeeLee's small sandals in one hand while he dug a set of keys out of the front pocket of his jeans. "It's okay, he can't hurt anything back there."

She gave him an annoyed look. "It's illegal to ride in the back of a truck."

Grant's wide mouth quirked. "Don't worry, my uncle's still the sheriff." He laughed as Jana opened her mouth to protest. "Haven't you ever let this boy ride in the back of a truck? That's a crime in itself."

She tried to think of an answer that wouldn't make her sound like an overprotective mother. "Who do you think you—"

"Look, we're way out in the country. He can sit close to the cab and I'll go slow as my grandma." He shook his head. "On second thought, Granny's not such a great role model. Make that slow as your grandpa."

She could stand here arguing all afternoon, then wind up having to call her grandfather after all. The stubborn glint in Grant's brown eyes was all too familiar. He'd made her get in his truck once before, then proceeded to humiliate her. But that was a long time ago. She was an adult now, and she'd had a lot of experience taking care of herself.

Some battles weren't worth fighting. "All right. Sit down, Ty, and I'll let you hold the fawn—but only if you promise to be still! No arms or legs or any other part of your body hanging over the sides." She turned to Grant. "And remember you promised to drive slow. *Real* slow."

"Yes ma'am." He stowed LeeLee in the backseat of the cab. "I hear and obey."

Grant had been hunting the woods of Jackson County since he was eight years old, but hauling out a beautiful woman, two kids, and a live deer was a first.

He glanced at Jana. Good night, it had to have been at least ten years since he'd seen her. No wonder it'd taken him a minute to recognize her. Back then she was a tall, leggy wild child with a long gypsy mane and too much make-up. Eye-catching, for sure. But look at her now—dark hair floating around her face in short, glossy waves, dark blue eyes brilliant as gemstones, mouth full and curling at the corners.

There was something different in her expression too, that he couldn't quite put his finger on. She sat crowding the door, hands clasped in her lap and narrow feet straddling the hatchet and industrial-size flashlight he'd left on the floorboard. He couldn't help wondering at the tension that all but vibrated from her slim shoulders. Surely she didn't still hold it against him that he'd bloodied her boyfriend's nose at the prom.

He could hardly believe she'd married that yahoo.

Curiosity sneaked under his guard. "So, what's old Richie up to these days?"

"Daddy's in heaven, playing guitar with Jesus," LeeLee lisped, right into his ear.

Grant nearly ran the truck off the road.

"LeeLee! Sit down and put your seatbelt on!" Jana glanced through the back window, then frowned at Grant. "You promised you'd go slow."

"Sorry." He gave her a cautious glance. "So Richie's, uh ..."

"Yes." Her voice was tight. "Three years ago."

Grant glanced at the dark-haired little widget in the rearview mirror. She was singing what sounded like a list of eastern European countries. He shook his head. Surely not. She couldn't be more than four or five.

Jana cut a glance at him. "LeeLee never knew her daddy, but I told her he's in heaven."

Lifelong acquaintance with the Cutrere clan made Grant seriously doubt that, but he kept his reservations to himself. Already he'd betrayed his favorite motto: Never ask a woman questions, you'll get way more information than you need. He wasn't about to break rule number two: Never let on how much you know or you'll wind up with an extra job.

"Hmph." He returned his attention to the zigs and zags of the winding county road. There was a moment's quiet, except for the little voice warbling in the back seat.

He was trying to think of a safe topic of conversation when Jana cleared her throat. "So which one of your sisters married Tommy?" She still didn't look friendly, but at least she seemed to have reined in her overt hostility.

"He hooked up with Carrie."

"Tommy's my age! Carrie's older than you, isn't she?"

Grant glanced at her, amused. "There's only about five years difference between them."

"But Tommy was even wilder than—"

He knew what she'd been about to say. Tommy Lucas and Jana Baldwin had both been known as "hoods." Initially Grant hadn't been thrilled with his sister's choice of husband, but Tommy had turned out to be as grounded as a Mississippi live oak. The guy worshipped the ground Carrie walked on.

"He became a Christian." Grant glanced at Jana to gauge her reaction.

A radiant smile bloomed on her face. "Did he really? So did I!"

That explained the difference he'd noticed in her eyes.

"Then you'll have a lot to talk about." He hesitated. "I noticed the U-Haul. Are you moving back here after all this time? I assume you're gonna stay with your grandpa for a while."

She didn't answer for a long moment. Then, "Grandpa's getting older, and I felt like he needed me."

"I know he'll be mighty glad to see y'all." He slowed to turn into the driveway of the veterinary clinic and smiled. "I'm glad you're back too."